Death in the South of France

Death in the South of France

Jane Jakeman

First published in Great Britain in 2001 by
Allison & Busby Limited
Suite 111, Bon Marche Centre
241-251 Ferndale Road
Brixton, London SW9 8BJ
http://www.allisonandbusby.ltd.uk
Reprinted 2001
Copyright © 2001 by Jane Jakeman

The right of Jane Jakeman to be identified as
author of this work has been asserted by her in
accordance with the Copyright, Designs and
Patents Act, 1988

A catalogue record for this book is available from the British Library

ISBN 0 7490 0555 6

Printed and bound in Spain by
Liberdúplex, s. l. Barcelona

JANE JAKEMAN is an author, freelance journalist and art historian whose previous trilogy of historical crime novels featured Byronic detective, Lord Ambrose Malfine. Born in Wales, she has travelled widely and is a great lover of French culture. She regularly reviews crime fiction for *The Independent*. *Death in the South of France* is her first modern novel.

Chapter I

The gulls swoop and scream over the long glittering expanse of the Croisette, over the absurd white wedding-cake of the Carlton Hotel, over expensive sand, luxurious blue water and brilliant red flower-beds. The sand is imported freshly every winter, when the town is deserted - otherwise, there'd be pure rock all the way along the coast. But the effect looks good, the authentic gold of the glamorous resort. The blue is bluer than blue, the red straight off the canvas of Miró. The fronds of palm-trees trail in an early morning breeze as Cannes, *la ville fleurie*, awakes for another day of dreams and sleaze.

But not yet. Another hour yet before the tourists emerge for the sun-tan slather, and the out-of-season starlets are still dreaming on, of shadows flickering over silver screens, of the never-ending dazzles of flash bursting into their eyes. The only sign of life is on a tennis-court, where some early-morning enthusiasts are knocking a ball back and forth, and out to sea, where a dog is swimming reluctantly for a yellow ball thrown by its master, who idles on the shore.

Further inland, in a cramped office, a man is listening to a voice on the phone.

'Oh, she's tough. Yes, that's all true. Came to work on a motor-bike. Not a dyke, though - at least, never heard of a girl-friend.'

The Marseilles accent was as strong as raw garlic.

Maubourg shifted back in his chair. The air conditioning seemed to have broken down and his shirt was already sticking to him.

Outside he could see two gendarmes hustling a kid out of a car. The kid's sunglasses fell off in the struggle and the cops considerately let him pick them up and put them back on again. After all, thought Maubourg, this is Cannes, film city, Mecca of the famous and the not-so-famous. Wearing sun-glasses is the ultimate human right.

A cop thumped the kid.

His sunglasses fell off again.

One of the not-so-famous.

The voice at the other end of the line wanted to know why Maubourg was asking about the woman.

'She's going to be the new examining magistrate here - at least, that's the word. Getting old Rigaud's case-load.'

'Shit, that's a tough one - you got the psycho there in Cannes, no? Cuts them up and chops the little bits off?'

'You think she'll cope?'

'Oh, sure. That is one determined female. Anyway, she won't take fright. She looked at all the floaters out the docks here. Even the ones bursting open and falling to bits so we got to hold them together with a net just to fish them out. Madame the judge goes down to the morgue, holds her nose, takes a good look. Don't make any mistake, boy, she'll sort it out. She hangs on to everything - doesn't let anything get past her. But what the fuck, this is Marseilles I'm speaking from. We got bodies here, we got crime, we got killers. No secret about that - hell, people expect it! But you, over there - it's a different story, eh? All golden sands and palm-trees and film-stars and that. The Cannes Mutilator - isn't that what they call the killer in the press? Doesn't sound too good for business!'

No, thought Maubourg, it doesn't sound too good. Don't frighten the tourists packing into the glitzy hotels. Don't frighten the starlets parading along the Croisette or the wattled Americans in the Carlton or the tuxe-doed gigolos who trawl the bars. Because this is Cannes, dreamtown, and we don't have murder here. And if we do it's just a few mobsters killing off their own kind, or a couple of druggy kids who deserve it. But we certain-ly don't have any nasty Grimm's-Fairy-Story bogeyman who slashes people into sushi. Bad for the image, bad for tourism, terrible for commerce ...

He says aloud: "Yes, they want to keep that word out of it. Mutilator. Just something the English papers started. They'll want the new *juge d'instruction* to keep the lid on it."

"Well, like I said, this one's real strong - she never gives up. Best of luck!"

Maubourg put the phone down and ran a finger round his shirt-collar. He wished he'd brought another shirt to the police station to change into, but he didn't seem to get that organised. He considered going home, thought longingly of a shower and the feel of a clean shirt on his back.

On the other hand, if you don't know what you're going to find, you don't want to go home.

Chapter 2

'I'm sorry.' The young inspector amended this, his eyes looking downwards in embarrassment. 'I'm very sorry to have to tell you this. We've just been in touch with Cannes to confirm it. There's no doubt.'

Charlie felt drained suddenly: it was the shock, he supposed, almost as if he were observing a stranger, standing there on the Thai rug in the dark living-room, listening to the story of a death.

'How did you find me?' It was really the least important question, he supposed, but it was the first that had come into his mind.

'The information was in the back of her passport,' said the plainclothes man. 'You were entered as the next of kin and the French police contacted us.'

She must have felt closer to him than he had to her. Charlie felt a sudden wave of guilt.

The uniformed policeman, who was older, quieter, had been present, Charlie guessed, on many such occasions. His voice was slow and gentle. 'Is there anyone you want us to contact, sir? Any other relatives?'

He had a notebook ready.

Charlie answered carefully. It seemed important, a matter of respect, to speak in this way, for the record. 'Rosie's mother is still alive, but she's in a nursing home in Australia. She has Alzheimer's. I doubt if she would understand anything.'

And he knows the picture comes into all their minds: a woman, sitting in a chair, staring into space. A nurse bends over her. Her child is dead: she stares on: it means nothing.

'That was the lady who owned the villa, as I understand it.?'

'Yes. Rosie was my half-sister. My mother died when I was twelve and my father got married again, to Rosie's mother Anna. - he died a few years ago. The villa in Cannes belongs to Anna. She had it before they got married.'

He sat down suddenly. The room seemed to have filled with dust, the air was choking him. He put a handkerchief to his mouth.

'I'm sorry, I can't seem to think any more? What were you saying?'

'I think we should call somebody, sir. A neighbour, perhaps?'

That seemed a quaint idea. They didn't have neighbours in suddenly fashionable Bankside, a stone's throw from Tate Modern.

He didn't really understand why, what anyone else could do, but he said mechanically, 'There's my cousin, Martin Hollingsworth. He's a solicitor. He handles all the family business.' He gave the sergeant the address of Martin's firm in Victoria.

'We'll contact him, sir.' The sergeant moved to the phone.

'Oh, yes. I suppose he could help.'

'You will need some help, Mr. Cashel.'

Was there something threatening in the Inspector's voice? Somehow, Charlie recalled the procedure of cautioning the subject in television police series. But of course, it wasn't anything like that.

He said, painfully, fearful of the answer, 'How, exactly how ...was she ...'

'Killed, sir?'

Killed. Murdered. That was what he meant.

'We have had no details yet, sir, from the French police. Only the information that your sister's body was found yesterday evening and they are treating the case as murder.'

The sergeant had been talking into the phone.

'Mr. Hollingsworth will be round straight away.'

'Good - he can help you pack.'

Inspector Willis, wasn't that the plain-clothes man's name? He had introduced himself when they came in to the flat. He didn't look as though he had done this sort of thing very often, looked uncomfortable, perhaps that was why he seemed unsympathetic. Shiny, red scrubbed face, turning now to peer out of the window at the traffic roaring through Bankside. 'Location, location, location!', Imelda had said, when they moved in.

'Pack? Oh, yes, I suppose - I'll have to go out there ... I'd better see if I can get on a flight ..'

'We can arrange that for you, sir. To Nice?'

'Yes, that's the nearest airport.'

'The French police will send someone to meet the flight.'

'Oh ...?'

'They'll ask you to identify her, sir. Just a formality.'

He said this more softly. But it made Martin feel worse.

The sergeant had his notebook out again. 'Do you live here alone?'

12

'No - I have a partner -' Oh, God, they probably thought he was gay. 'What name, please?'

'Imelda Shoesmith.'

It was a more interesting name than most, but then, Imelda was a very interesting person, though she didn't like the Shoesmith part, always said it sounded horrible and horsy.

'Where is she now, Mr. Cashel? Does she work? We'll get in touch with her.'

'Yes, but only in the mornings. She works in an art gallery in Cork Street.' He looked at the clock. 'She'll be home in an hour anyway.'

He hoped they'd have left before then.

They did go, once Martin had arrived. He was a big man, and seemed to fill the room, as he introduced himself, told them he had Anna's power of attorney, yes, he had always acted as solicitor for the Cashel family.

He said all the right things, the things Charlie hadn't managed.

'What a dreadful thing! Poor little Rosie - she was only nineteen. Have they caught him yet? - I assume it is a man, Inspector? Let's hope they get a move on. Charlie, I'm going home to get my passport and a clean shirt - I'm coming with you to Cannes, of course. Will you be all right - Imelda'll be home any minute, won't she?'

Yes, she would. In fact, he had originally thought that was what the police were calling about, when he had opened the door and seen the uniform, the warrant card held out.

The night before, they'd been to a party for an artist in kaleidoscopic multimedia, Imelda wearing a black dress with complicated bondage-style straps.

'Mmm!' Tibor Henschore, the owner of the gallery where she worked, flicked at the tattooed wasp on her shoulder, then kissed it.

She was very beautiful, Imelda, with long black hair and golden eyes, really golden transparent pupils, like yellow stained glass. That was probably why Charlie had taken so long to realise what she had been doing, but now he knew, he was eaten up with anxiety.

Sometimes he'd found shiny packets of tights strewn round the bedroom, or new cashmere scarves and sweaters stuffed into drawers. Once there had been two identical handbags with gilt chains lurking in the wardrobe. None of it was the kind of stuff Imelda actually wore, which came out of whitewashed basements where young art-school designers piled their stuff on steel shelves. Imelda would never have been seen dead in public clutching a quilted handbag with a chain.

At first, puzzled, he'd thought she'd been given the stuff, but she laughed at him, without saying anything, just laughed, with her fine chalky-white teeth on show.

Gradually, Charlie had come to realise a few things. Some of the things still had store-tags. None of them ever had any bags, with the swirling logo of some expensive shop - and there were never any receipts fluttering about, those irritating little bits of paper.

When he tried to tackle her about it, she burst into a rage. 'So you think you're God almighty, do you? Never put a foot wrong? Well, mind your own bloody business for once. You're such a fucking bore, Charlie! Look at you, you're really worried!'

Well, he thought, it's true. I am. Living with a shoplifter frightens me.

He thought she was a kleptomaniac, without being quite certain of what it meant, but knowing that she came back sometimes with an extra laughing excitment, as though she were on a high.

The evening before the party, he'd come home to find a pile of expensive brocade ties lying on the bed. They lay there in a tangle, their brilliant reptilian colours glistening like snakes.

When he came into the room, Imelda snatched them and thrust them away into a drawer of her dressing-table.

He looked at her, wondering if he could go on with this. He wondered all the time now if she'd been followed, if she'd be caught, if he could be charged with something even though he would never have stolen anything from a shop in his life, felt he would have rather died. But the rent was paid in his name - maybe that meant he was a receiver of stolen goods - he didn't know, felt only some wretchedness and shame that made him begin to hate her.

And, after the party the previous night, when they got home, matters had come to a crisis. Fired up by the drinks, perhaps, the edge sharpened by jealousy of her flirtation with Tibor, Charlie had pulled the nest of ties out of the drawer.

'You have to stop doing this! Don't you understand? It's mad!'

'Oh, there speaks the little bourgeois!'

'Well, I pay the rent, call that bourgeois if you like.' And then, softening, because she was tense and trembling, 'Look, you've got to do something about it! It's dangerous - hell, you could go to prison!'

She was angry, and pretended there was nothing wrong. But he was afraid for her and knew that even if the store detectives didn't catch her, it was over between them. In fact, if the police did get her, it would be worse, then he would feel he couldn't leave her, had to stand by her. Better to make a break before that.

He'd been certain, when he saw the warrant card, that they'd come for Imelda.

Chapter 3

Charlie didn't remember much about the flight. Martin was sitting beside him, and the air hostess, solicitous, had been evidently forewarned that she was dealing with the bereaved, asking if he wanted anything, if he was comfortable. No, yes, numbness.

He found he was still worrying about Imelda. If the police came round again, which was surely possible, then they might spot something odd, something left lying round.

'Martin', he said, 'there's something else I want to talk to you about.'

Martin was horrified. 'Is she crazy? As a lawyer, I have to tell you this could be very serious. I don't deal with the criminal stuff myself but I could get you on to a good man if the worst comes to the worst. But you should finish it with her, Charlie, right away. You've got to protect yourself.'

'I think she is a bit crazy, Martin'.

'Can't you get her to stop? Have you tackled her?'

It was the way Martin spoke, 'criminal', 'protect yourself', that seemed so alien. Lawyer's talk, Charlie supposed. Not real.

'She won't stop.'

That was all he felt like saying.

They were met at Nice by a big black Peugeot, and there were several French policemen, but not the picturesque blue-caped gendarme sort. One was a big tough man, with rolling fat and bristly cheeks. The other, his superior, was smaller, with a crumpled face and small shiny dark eyes. He introduced himself. 'Maubourg, Pierre Maubourg.' Inspector Willis in London, Maubourg in Cannes - he seemed to be collecting policemen's names.

On the road to Cannes, there were posters outside the little kiosks selling newspapers and tobacco. 'Encore une victime!'

And then, horribly, something about 'Mutilée'. He began to feel very sick and tried to ask the policeman, 'How did she die? What happened?' but then Martin was intervening, leaning over and trying to prevent him from seeing the placards.

Charlie had thought they would go straight to the Villa Bleue, but the car swept up to a long low white building. There was a constant electrical humming sound as they entered the door, and it bothered him.

16

Martin was saying, 'Do we really have to do this straight away? Couldn't you let Mr. Cashel have a rest?'

And then the senior policeman, careful, good English, 'It's better now. Afterwards, he can rest.'

And then there was a long table, nothing coming rolling out of the wall, as he had pictured. It was all ready for him.

Her face was already uncovered, blotched, swollen, her eyes shut, but there was a white thing pulled up to her neck.

He was going to stroke her cheek but they pulled his arm back.

'Yes, that's my sister. Rose Anne Cashel.'

He was in horror of what lay beneath the white thing.

The word on the placard stuck in his throat. 'Mutiléé'.

He said it aloud.

'No, Monsieur Cashel.' The policeman had taken his arm. 'No, no. Your sister was strangled. Her body was not marked. No ... mutilation.'

He was getting out of the room, only it was really a shed, a kind of white hygienic shed with a dreadful smell, and then being led to a sink, and vomiting. They seemed to expect this, though he tried to apologise. Someone gave him a paper cup of water and a thick paper towel. He was offered cognac from a flask in the police car, but the smell seemed sickly.

They were driven to the Villa Bleue.

The villa lay through a suburb, a dusty row of shops lining wide pavements, more salubrious than the district through which they had just come. Beyond this, winding up a steep hillside, were high walls which discreetly hid the houses from view. The walls were punctuated here and there with the twirling iron grilles of gateways, but it was noticeable that here, in this remoter outpost of the seedy glamour of Cannes, there were fewer security cameras protruding their black popping eyes over the walkways, there were some deserted empty swimming-pools, some dried up lawns. This was not the area most favoured by the new Riviera aristocracy, the orthodontists.

The car turned into the short drive, between unkempt date palms. The lavender blue paint was flaking off the walls, peeling and blistering here and there. Like Cannes, itself, the villa was all vaguely familiar to Charlie, part of his youth, something out of his mind for fifteen years or so, nearly forgotten. Those odd turquoise-coloured ceramic roundels set for ornaments high up into the walls, yes, he remembered those. They seemed to have survived the seasons of heat and cold. The villa still had shreds of its old charm, rather like Anna, Rosie's mother, who had fluttered about in full skirts when all the other females round here were sporting loon pants or black jeans.

Villa Bleue. Quite simple, but somehow it hinted at the Train Bleu winging its way down from Paris, it sugegsted hibiscus and oily perfume sold in little dark blue bottles. Like one of those old-fashioned heavy scents, the villa conjured up a certain atmosphere: the South of France in the era of blonde starlets and leopardskin bikinis. Charlie had stayed there when he was a student, during the long summers. Rosie had been a child still, and Anna had the outside painted with a hazy blue wash, against which grew pink and white clumps of oleander. There were blue hydrangeas around the garden, and the paths were lined by tubs with strawberry plants spilling out of them.

All gone or run to seed.

The senior policeman pulled a key out of his pocket and unlocked the front door. It was stiff, but the door swung suddenly on its hinges. A stray cat fled from the garden as the door banged back against the porch.

Within, the shutters were drawn. Martin walked in and went round flicking switches, but Charlie stood at the doorway.

He said, 'Where was she?'

'Not inside the house', said the senior policeman. 'Here, just outside, in the garden. She may have known the attacker, or he might have been a stranger. Nothing in the house seemed to have been disturbed.'

Martin said, 'I arranged for the woman who comes in to clean to leave us some food. She was the one who found her ... found Rosie, apparently. Quite a shock for the poor old thing.'

The food had been left out on the kitchen table, neatly covered with foil. They ate a little, some rolls with chicken and mayonnaise, and had coffee, which was standing ready in a percolator. Charlie began to feel slightly better, steadier.

'Do you still know anyone round here?' asked Martin.

'No, I haven't been here for years. There's old Monsieur Arthuis across the street, I suppose. He's been there since Anna bought the villa. But he's an invalid, I think.'

The house across the road, visible from the kitchen window, its grey-painted Venetian blinds closed, was taller, older and more restrained than the Villa Bleue, which belonged to the brash era of the fifties.

'We would like you to come to the police station to make a statement now, M. Cashel,' said the Inspector, who had followed them in to the villa and waited while they ate, his bright eyes following them.

'Really, is that necessary?' Martin was a pompous ass, thought Charlie, but he was taking care of things.

'Yes, I'm afraid it is.'

The police station was very close to the sea, just off the Croisette in fact, a discreet building. As they went in, there was a bustle of tourists at a counter, reporting something, American voice calling something indignant. 'But it was right there, under my arm! Then he had it in his hand!'

They led Charlie past this into a small, quiet room, presumably sound-proofed, for none of the babble in the outer office penetrated. Then the room seemed full of people suddenly, a policeman tapping at an ancient typewriter (Charlie's mind registered that it wasn't a computer), a civilian with round John Lennon specs from the office of the *juge d'instruction* according to Maubourg, a woman introduced to him as an interpreter. Their faces were all composed into blank masks of official sympathy.

Maubourg sat opposite him. He saw the policeman's face clearly, as if it had been for the first time, its crushed-looking bones and the small shiny eyes like sloes. He offered Charlie a chair and indicated the interpreter, but Charlie said, 'No, I don't think I'll need it.'

'When did you last see Miss Cashel?'

'Oh, it must have been, about six months ago.'

'That's a very considerable time, surely?'

'We weren't very close. We lived quite separate lives, really. Of course, there's a big age difference: I'm twelve years older than Rosie.'

'And where were you the night before last?'

Charlie's brain refused to work for a moment. 'In London, all the time. I was at work - and then at home.'

'And during the night?'

That must have been when Rosie was killed. God, he was being asked for an alibi! Maubourg's face suddenly seemed much closer, and the room full of hostile faces. Perhaps he should have had the interpreter. Perhaps he would have felt there was someone on his side. He looked round, but Martin hadn't followed them into the room.

But the answer was simple, anyway.

'I was at home. All night.'

'You have a witness?'

'Imelda', murmured Charlie, thinking, frantically, yes, oh hell! - Imelda, liar, shoplifter - alibi witness? He felt sweat breaking out on the palms of his hands. Wasn't that an indication of fear? He thought he remembered someone telling him that we sweat over all our bodies when we are overheated, but through the palms when we are frightened.

'Your wife?'

'My girlfriend.'

'You do not seem especially keen on family life, M. Cashel. You hadn't been in touch with your sister, for a long time, after all.'

What could he say? Charlie felt another surge of guilt towards Rosie. Damn this man, was he playing on it?'

Maubourg paused and tapped a sheet of fax paper in front of him. It looked as if it was in English; something from the British police, the result of Inspector Willis's visit, perhaps. Charlie felt as if he were caught between two pincers.

'Your sister, now, I understand the Villa Bleue belongs to her mother?'

'Yes. My stepmother.'

'And at her death you can expect to inherit your sister's share in a very valuable property, assuming she made no will, which would be very unlikely?'

'I ... suppose so.'

Another long pause. Charlie suddenly blurted out, 'But I loved Rosie! English families are like that. I didn't see much of her, but I would never have harmed her.'

Maubourg signalled to the man with the typewriter, and the painstaking recording of a formal statement began.

It was a long one, it seemed to Charlie. No, they had definitely not quarrelled, they were just not very close. Rosie liked the Villa Bleue, came out to stay quite often. No, he didn't know of any particular friends here, didn't know about any men friends. Address where she had worked. They might know something ...

He suddenly felt he wanted to say something very important, and broke off from the orderly pattern of the statement. 'I want her brought back to England. For the funeral.' He was surprised by his own feelings. 'I will take a formal note of your request', said Maubourg, coldly. 'In the meantime, you may return to England.'

Charlie felt another shock of fear. It hadn't occurred to him, till then, that he might not be allowed to do so.

Then he was signing the typed pages, and getting up, feeling stiff and cold, in spite of the heat of the day outside. In the outer room, Martin was waiting, saying he would take care of the formalities. The Inspector was explaining something, in official-sounding language, humanity ironed out of it. 'There have been other deaths in the district ('mutileés', thought Charlie, in a surge of nausea) and it is possible that the crime committed against your sister is related to them. The matter will be referred from the Prosecutor's Office and placed in the hands of the *juge d'instruction* - the examining magistrate - to decide whether your sister can be released for burial. But you can go back now and wait.'

Yes, all he wanted now was to get home. Even to Imelda.

'It's important we stay in contact with you, M. Cashel.'

'Shall I stay on here for a couple of days?' said Martin. 'There'll be some more formalities, I expect. I can get in touch with you if you need to do anything, Charlie.'

He went back to the Villa Bleue and the French police drove Charlie to the airport. As they got out of the car, the inspector said, 'M. Cashel, there is a problem at the moment - the examining magistrate, M. Rigaud, to whom serious matters such as this would have been referred, died of a heart attack very recently. His successor has not yet taken over.'

Charlie felt the obscure sense of warning that he had experienced when Willis had talked to him in the stuffy little room in London.

'I tell you this because matters may be delayed. But there will be a new *juge d'instruction* on the case.'

It didn't mean much to Charlie at the time.

Chapter 4

A fair-haired woman in a room high up, further inland, away from the golden fly-trap along the coast, walked towards a desk where four white envelopes were set out in a row, and picked up a photograph. The clear early morning light of the South of France flooded into the room through the slatted blinds and fell remorselessly on the picture in her hand.

Difficult to recognise, unless you knew. Dried blood and macerated flesh, colours like bruised fruit, soft-looking, with white streaks of exposed muscle and muzzy nets of ripped pubic hair.

Easier to look at the close-ups. She had got more or less hardened to this, by now. The close-ups were nothing, just shapes and colours, a thick and meaningless impasto of human debris.

Cecile began reading the medical summary of the cases.

'An obsessional hatred of women is clearly manifested in the genital injuries inflicted on two of the female victims, Constantinou and Auvers.'

No great professional training required to deduce that. Words, verbiage, masking the realities and intensities of hate, neutralising them, reducing them to marks on a page.

More interesting is the analysis of Chief Inspector Pierre Maubourg, which she was leafing through.

'Identical patterns of facial injury appearing on both male and female victims and apparently inflicted with the same weapon (pathology report appendix A para 2.1, microscopic analysis of parietal and tissue damage and intruded particles, attached herewith) lead to the conclusion that one killer is responsible for four murders in the Cannes district. (Locations map attached).'

He's efficient, Maubourg, she thought, scanning the street-plan, with the red marks scattered close to the shore. No particular pattern or grouping, apparently, except that the taxi-driver and Véronique Dupuis had both been found on the Croisette, Mayleen Constantinou in the Rue D'Antibes and the fourth victim, Jeanette Auvers, near the Place Mistral. In other words, all in the most desirable and luxurious part of the town, from whence none of the victims had originated. She read on. Another half-hour, perhaps before Marc arrived. She made an early start this morning, since there was no child to feed or drive to nursery school. Florence was with Louis's mother.

Don't think of Florence. Put a barrier up between your child and what you have to do now.

Maubourg's summary.

'The weapon which inflicted the injuries is most likely to be a long-bladed knife of the type made for professional restaurant use and known as a boning-knife.'

No need to elaborate on that.

'Microscopic analysis of the perimeters of the wounds would appear to indicate some minute notching or scoring on the edge of the blade close to the hilt, which would be an important factor in identifying the weapon.'

If we ever get our hands on it.

Cecile tried to suppress her silent mental commentary and concentrate solely on the report.

'Two female victims display both facial and genital injuries.'

They would be...she turned over the photographs...Mayleen Constantinou and Jeanette Auvers..

'The most distinctive feature in these cases is the removal of large areas of flesh. Another female, Dupuis, and the male victim, Barsi, were subject to facial mutilation only. Little blood was in the area of the find-sites. The victims were therefore presumably killed elsewhere and subsequently deposited where they were found, a pattern consistent with the uneven settling of blood in the underlying parts of the bodies.'

'Patterns of blood smears and forensic tests suggest that plastic bagging or wrapping was used to cover the bodies at some stage before discovery. No witnesses have come forward to give evidence of seeing anything relevant in this regard.'

An interesting turn of phrase, 'No witnesses have come forward.'

Did that mean that Maubourg thinks someone might have seen something but be too frightened to speak?

Cecile crossed the room and stood looking down through the slots in the blinds, at the city street below, getting busy, where the sunshine gleamed off the long shiny lozenges of car roofs. Normal life. People going about their business. Down on the pavement far below, a young woman in a thin white dress posed against the bonnet of a car and a photographer sprayed water over her so that the long folds of the dress are plastered glistening and crumpled against the metalwork. The photographer began to click furiously and the woman to turn and twist for the lens.

Of course, Cecile had to admit, Cannes was the kind of town where normality itself has a special meaning.

Back to the dossiers.

'The immediate question to be posed, given the influx of organised crime into the area, is whether these deaths are the work of gangland mobsters operating systematically for conscious self-interest or a psychopathic serial killer working from alone from compulsive emotional drives.

'Pointers to the former theory, that of gangland killings, are: of those victims not subject to genital mutilation, the male, the taxi-driver, was found to have traces of illegal narcotic substances in the bloodstream (pathology report appendix C) and injection punctures and traumas on the upper arms and thighs. One of the females, Véronique Dupuis, had extensive partly-healed injection traumas and a record of involvement in petty crime, though no actual traces of narcotics were discovered.'

'Pointers to the latter, that there is a psychopathic killer at work, acting in response to his own needs, the 'Cannes mutilator' of whom the press has made so much: the obsessive and repeated nature of knife-wounds to the genital areas of two of the female victims and the removal of areas of flesh and pubic hair of which no traces have been found, and which therefore may be presumed to have been destroyed or hidden by the killer. The latter is probably correct. Trophyism, that is the removal and retention for the criminal's own gratification of portions of the cadaver, is a common feature of psychopathic sexual killings.'

Cecile sat back in her chair for a few moments. Already the sun is getting higher. It will be a warm Easter.

Another sentence in Maubourg's summary. 'I have been asked to consider whether the death of the English girl, Rosie Cashel, is in any way connected with the four cases outlined above. In my opinion, it is not.'

The phone rang - her private line.

'Cecile? - Darling - I didn't think you'd started the job yet, but Daniel said you'd be there.'

'Yes - I have to get used to things as fast as possible.'

Babette sighed. 'Then I won't see you for a while? Or Florence, I suppose. Of course, she's much better off up in the mountains, really.'

24

'No, Maman, I don't think I'll be able to get over for a while. I'll have to spend the weekends catching up on the files.'

Damn, she was smitten by the thought of Babette, who felt lonelier than ever when Florence, her only grand-child, went to stay with Louis's parents. But it was quite true that Louis' parents could give the little girl a much better holiday on their country farmhouse than could Babette, in her hot Marseilles tower-block.

It was no good offering yet once more to buy her a nice little apartment, Cecile, supposed, somewhere outside the city in a safe clean suburb. They could probably manage it without too much difficulty, but Babette would never believe that. She had lived with poverty so long it was almost impossible for her to believe that it wasn't necessary any more: her store-cupboards hoarded tins past their sell-by dates, her jumpers always seemed too thin. After Guillaume's horrible death, Babette had clung to her world more than ever, as if for safety. His loss seemed like a black reservoir of emptiness within her, that could never be filled.

'I'll have to take her shopping', thought Cecile, knowing she could not give her mother anything deeper. 'She'll let me buy her a few things.' Aloud, she said, 'Maman, I'll come to see you as soon as I can, I promise.'

'All right, darling. I'm proud of you, remember, I really am. Just wish you didn't have to work so hard. I'll ring you at home in a day or two.'

It wasn't that in Babette's world they didn't work hard - they did, back-breaking work, serving on their feet all day in shops or cleaning hospital wards. But when they stopped, they stopped altogether, put their feet up. Or else they went out and spent their bit of money with their friends. Babette could never really understand the pattern of life that Cecile and Daniel led - Daniel working at home, being a house-husband, both of them often spending all their spare time reading or working at the computer. She loved Cecile both unconditionally and uncomprehendingly.

Better for Florence in the farmhouse in the mountains than anywhere in the city. A picture formed in Cecile's mind of her small daughter, in her sun-hat, stumping up a rolling hillside clad with grey-green shoots of lavender. Sentimentality? Didn't Louis say they had grubbed up the lavender fields? No, only that there had been talk of it, surely.

Cecile gazed at the blank wall opposite for another moment: its very emptiness was a relief. Then she turned again to her work.

Chapter 5

Another town, another day.

In an office near Victoria, a secretary was contemplating the possibility of slipping out for a sandwich to the little Italian place near the tube entrance. Shouldn't be a problem - it would only take five minutes. The street was comparatively quiet - it was only just after twelve. Wouldn't be much of a queue. She'd get a bottle of orange juice, too. The air was so filthy - the window looked out on the double-decker buses swinging round into the bus-station, the fumes rising bluish on a fine day, brown wet muck splashing up in the rain. The windows had to be kept closed all the time, really, but then she got so dry and thirsty in the office.

She could hear Mr. Hollingsworth's phone ringing in the room next door, and his quick voice as he answered the call. This was once a big room stretching across the front of the building. Now it's been divided up by thin partitions.

'Martin Hollingsworth.'

There was a pause, then Mr. Hollingsworth's voice said something in French. He had originally advertised for a secretary who spoke French, because, as he had explained to the agency, his family had some property in the South of France. 'It belongs to my aunt, she's in Australia now, and I look after things for her. It would be very useful to have someone who could deal with telephone calls and so on.'

But the agency hadn't had anyone who spoke French, and he rang up again and said he didn't need French after all, he'd changed his mind, but he really wanted someone straight away, Carol was right there in the office when he rang, so she got the job, on a temporary basis. She had the legal experience, which was the important thing, the woman at the agency had said. 'Lucky for you!'

Now that she could hear his voice on the phone, Carol got her purse from her bag, safely stowed in the back of her desk drawer. She'd worked in a lot of offices.

He'd had a quite a few long calls from France - it should keep him safely out of harm's way for five minutes at least, judging by what's happened in the past few days. Carol slipped out of her office, bending her ear towards his door as she went past. He was still talking, all right. She heard the click as he put the phone down. Damn it, he might come and look for her ... no, he was talking again, in English, now. Must have made another call.

As he talked, she waited to get unnoticed through the outer door, with the gold lettering on grey sandblasted glass. 'Hollingsworth and Creedy. Solicitors.' There was no Mr. Creedy, apparently. Just the one partner.

'Charlie? Yes, it's Martin. I just had a call from Cannes. We can go ahead at last. They're releasing her. Yes, there's a new magistrate - a new *juge d'instruction* - on the case, taking over straight away. A woman. Maybe it's her decision - I' m not sure. Anyway, I talked to her just now. It can all go ahead - no, there's no need for anyone to go there. The French funeral people will do the necessary there, and the London funeral directors will have someone take it off the plane. Yes, they can take it straight there. I don't think you need to be at the airport - no, I'm not going. We've done our bit ... oh, that's all right, don't worry about it. Anyway, this woman seems more reasonable than the previous magistrate - Rigaud. Oh, I wouldn't trouble about it, Charlie. There's no point in flying Anna half way round the world - she won't know what day of the week it is, let alone what's happening.'

Carol was only moderately interested in all this. She was hungry now, but thought she'd better not risk slipping out, not without asking him.

Resigned, she went back to her desk and sat down, but heard her boss's voice still droning on.

'No, that's my advice, as a professional, as well as a member of the family. No need to tell Anna - doubt if she'll even understand what's happening - and anyway she can't possibly come out from Melbourne. You and I will be there, after all.'

Martin Hollingsworth put down the phone and went into the secretary's office. He drummed his fingers on her desk in a way she really didn't like. Her heart sank. He wasn't the kind of man you can just tell you've had no breakfast and you're starving.

Three weeks later, Charlie stood at the front of the awkward little undenominational chapel attached to the crematorium.

'Too small,' he was thinking, but he himself was not certain what he meant: the chapel was too small, so that he felt pressed up against the coffin that stood on a kind of absurd little stage before his face. But the coffin was also too small, tiny, really. Perhaps people always seemed smaller when they were dead than when they were alive, the body gave out a sort of penumbra of vitality and movement that seemed to shrink into a sort of crumpled space when they died, so they could be fitted into these shiny veneered boxes.

Horrible to think of her poor face there, just a few inches beneath the lid.

The minister, with a pale, sweating face, wearing a collar and black suit, a kind of unobjectionable universal god-person for all denominations, had uttered a few sentences about the metaphysical transformation that might await the inhabitant of the shiny bevelled box, whom he had never met, and about whose much-publicised death he knew only what he might have read in the newspapers. But Charlie felt an obscure gratitude, nevertheless. The man had managed to say something about Rosie.

'I hadn't seen her for a long time,' Charlie had said, when they had talked briefly before the service - if this curtailed little travesty of a rite could be called that. 'I don't think she believed in anything in particular.'

'Is there anything you would like me to say about your sister? Any special qualties she had that we ought to remember?'

Charlie tried.

'She was kind,' he said, and stared at the man, and then looked away.

It was this man's task to make a five-minute oration from any little scraps culled up from the depths of memeory by shame-faced relatives. 'I hadn't actually seen much of her ...' the man must have heard it a thousand times.

But not, Charlie supposed, about someone who had been strangled.

He felt awkward, standing almost alone in the front row of the chapel. Only Imelda stood next to him; he could smell her perfume.

He looked away from the coffin on the dais, down to the purple tufted carpet, to Imelda's grey snakeskin shoes. Behind them, someone was sobbing quietly. One of the girls from Rosie's charity shop, he guessed.

In the crematorium garden, with its spindly rose-bushes and rashes of little plaques, there was a plump girl with her face streaked with tears. A shiny bronze angel, or some other winged being, vaguely Christian, nothing too god-like, was suspended over the clean brick entrance to the crematorium. Charlie looked up, but a soft rain was falling in his face and he turned to the other mourners. One of them came over and held out a hand.

Charlie thought he recognised Rosie's boss, the head of the charity organisation. She had a black suit and straight brown hair in an expensive boarding-school cut, and her face was composed and distant. There were several women with loose drab-coloured skirts and a man with an incongruous bright blue sweater - probably volunteers from the shop. They were drifitng away, murmuring, 'how sad, so sad, such a young life ...'

There was Martin, of course, looking serious, his face well-scrubbed, his suit immaculate, his blackish-grey curly hair carefully combed.

He came over now, and Charlie was suddenly aware that his cousin was not just a big man, a bulky man, but someone who had already a powerful presence, the kind of aura that successful lawyers develop.

'I've got the legalities all sorted out,' he said, and shook the hand of the clergyman, thanking him, which Charlie should have done, but realised too late.

Charlie and Imelda went to an opening that evening, an exhibition in a small gallery off Marylebone High Street.

In a back room, there were white trails on a mirror. 'We need it! We've been to a funeral. Charlie's sister, you know. They've been keeping her in a morgue in France.'

'Oh, darling, whatever happened?'

'Oh, terribly sad, she was killed, you know. Someone killed her. They're still trying to find out who it was.'

When they got home, Charlie lay for a long time with his eyes open, staring up at the ceiling by the dim yellow light from the street below. Eventually, he got up and read a copy of The Face till it was dawn.

Chapter 6

The roll of film fell out of the envelope and slithered down, black and shiny, futuristic.

Charlie picked it up from the floor. The bright yellow tab stuck out of the side of the roll.

The early morning sun poured through the window. It was the nervous sunshine of London, unconfident, easily seen off, but Charlie usually enjoyed this part of the day, unless he'd had a heavy night.

Who the hell was it from? It would be lucky, he thought, if the film wasn't too badly damaged to be printed; the envelope was torn and dirty, with French stamps stuck on it at odd angles, dull blue and mauve depictions of some national bore with large whiskers.

He put the package on the table and found that he had a reluctance to handle it, a reluctance which was slowly overcome as he drank his coffee, eyeing the envelope over the white edge of the cup.

Charlie never had breakfast - that was practically an article of faith with him. Two mugs of coffee laced with brown sugar was all he could take first thing in the morning, apart from sex, of course, which hadn't been on offer at this particular wake-up call. Imelda had gone determinedly back to sleep.

He shook the envelope, but nothing else fell out.

Putting it down on the table, he peered at the French post-mark.

'Cannes', date undecipherable. No return address on the envelope, no enclosure.

Nothing but the film.

Imelda walked into tthe room and came over to the table, yawning. She was wearing a grey kimono.'God, you made a scene last night, Charlie. Getting pissed and shouting the odds at the boss! What's that?'

She picked up the envelope and saw the French post-mark.

'You got some tart in France then, sending you dirty pictures? Oh, sorry, this must be something to do with poor little sis.'

He couldn't think of anyone in France who would have sent him the film. Not anyone in authority, surely - it would have been accompanied by some sort of official communication. And he had barely encountered anyone there outside the ranks of the police.

He had a bad feeling about the film, as if it were going to decide something in his life. There was no reason why someone should send you a roll of film out of the blue. 'They should have put a letter with it.' he found himself saying. 'They should have warned me.'

It was the wondering that was so unpleasant. Wondering what the pictures would show, whether it had anything to do with Rosie's death, whether they were of Rosie and if she had been dead or alive when they were taken.

The woman magistrate had phoned Martin up, not Charlie, when Rosie's body had been released for burial. So maybe someone had contacted Martin about the film. Rosie's things had all been returned to him, in a sad little bundle, and he had passed them on to Charlie.

'Well, what are you going to do?'

Imelda was standing, watching him.

He went and raked among various pieces of paper and shiny plastic cards, found the bits he needed, went on into the bedroom, pulled some shirts and underpants out, noting as he did so that there was nothing peculiar squirrelled away among them at the moment, anyway.

He'd quarrelled with his boss, Ivor, the night before, and if he went in today to the publishing company where he'd led an uneven career for a year or so, he thought the chances were he'd be shown the door.

There was really nothing at all to stay for.

In the Underground the Central Line train seemed to be roaring in his head, jolting and jerking his body as he swayed and looked at his image, darkly reflected in the black mirror of the opposite window. It screeched to a halt at Victoria and people with suitcases struggled out past him, but he got up and made for the doors in time.

Martin's office was up three flights of stairs. There was a security entrance at the bottom and a new voice squawked out in answer to Charlie's buzz. 'Mr. Cashel?' the voice repeated the name carefully and then the door clicked open.

The carpeted stairs muffled his footsteps. The carpet looked new, and there was that indefinable smell of new carpet in the air, a sour sort of smell, like rope and wool, and Martin's office door was clean and shiny.

A girl was sitting at the desk just inside. 'Pleased to meet you, Mr. Cashel. I'm Carol Bassett, Mr. Hollingsworth's new temp.'

She had a good, warm, Black Country accent, odd and likeable in the cold dirty heart of London.

Carol Bassett must have heard about Rosie, because her eyes were big and round as she leaned over and said confidentially, 'I'm ever so sorry, Mr. Cashel. About your sister, I mean. Terrible, isn't it? Of course, I read about it. They haven't caught him yet - when was it, several months back?'

'Three months ago.'

Charlie supposed it would be quite something in Carol Bassett's life to meet someone related to that poor girl who had been murdered in France, a death which had been splashed all over the papers.

Rosie's case had made some trumpeting headlines in the British press, with that current of suspicion underlying everything, that the French police were not doing all they could to find the killer. This was just as had been suggested in the reporting of other English victims in France - that poor schoolgirl, for instance, who had apparently been murdered while only a few feet away from the beds of her school-fellows in the dormitory which they shared. There was the student murdered on a train - and the uncon-victed killer had escaped from France and evaded justice altogether in the end.

When it had happened to Rosie, Charlie suddenly came aware that there was a long history of these unsolved or unstatisfactorily resolved cases, begining with Sir Jack Drummond and his wife, who were killed on a caravanning holiday in the fifties. The British papers always implied that there was someone behind it who was far more sinister than the mad old farmer who was eventually convicted of the Drummond murders. It was as though there was something inherently unstable and dangerous about the land of France, through which stout British citizens passed in peril of their lives and the French police force was manned only by so many Inspector Clouseaus.

The British press at first had a field day over Rosie, whose pale face with long straggling hair - a photograph they had got from a schoolfriend - appeared in the tabloid newspapers, a childish Rosie, a young teenager who had ceased to exist even before her death. And the dusty villa became a glamorous residence, even figuring in some upmarket papers as a chateau, and in the English papers Charlie appeared as a grieving brother, a hero of some sort.

But Rosie was not among the victims of the 'Mutilator'. She had been permitted a quieter death, and could not appear in the lurid light that overcast his victims. The British papers had soon dropped the story.

Carol Bassett's eyes, which were pale greyish-blue and bulging, did look quite genuinely damp.

Martin's door opened. 'Ah, Charlie, come in. Sorry I've only got a moment, but any time, of course, any time. What is it?'

Martin produced a bottle from somewhere under the large oak expanse of his desk and a glass from a cupboard.

Good Scotch, fiery, giving courage.

'No, I'm not having one myself, but you look as if you needed it. If you want to know the legal position, Charlie, then technically Anna still owns the Villa, and it will come to you eventually, as the only remaining heir. Of course, even in its neglected condition, it's worth a great deal of money now. Or did you want to see me about the other thing - Imelda? That business?'

Martin didn't like to use words like 'shoplifting'. Too crude, thought Charlie. Murder is a respectable thing to have in the family by comparison.

'No, no, something else.

He fumbled in his pocket.

Martin took the opportunity to speak into the phone on his death, but quietly, as if doing homage to the presence of the grief-stricken. He had never been very close to Rosie and children when they had all been younger.

'Miss Bassett, perhaps you would get that file we talked about this morning. With the draft conveyance. I want to take it when I go out.'

Charlie put the roll of film on the desk between them.

'I had this in the post, this morning.'

Martin peered at it suspiciously, sideways, like a blackbird.

'What has that got to do with me?'

'Oh, sorry, I should have said. The envelope was postmarked 'Cannes'. I thought it must be something to do with Rosie.'

'Well, I can't think what on earth it's about. I suppose - was there a camera in Rosie's things?'

'Yes. There was no film in it, though. I gave it to the charity she used to work for and the chap checked.'

'Surprising how many people leave the film in the camera when they give it to us', the man had said. 'Like leaving things in pockets and handbags. We always have a look'. The back of the cheap camera had clicked open. Empty.

The film looked very small and somehow tacky on the vast polished surface of the desk. Martin put out a hand to pick it up, but Charlie reached out and took it back.

'That's all right. I'll have it developed.'

'Why not leave it to me? I'll get the girl to drop it in and let you know what it is.'

'No, it's all right. I'll see to it.'

Martin showing him out, the girl's pale, avid face, the windy street.

A photographer's near Victoria Station had an express service. They could develop the film in an hour.

He wandered round the peculiar network of shabby streets behind the station, stretching down to the fashionable blocks of Pimlico: Italian take-aways, alleged bookshops, boarded-up houses, rough pubs, art students straying from the Tate. The flotsam and jetsam of life washes round Victoria: Charlie peered into the window of a pawn-shop displaying brooches with half-sovereigns, gold chains and old wedding-rings, crucifixes and red-gold bangles, the desperation that flushes the hoarded treasures of poverty out into a shop-window. Rosie had needed him at some time, he knew that now, obscurely but painfully enough. They had once shared a life, the experiences of the same chilly little British seaside town where they had spent the first years of their lives, in that strange world called childhood, in the shadows of the same trees and under the same cracked ceilings. They had each lain there and watched the reflections of sunshine on water rippling over their heads.

But Charlie had become so preoccupied with Imelda that he had scarcely noticed when Rosie had dropped out of his life. Even after her death, he hadn't had time to think of her much, because they, Imelda and Charlie, were always going to some gallery opening, shaking drinks about in thin-stemmed glasses. In the middle of it always was Imelda, thin and brown, long-legged, her mouth outlined with red pencil.

Eventually, he looked at his watch and went back to the shop. The girl said as she handed over the packet, chanting automatically, 'We don't take responsibility.'

He stopped for lunch, which was a bacon roll and a cup of coffee in a little Italian café, as long and narrow as a railway carriage. Charlie wondered if the proprietor was from the south of Italy; he looked as if he might be, a short stocky man, his arms folded over his apron.

Looking out of the café window, there was the soft damp greasy rain of London at its worst, the micro-moisture that soaks through your clothes and smells unplesantly of damp wool. The air in the little place was heavy with the dampness of the rain, the brown lino that covered the tables had a wet bloom.

He opened the envelope and the shiny photograph spilt out in bright pools of colour across the brown surface. The unmistakeable brilliant blue of a southern sky.

One print only. He picked up the negatives. It was a film of twenty-four exposures. Twenty-three were solid black. 'We don't take responsibility', the girl had said. Presumably, there had not been a mistake in the laboratory and the film damaged in some way. Those black negatives were not the result of failure in the development process. They were there because the whole of the film had been sacrificed to one shot.

He oriented the photograph. Triangles of white fluttering across the blue, oily dabs of shiny cobalt and lapis. And below, an expanse of sepia with harsh black shadows, the deep green of cypress, and low stone walls with overgrown ornate grilles and what looked like small decayed houses, but absurdly small, like grotesque doll's houses. In the foreground, projecting out of long mounds, flat white rectangles like teeth, with shadowy lettering indocated upon them.

The separate items of the picture began to fall into place as his brain tried to make sense of what he saw. He was looking at a photograph of a painting, apparently a sketchy modern oil-painting of a cemetery on some arid hill-side.

The owner of the café and his wife, looking from behind their plastic-shelved counter, could see the photograph on the table before him. Another world lay there, on the table of the dingy London café. A world like the one they had left, perhaps.

The man was wiping his hands on a cloth and he and his wife came out towards Charlie. He pushed the photograph to their side of the table and the two of them studied the shiny little rectangle.

'I don't know where it is', said Charlie, helplessly, and yet, somehow, he knew it, without ever having seen the place. But he had never seen the painting before, he was certain of that. It had certainly never been in the Villa Bleue - at least, not when he had been there, and it was not to Anna's taste at all. She had favoured water-colour landscapes.

'It is in the south, of course', said the woman. 'That sky - and there is some sea beyond. It is a Catholic - what you say? - burying-place. You can see the tombs for the families, with the holy Jesus.'

She meant the crucifix, sketchily but unmistakably rendered, on a tomb in the foreground.

The man nodded in agreement.

'I don't know where, exactly', he said, 'but maybe is in the South of France. Yes, I t'ink you can just see some name on the stones. French. Provence? I don't think it's Italian. Is a nice picture, if you have someone buried there, nice place. You have been there?'

'No, no, I have friends there.'

'They must live in a beautiful place.'

They smiled politely, formally. Charlie picked up the photograph and put it back into the envelope.

Rosie had not been buried in that exotic place, the cemetery in the picture. She had been cremated in a drab London suburb on a windy day when leaves whirled past neat brickwork and the sketchy bronze wings of an inoffensive ecumenical angel.

Chapter 7

Maubourg walked into the examining magistrate's office and saw the woman behind the desk get up and cross the room towards him. They shook hands formally.

'Chief Inspector Maubourg? I've been reading your reports. They are remarkably clear.'

'Thank you, Madame.'

'Please sit down.'

He took the chair opposite her desk and looked carefully at her as she swung round and seated herself.

Her honey-coloured hair hung in a bob, falling into place as she sat down. She was wearing a suit of some dark reddish colour. He wasn't good at women's clothes, but it looked like the kind of thing that would have come from one of the expensive shops. Harder and tougher looking than the things Violetta wore, but it had probably cost more.

'Of course', she was saying, 'I could just have sat in my office and read the files, but we're going to have to work together so I thought we should meet.'

'Oh, yes, of course.' But he thought to himself, I bet it's nothing so vague. There'll be a reason for this. You don't look like the kind of woman who acts on a whim.

'You'll naturally think I have some particular reason for wanting to see you now.'

Blast her! She'd read his mind.

'I have, of course, but I also thought you should know the methods by which I personally prefer to work.'

So she was going to tell him something, and not the other way around. He didn't mind, he found, as he watched her. There were sparks in the air around this woman.

'There is something I wanted to talk to you about first: the case of the English girl, Rose Cashel.'

' She was not one of the mutilation victims.'

'No.. It was why I was prepared to release the body - all the requisite samples had been taken and sealed, and there seemed no reason why this murder should form part of the Mutilator case. There is a statement on file here from the brother. He stands to inherit the Villa?'

She ended with an interrogatory note.

'Yes, he was an obvious suspect. There was an alibi - '

'Ah, yes. An inspector in London took a statement from the girlfriend. She was with Cashel all night in London for the relevant time.'

'But I talked to Scotland Yard on the' phone. His personal opinion - just privately, you understand - was that the girlfriend - Imelda, was that it? - was hiding something. Just a feeling, but they both thought that - him and his sergeant. He hinted that she might be easy to break.'

'So that means the brother's alibi is pretty insecure?'

'It was just - just a conversation, madame. Only his opinion, nothing more.'

'There is another suspect, isn't there, Inspector? Rosie Cashel had a boyfriend, here in Cannes. No one in London seemed to know anything about it. I think we need to focus on him.'

'We couldn't find any evidence there, madame.'

There was a silence. She got up and walked across the room, turned away from him, seemed deep in thought.

He broke the silence.

'You were saying that you had something else to tell me?'

'I am reading through the dossiers of each of the Mutilator victims and reviewing all the evidence. I may from time to time phone you and ask for extra information. Please be prepared about the matter.'

It sounded sharp, almost rebuking.

'Very good.'

Perhaps he would needle her a little.

'And when you have finished reading, Madame?'

The energy of her response astonished him.

'Well then, Chief Inspector, I start doing.'

After he had left the room, Cecile sat down at the desk and put her head in her hands. 'I was a cow to him', she said to herself. 'But he doesn't see what's coming.'

She'd worked it out straight away, as soon as she started to consider whether Charlie Cashel might have killed his sister.

As far as the authorities here were concerned, that would be the most satisfactory solution by far. The brother had come over, say on a night-flight or a Eurostar, he had gone to the villa and killed the girl, he had fled back to England.

Then there would be no involvement with anything French, nothing that might damage the glamorous Cannes image. It would simply have been one British citizen killed by another: it could have happened anywhere, in any country. Of course, it would have to be tried by a French court - but no doubt, eventually the prisoner could be transferred to a British gaol.

So they had to guard against any political pressure to get an extradition move and pin the blame on Cashel.

The opinions of Willis as to his alibi would be singularly unhelpful if they were recorded in black and white, or known beyond this room.

Maubourg hadn't thought of that.

Cecile felt like someone trapped alone in a maze.

Chapter 8

Take it easy, she said to herself. Take it one at a time. One victim at a time. Maubourg had departed and Cecile was alone with the files.

This was the first victim.

From the white envelope furthest to the left, Cecile took out a photograph. A young, freckled face, with springy dark brown hair, the edge of a sports top just showing at the bottom of the picture. Cecile held it up, peered more closely. The white light was flooding through the window now, falling directly on to the little square of paste and emulsion. No make-up, but the skin looks deeply, evenly tanned, the eyes already have fine screw-up lines.

Mayleen Constantinou. Aged twenty-two. Australian. Third generation Greek immigrant family that had picked up a few ginger genes somewhere along the line, giving her that red-head skin type. Would probably have got skin cancer, if she had lived long enough.

This is the bit that hurt, looking at the face, when you could still see someone. Someone who played a lot of sport, who didn't try to cover anything up, who looked straight at the camera, a small lop-sided smile turning up one corner of her mouth, for this passport photo, the first step along the road that would bring her around the other side of the world, to wander round Europe and then to the Riviera, and then to Cannes, palm leaves and postcards and film-dreams.

And then to this. Pain, blood. Fear, presumably; death, eventually. And photographs in a still-open police file in this unforeseen Cannes, the tacky, glitzy place of her dying.

I suppose Rigaud didn't want to have these scanned in, thought Cecile, who had trawled through her computer files to catch up with some at least of the mountainous case-load she has taken over from her predecessor. The photographs of the victims of 'The Cannes Mutilator' had been in a drop-file, not held on the computer. Probably Rigaud was of the old school and did not trust the new equipment to accurately reproduce the photographs of the victims. Another possibility: Rigaud was so sensitive he couldn't face having them transferred to the computer screen, the possibility of calling up these images confronting him every time he looked at the file.

Unlikely. Not that she thought he had been particularly callous, but any experienced *juge d'instruction* would have seen a lifetime of such photographs, torn features and mutilated limbs, of contorted torsos and slashed faces. She herself, in three years in Marseilles, had seen swollen and bloated corpses brought from the waterfront, rotting cadavers, flesh burned in warehouse fires and blown apart in drug killings. Admittedly, she had been an exception in insisting on seeing every corpse investigated under her jurisdiction: there was no actual compulsion on the judge to view the body. Theoretically, she could have stayed in her office and studied the pathology reports.

After Rigaud's sudden fatal heart attack, when Cecile, her three-year appointment in Marseilles just completed, had been hastily drafted in to succeed him, the Department of Communications had to be called in. They had to get into Rigaud's computer files, to change the dead man's passwords and give Cecile access to his material. There weren't any visuals with the on-screen 'Mutilator' documentation.

At first she had thought, as she slid out the grey metal drawer of the cabinet in a corner of her office, that the old man had hidden some collection of pornography. She could see straight away that the packet of white envelopes inside the unlabelled drop-file held photographs of some sort. They all had names and numbers across the backs of the photographs and were stamped with the dates and times they had been taken. There was something curiously mundane and bureaucratic about this routine treatment of the hideous subjects on the other sides. She had transferred the photographs to the other files on the Mutilator's victims, re-uniting them with the verbal descriptions of horrors.

All the material should eventually be scanned in to a computer so that it could be easily accessed, she had thought, but it would probably be necessary to get some special equipment grants and that would mean wrangling with the bureaucracy here. The more successful a department, the better the equipment it got, but without good equipment, it stood little chance of success in the first place. Somehow she would have to break through that, use levers if she found them.

Cecile had long ago learned her lesson as far as political games were concerned: you wanted to get things done, you played the games.

Now she glanced at the clock. Nearly nine. Marc Lenoir, who had been Rigaud's clerk and was now hers, would be in the outer office any minute.

'Good morning, madame.'

He had a cherubic face, curly hair and quick eyes behind small round John Lennon-style spectacles: Cecile thought it was an odd concession to trendiness in a young man who was otherwise totally conventional. Maybe Lenoir's got hidden depths, she thought.

He had a very even, quiet voice. Cautious.

'Ah, I wondered where he had put them.'

'All the photographs of the case? This is the first one - the Australian girl.'

'Ah, yes, last February.'

'What was she doing in Cannes in February? Hardly a holiday month.'

Lenoir shrugs. 'It's cheap here then. At least, cheaper than usual. And the German girl she shared a room with in London - the one the British police interviewed - she said that Australians missed the sun terribly. They can't bear London in the winter, apparently, all the rain and fog. She was going to try to get some work if her money ran out.'

'Not on the game? She doesn't look the type.'

'No, not an aspiring starlet either. That's what we get most of here in Cannes.'

Hmmn, Cecile thought to herself. That's scoring a point neatly. Madame the examining magistrate has just been transferred from Marseilles, where things are rough and crude and dangerous and they have tarts and drugs and gangs - but here in Cannes we are accustomed to glamour all around us. This is the heart of the Riviera, after all - this is what Cannes means. Blue skies, glossy women, golden beaches, palm trees ... all the clichés and they're all true. So is a lot more, the Russian prostitutes, the drug scene round the station, the mangy white bulldogs with advanced skin cancer that trot along the pavements with the old male whores ...

She looked at Lenoir sharply but his face registered nothing behind the round wire spectacles. Probably Armani. Not like John Lennon after all.

Aloud, she said, 'I'm going to study them in order, the Mutilator victims. Mayleen was the first, right?'

'Yes.'

Damn him, couldn't he say anything more? Always the absolute minimum.

Well, all right, you don't want to add anything to what I've inherited. No extra friendly titbits, no comments about what might have happened to poor little Mayleen who ended up like a bloody mess of minced meat - nothing to eke out the cold records of the dossiers and acknowledge this was a human being who got cut up here like a rabbit in a butcher's shop. You're a cautious little sod. Well, I'll just have to read it all through, work it all out. You want it that way, Lenoir, I'll play it like that and you can take the consequences. If that's what you're like, I'll get rid of you in the end. After all, I'm the boss. I can change the tune here. You can't.

'The photographs were in that cabinet,' she said aloud.

'I didn't know that. He never told me he was putting them there.'

He sounded almost indignant. Ah, that caught you on the raw, Mr. Armani specs.

'Was there anything with them?'

She doesn't answer him directly.

'I'll have to go through them systematically. Do you know why he had them separately from the files?'

Lenoir was surprising. 'I don't know of any reason connected with the photographs. More of a reason in him, if you know what I mean, in his mind.'

'Can you explain that, or is it just a feeling *you* have?'

She was aware that she sounded too sharp. Don't start by alienating him, she said to herself, even if you're afraid he'll turn out to be a woolly-minded psychic freak.

But he wasn't.

'There were the death threats, madame - I understand that's been explained. From White Boy - from the mobster. I think M. Rigaud had things preying on his mind. I don't know exactly what. There's nothing more I know.'

She took particular care to thank Lenoir for his help as he left.

Australian passport, immigration visa.

Cecile went on through the brief life of Mayleen Constantinou.

Statements made to the Australian police by the parents. There had been a boyfriend, but Mayleen's mother didn't rate the relationship very highly.

'She wanted to travel,' she had told the police in Sydney about her daughter.

43

The Australian police had investigated the boyfriend. Mayleen wanted to travel, but he was the stay-at-home type. Had been in Melbourne all the time Mayleen had been in Europe. They'd been thorough - checked at the bar where he worked, checked French immigration. A solid alibi on the other side of the world. 'G.S.P.G.' was the note at the end. A phone-call to Melbourne made by Lenoir had elicited the meaning of this. 'Grief-stricken, probably genuine.'

Statement from the German girl with whom Mayleen had shared a room in Earl's Court, London. No, Mayleen had never mentioned anyone in the South of France. She wanted to go there because February was so cold and wet in London and she couldn't stand it any longer and she'd seen a picture of Cannes which reminded her of Australia. Yes, the picture had been in a travel brochure. She couldn't remember which one. Mayleen had sent a couple of postcards, one from Paris, one from Nice. Nothing from Cannes, where she had arrived three days before she was found, early one morning at the back of the Rue d'Antibes in a black plastic bag which was bursting open, by the owner of a guest-house.

Cecile paused. The police photographer had taken shots of the bag, lying open in the street. Mayleen's horrific injuries stared up at her. The face obliterated, the pubis skinned.

This had been the first time he had struck: the first catalogue of the bloody business of hacking and slashing and missing pieces of flesh, the first warning that there was a creature loose here. Nothing that could be called a man, Cecile thought, just something to be tracked and caught. Yes, think of it like that. It made it easier.

She bent to look closely at the photographs.

Chapter 9

The second folder. The second victim.

Cecile crossed the room and pulled the cord of the Venetian blinds so that the light didn't fall on the computer screen.

She had just driven through Cannes in streets that were almost empty, except for the early morning dustcarts. On a fresh morning like this, she would have liked something of her old anarchic life, to have worn leathers and ridden the bike, as she did once upon a time, but she had been warned that here in Cannes she must have an official car with bullet-proof glass.

The reason for this was not a vague notion of convention or status or theoretically estimated risk. The reason was quite specific: it lay shut away in the files in this office. Not these: not the records of torn and tormented flesh that is the work of the Mutilator, but other threats, less macabre and tormenting, less the stuff of nightmares, but more likely to come to pass.

Cecile delayed for a few minutes. She was unwilling to give up the morning. There was a small mirror hanging in the office, the kind of thing that is thought of as more of a bit of bric-a-brac than a mirror. In fact, the only object there that was not official issue was this piece of gimcrack - she wondered how it had got in. It was so well hidden in the corner that she hadn't noticed it for a day or two.

It served Cecile well enough to see herself now, so that she didn't have to go along the corridor and gaze into the cold reflection in the lavatory and washbasin provided for the judge's office. Although she had to take the mirror off the wall and hold it at an angle, because it had been consigned to that shadowy corner. Maybe that was how it came to be overlooked.

She got out a comb, checks her hair is smooth. Professional image, tidy hair. Damn it all, how could it not be, these days? Cecile had the marks of success: her hair had been cut by an expensive hairdresser with express instructions to style it so that it would cause her no trouble. And she came to work in expensive air-conditioned transport so that her hair now never got blown free in the breeze, nor sticky with the whirling dust of city traffic.

More fun in the days of two wheels, she thought, smiling for a moment, as she hung the mirror back on the wall.

She taps the computer alive, enters passwords. Warning signs flash up on the screen: she navigates them safely, puts in codes and numbers.

First task of the day: she checks her electronic notebook. Their lives were set out there, arranged partly by her clerk in this office, partly by Daniel at home, intermeshing in complex patterns, a choreography of obligations and pleasures. Daniel will take Florence to meet Louis at the station and then take the car to the garage. Cecile will collect the dry cleaning and continue to study the dossiers on serious crime which she has inherited from her predecessor. Trivia, life, death, dry cleaning: compulsions driving her on, the serious and the silly intermingled in a constant restless, relentless, series of demands.

'You chose it!' she said to herself. Meaning her life. Yet she knew this is not really true, for it was a choice that forced itself upon her. She could not reject it, could not refuse what she had wanted and needed and worked for.

Once more, she opened one of the four files in front of her.

The next woman was more predictably a victim. Not a strong young clean-limbed Australian backpacker, but someone who had lived on the fringes of petty crime. Véronique Dupuis, aged thirty-two. She was from the Cannes district. Had a kid, now aged fifteen.

Véronique was the kind of woman you might expect to end up as a murder victim. She had kept bad company: a drug habit, funded from prostitution and petty theft. Not one of the young Russian prostitutes brought in by the Chechin mafia, but an older woman, French nationality. Older, but not wiser. Conviction for theft of a tourist's handbag - the woman had chased after Veronique down the Croisette and caught up with her. The medical report, however, included analyses which showed that she was free from drugs at the time of her death and though there were injection traumas on her arms they were partly healed.

'My mum was trying to stay clean', the daughter had told Chief Inspector Maubourg. 'She said she wanted to stay off it all, anyway.' This death promised much more fruitful investigation than the last. After all, Véronique was known in Cannes, she had connections with the criminal world. Somebody called Montvallon, presumably Maubourg's sidekick, had gone into bars and hauled in known drug dealers and petty thieves.

Nothing. There had been a pimp: mugshot of one Louis Gironde, black sideburns, neck-chains, playing the part only too successfully since when Véronique died he had already been in jail in Marseilles.

Véronique was evidently part of a shoal of petty criminals, little fishes who swam in and out of the nets when the trawlers descended. But at the end she had done a spot of free-lancing, away from the companionship of the darting, drifting throng. On the evening of her death, she had left home telling her daughter she wanted to make the money for a new pair of shoes she had seen in a shop on the Rue Jean de Rioffe, off the Rue d'Antibes. 'Red, with flowers across the front.'

The shoes were still in the shop window when her body was found in a plastic bag the following morning. It was dumped in a flowerbed on the Croisette.

Bad for tourism. Very bad. But at least Véronique was a local. It wouldn't matter so much to the foreign press. Perhaps that was why there seemed to have been less investigation of Véronique than of Mayleen. The injection punctures on her arms, for instance. Partly healed - but had the process started when Gironde was imprisoned? Or had she gone on getting it elsewhere? The pimp was the normal source of supply: they used drugs as a means of control over the girls. Not that Véronique could be described any longer as a girl.

Cecile turned to the photographs. She had been strangled and then he had set about her with the knife. The mutilations in this case were all facial - to put it bluntly, Véronique had lost her face altogether.

Microscopic analysis of the wounds revealed the same knife had been used as in the case of Mayleen Constantinou. There was the miniscule but detectable notch in the blade, noted in Maubourg's summary of the four deaths, and the angle of the thrusts which had made the wounds appeared to be identical with those on Mayleen's body. But the killer had stopped there.

Véronique's wounds were confined to her face.

Why? Possibly he had been interrupted. But the pathologist estimated death had occurred approximately twelve hours before her body had been found - and it could not have been lying on the Croisette for long. There was a constant throng coming and going till the small hours - late night gamblers, dancers. Somebody would have seen something. Only towards dawn would it have quietened down.

So he would have had some hours with Véronique's corpse, but he had not inflicted on her the same extent of savagery as he had on Mayleen.

47

Chapter 10

Maubourg let himself in and crossed the hall of their apartment to the kitchen. He caught a glimpse of himself in the hall mirror. Almost a parody of the French cop, he thought: cynical, world-weary face with brown eyes and deep lines, the crumpled trench coat almost a uniform - at least the mirror didn't show the nicotine stains on his fingers.

His daughter would be back from school. Whether his wife would be home was not so certain.

But Violetta was already in the kitchen, standing finishing off a yoghurt.

Their daughter, Rachelle, was sitting at the table.

'But I don't see why she shouldn't wear it. What difference does it make?'

'It doesn't show ... well, it doesn't show respect for France. For the French way of life', said her mother, in an exasperated way.

Maubourg had been standing in the doorway of the kitchen, thinking how dark it seemed. He wished they could afford a better apartment, but Violetta had seemed to be happy just to live in Cannes when they moved here five years ago. The town had a certain image, after all, the sea was warm enough to swim in till November most years there were plenty of concerts. Those were two of Violetta's chief amusements and besides there was the TGV express to Paris, making it possible to go there just for the day if she wanted to, as she sometimes did.

Rachelle jumped up and gave him a kiss on the cheek. 'There's a Muslim girl in our class at school and she wants to wear a headscarf. They won't let her come into lessons with it on.'

Maubourg sat down at the table. The last thing he really wanted was a debate of some political or religious sort, but Rachelle was at the age when these things become of burning interest.

'But I think it shouldn't matter,' said Rachelle. 'What's important is to learn something, not whether you've got a scarf on your head or not.'

'Well, I think they should conform said Violetta. 'They should conform with the French way of life.'

'But they are French,' said Maubourg, and realised that he had been drawn into the argument in spite of himself. After a moment he was glad, as he saw Rachelle with a smile of what looked like relief on her face. She often counted on his support in domestic arguments, but was less sure of getting it in this kind of debate.

A daily newspaper, *Nice-Matin,* was spread across the table. 'Is this your school?' He picked it up. There was a blurred photograph of a group of girls, two of them with dark scarves tied round their heads.

Violetta answered him. 'No, that's a school in Nice. But it'll be theirs soon. I don't think it's good for the children, all this publicity. It detracts from their education.'

'But *maman,* this is education!'

Violetta wasn't prepared to carry on the argument. She scraped the spoon round in the bottom of the yoghurt pot.

'Go and do your homework,' she said to Rachelle, and then to Maubourg, 'I'm going out - there's a concert I'm going to with Denise. I'll be back about ten.'

'I'll come and pick you up,' said Maubourg. 'What time does it finish?'

'No, don't bother. Denise will give me a lift home.'

As the lock closed behind her, Maubourg found himself wondering yet again if his wife was having an affair.

'How can a policeman not know these things?' was the obvious question, but there was an answer to that.

Because he shuts his eyes to it. He doesn't come blundering home for a clean shirt, though he doesn't really believe Violetta would do that to him, have sex here in their flat with her lover. But he's careful never to check up on her, not to make that 'phone-call that would reveal that there was no concert tonight. He would never ask Denise when next they met how she had enjoyed the music, make sure never to do anything unpremeditated in their private world, like suddenly fishing for a set of keys in his wife's handbag. He treads warily, because to open his eyes might mean making decisions, mean having to make a choice, and then there would follow the whole pitiful process he thought of as 'dragging Rachelle into it.'

And also, because a policeman must face the truth sometimes, he knew he did not want to lose Violetta. He was still capable of being astonished by their marriage. Violetta was slender, with a cloud of dark hair round a pale high-cheekboned face. She took a lot of trouble with her clothes. He didn't think he had ever seen her in anything crumpled. He tried to think back to when Rachelle had been born - surely Violetta must have been groaning and sweating then - but the only picture he could summon up was of Violetta lying back in an immaculate white cotton dressing gown, with a small squalling red-faced bundle in her arms.

'Has there been another of those killings - the ones where he mutilates the face? I saw a newspaper placard.'

Rachelle's face was now serious, her round eyes anxious.

Maubourg swung between protecting his daughter like a piece of fragile china and telling himself that she couldn't escape reality. He'd seen too many policemen's kids go to the bad, usually with drugs, and always there had been parents who would have freaked out if their offspring had taken an aspirin too many. 'She's got to come to terms with it - it's her genera-tion that'll have to deal with the mess; we can't clean up the world.' That was what he had said once to Violetta, playing the tough guy, case-hard-ened, even when he was quaking with fear for his daughter and, in spite of what he said, he hated Rachelle to be out alone, never allowed her to go out after dark unaccompanied. He didn't even like to see the newspapers that specialised in banner headlines. Never used to care about them, but maybe Rachelle would see them, be frightened. He found himself thinking about it now. What the hell could he do about it, anyway?

He looked at his serious-minded daughter, who had inherited his own irregular features and thick eyebrows. 'Mustn't pass it on to her,' he thought. 'What I think of the human race - what I see of it. The underside. Policemen are like priests in the confessional, or cancer specialists.'

'Yes, there's been another one, but don't be worried. It's a gangland killing, like the others - they won't hurt outsiders.'

That was what he said aloud.

Rachelle got up and went into her bedroom with a pile of books.

He rummaged in the fridge and found some salami, tomatoes and olives, and, piling a plate, sat at the table and began to eat with a file of notes open beside him.

If there was one thing which an investigating magistrate should give pri-ority to, it was the White Boy file. The Mutilator was a freak, hideous, sen-sational, but White Boy was at the bottom of half the crime in the entire district. In the total load of human misery on Maubourg's patch, White Boy weighed heavily on the scales.

Chapter 11

No point in delaying, no gain in giving the mind a few more minutes respite.

Cecile Galant had arrived early again - there was no other way of catching up with her backlog of cases. Her mind was straying in the few moments before she opened her dossiers.

Then she caught her thoughts. No, not Florence. She did not want to associate even the idea of her child with the things she was about to read. There was no picture of Florence on her desk, for that same reason. Things from the outside had no place here. What went on in this room was not for the normal world. Better to keep them separate, to try and put a sterile boundary round her working life, as if she worked in an isolation hospital for diseases.

Think of something else.

The mind is begging now, longing for a postponement, twisting away from what it must confront.

Last night, they had gone to the ballet - the Kirov on tour. Spectacular, but somehow the Russian names on the programme, snatches of heavily accented French overheard here and there in the crowds in the foyer, had made Cecile think of the old South of France, the land of Russian émigrés forever expecting they would one day return. Their boxes at the Imperial Theatre, their carriages in St.Petersburg; they had been certain they would have them again, along with the violet pomades and astrakhan collars, the little Russian cakes and the silver samovars, which they could barely afford in exile. All gone now, along with the Ballets Russes, reduced to incomprehensible foreign names on tombstones in a French cemetery.

Thinking of the Russians had occupied the moments while she selected the dossier she wanted to study this morning. It was not one of the Mutilator files - there was another matter which demanded the attention of the examining magistrate.

This time, the first photograph was quite ordinary. This was not a murder file. It was taken full-frontal, the camera lens looking straight into the face of a tubby middle-aged man with dark hair. His features were very pale, highlights of shiny sweat on his cheeks and forehead appearing white in the light of the flash. She knew it had been taken with flash, because the picture suffered from a bad case of 'red eye', which would have looked quite sinister if it hadn't been so ludicrous. There seemed to be a fairly exotic background of lights and palm trees, and on the man's tuxedoed right arm was a girl with long ravelled blonde hair hanging to her waist. The glossy sheen on her, the gleam of her teeth and lips, were instantly familiar in the Cannes setting as the marks of the festival starlet.

Cecile didn't know who the girl was, but she recognised the man.

Jean-François Grandet, otherwise known as White Boy. Leading mobster, controller of organised crime, with his hands in the coffers of more bars, casinos, restaurants, massage parlours, than the starlet beside him had hairs on her head. The file had been opened six years previously, when the subject of this dossier had first arrived in Cannes, probably from Nicaragua. He was already in possession of a valid French passport. Grandet had survived police investigations and the scrutiny of several prosecutors and two of Cecile's predecessors. Traces from White Boy's web spread out in all directions: Cecile had never seen a file with so many cross-references to other cases, yet they had all led nowhere, all the related cases of drug smuggling or arms-running, even murder, all the evidence assembled against smaller fry, petering out to nothing when it got to the big boss himself. No one, but no one had given the slightest evidence that would implicate him.

It was thanks to Grandet that Cecile came to work in the special car provided to protect the magistrate examining this dossier. Grandet had a long arm ... there had been two attempts on Rigaud and White Boy was unlikely to let up on his successor because she was a woman.

What to do? The trouble with cases like this was that the initiative lay with the other side. Waiting and watching, hoping he would make a slip, that someone, somewhere, would experience enough of a grudge, a burning surge of hatred sufficient to overcome their fear and make them turn police informer, that was all the investigators could do.

In the meantime, Cecile hated being passive, reduced to a role where she could do virtually nothing. There was only one positive resource left to her and that was to scrutinise everything again, all the material her predecessors had looked at, with the most scrupulous care. Traps were set with hair-springs, she told herself, and she began the delicate business of searching for the fine and brittle mechanisms that might eventually catch a killer.

A note appended to the dossier on White Boy, with a signature at the bottom, interested her enough to try phoning Maubourg's office. There was a chance he would be in at this hour - from what she knew of the inspector, he too would like an early start.

He did.

'Cecile Galant here, Inspector. I'm reading through the Grandet file.'

His voice was cautious, non-committal. If he were surprised to be telephoned by a *juge d'instruction* at this hour of the morning, he did not betray it. She carried on.

'He seems to be at the bottom of half the crime in the district - prostitution, drug peddling, you name it. But we haven't been able to nail him.'

Maubourg saw his chance. 'He's the major crime problem here, Madame, - in reality, more serious than the Mutilator, though that attracts more publicity, of course.'

'That might seem a callous approach, Inspector, but I understand what you are saying. But we must remember that in a sense Grandet is less of a threat to a certain image - it is the Mutilator who gets the bad publicity for the city.'

Is that all she can think of, he thought, how it looks? But no point in trying to argue with her about that.

'Anyway, the problem is getting the hard evidence. He's an intelligent man, Grandet. Has eyes and ears all over the place - bribes lavishly for information. That's why... well, we've advised you to take extra security precautions.'

There had been quite a pause in that sentence. Her reputation for riding around on a motorbike must have preceded her, thought Cecile, with amusement.

'Difficult to get hold of, these gangland types. They've all seen too many movies.'

There was an answering laugh. 'You're taking on a tough case-load, Madame.'

'Varied, too.'

She could hear her clerk's footsteps in the corridor and looked at her watch. Eight-thirty. Lenoir and the secretaries would be arriving soon.

'Talk to you later,' she said to Maubourg and put the phone down. No point in having too many people know what she was studying.

Privately, she agreed with Maubourg. White Boy was by far the most serious crime problem in Cannes. But there was a race against time as far as the Mutilator murders were concerned: the deadline was the Film Festival in May. The local council wanted everything cleared up by then - they wanted to see 'Mutilator' caught - Cannes safe for tourists' in the newspaper headlines; they wanted the rich and the greedy, the young and sexy stars and the Viagra-shagging oldies, to stroll happily along the glorious boulevards of the most elegant town in Europe without stumbling over a mess of blood and guts. Or worse still, becoming one.

The third murder.

This victim broke the pattern - he was a male. Paul Barsi, a taxi-driver in his early forties. He was French, but not mainland. Born in Corsica.

Cecile scanned the page, looking for reasons. Firstly, why had this file been placed with the victims of the Mutilator?

Answer: because, like Véronique, the face had been slashed off. And apparently with the same knife.

Running her eye down Maubourg's summary of this investigation, she frowned. How did this killing fit into the picture? There seemed to be no sexual motive, no trace of sexual assault had been found. But then that had been the case with two of the others, Mayleen and Véronique, so it was impossible to infer that the Mutilator preferred women to men. Did he just get his kicks from carving his victims up, irrespective of their sex?

Barsi's life story had been investigated, laid out neatly on the paper in front of her. Conviction for drug-smuggling: sentence served, released. That had been two years previously. Barsi had looked older than his years, perhaps as a result of his incarceration. There was a police mug-shot of a thick-browed middle-aged male, application for taxi driver's licence with photo attached. He had lived with a woman, Angélique Berois, in a small low-rise apartment, where she had been interviewed by Montvallon. No, she knew nothing that could help - Paul had gone off as usual the previous afternoon. He didn't have any special customers that she knew of - just tourists mostly.

She had sobbed and shouted and sworn at Montvallon when he suggested that Barsi might have known some drug dealers.

'No - he'd given that all up! I know you never believe that, you fucking policemen, but in this case it's true! He did want a new life. He did!'

The autopsy had found no drugs in Barsi's system, except for a small

54

quantity of alcohol, which accorded with the glass of pastis and the beer Angélique said he had drunk at lunchtime. He had clattered down the stairs of their apartment block as he always did (she had cried again because she remembered how she used to tell him to shut up and not be so noisy) and the sound of his clumsy footsteps banging on the stairs had been the last time she ever heard him. He didn't come home that night.

Like Véronique, Barsi was found early in the morning. In a plastic rubbish bag.

Chapter 12

Cannes, twinned with Beverly Hills and the Royal Borough of Kensington and Chelsea, is a long way from the days of its film star glory in the nineteen-fifties. The yachts still ride at anchor in the harbour, but they no longer belong to the likes of Errol Flynn or Aristotle Onassis: they are owned now by balding, jean-clad, microchip billionaires, or dark-suited men who control the huge warring drug fiefs which sprawl out from the docks at Marseilles. During the film festival, the starlets still gather in frantic clusters before the all-devouring photographers, but it is tacitly understood that no big time Hollywood future lies ahead for the girls, only a short life of spreading open their legs for the video rollers.

But here and there, it is true, Cannes almost lives up to its hype. It keeps some traces of former grandeur, of the days when kings and moguls had ruled their retinues from red velvet couches in the orchid-filled rooms of their suites in the great hotels.

The sky was as blue as promised in the brochures, and the sea glittered as brightly, when Charlie walked out of the station and towards a waiting taxi. The Croisette stretched elegantly away, its wide spaces still comparatively uncluttered with tourists. A few well-dressed high-heeled women walked small dogs with smart little canine overcoats tied about them lest the dreaded chills of early spring bite through the blow-dried puffs of doggy fur. On the beach, a group of determined sun worshippers sat under striped beach umbrellas; something about their white skin and innocent haircuts said they were British. Charlie's taxi slid along the wide boulevard, past a big white-stuccoed hotel, with a plush carpet spread over its steps and beside them a liveried chauffeur nosing a great gleaming bonnet into an underground garage. The taxi driver spat on his thumb and jerked it obscenely in the general direction of wealth.

There was the over-the-top fantasy of the Carlton Hotel. Its twin domes were supposed to be modelled on the breasts of the courtesan, La Belle Otero, said the driver, laughing, his hands for a moment off the wheel indicating enormous pigeon-pouting scoops on his own chest.

Charlie briefly glimpsed the glittering shop fronts as they turned inland and drove up the hill towards the township of Le Cannet, and then branched off to the left. They went into a part of Cannes the tourists don't wander through and never have done - the back streets, now with Arab faces and shop signs and sometimes with posters showing the unashamed face of racism gazing down at the enemy. Prime National Front territory, Cannes, stuffed with old blonde female 'haves' clutching on with their red-lacquered claws.

'Villa Bleue, s'il vous plaît.'

The driver had known it, without an address. Not surprising, after all it had been notorious when Rosie's body was discovered there. It had been a nine days' wonder in the local press here, as well as in the British tabloids, but in Cannes the murder had been attributed to the influx of tourism and the consequent flood of riff-raff, this being understoood to include British visitors. The underworld of extortion and drugs in the South of France, although it lies behind most of the serious crime, is rarely mentioned in the local press. The conclusion in this particular case had generally been that it was a crime committed amongst the footloose expatriate community, or even among the deceased's own family, and that the murderer had proba-bly disappeared out of the country amidst the charter flight crowds head-ing for the airports. And perhaps in this particular case the papers were right: all sorts of unsavoury types arrive in Cannes every year, for events like the jazz and film festivals after all; some never leave, but drift like flies round the honey pots of fame and wealth that still cluster in the mirrored bars, the casinos and night-clubs, and anyway who knew what the English girl in the Villa Bleue might have got mixed up in?

Charlie found himself easing up on the headlong rush that had so far fuelled his journey and he started to make calculations in a colder order of reality.

He had booked the ticket from a bored woman in the Eurostar office at Waterloo and taken the train to Paris and then made another booking to Cannes.

When he had met Imelda, Charlie started to live a life that revolved round her and her alone. He had made almost a complete break with the past, with everything and everyone before Imelda. Ivor, his boss, and the others in the office where he had worked knew little about his private life. There had been a few convivial evenings in the pub with his colleagues from the publishing company, a couple of big, mindless parties, no mutual secret invitations or drunken confessions. He had been anonymous during most of his London existence - and he could effectively vanish out of it for a while. He didn't think there would be much chance of carrying on working for Ivor, anyway: he and Imelda had a terrible row one evening, and Charlie had felt he had to back her up, seeing all the time the anger on Ivor's face. London seemed a long way away.

Chapter 13

Somewhere, thought Cecile, there was a world where human beings did not drill holes in one another, or beat their children to death, or think betrayal a cheap price to pay for their next shot of heroin.

She had thought it might be Cannes, that clean, flower-filled city. She remembered coming here before she accepted the job, and walking through the Marché Forville at the Porte de la Miséricorde, the scrubbed brick floor, the stalls filled with heliotrope and mimosa. And the beaches, so clean, the water transparent, the little coloured sails of windsurfers out between the mainland and the Île Sainte Margeurite. It was, she thought then, a place to bring up a child. She had said that to Daniel, when they were in Marseilles.

'It would be so good for Florence. When she's a bit older - all the water-sports. We can't even let her go out on her own here.'

Well, there was a serpent in paradise - more than one, it seemed.

Marc Lenoir came into the office and took his chair at the other, smaller, desk. She looked up and rubbed her eyes.

No point in pretending she wasn't after someone. She couldn't hide it, when she felt hungry for finishing it, couldn't conceal the drive to get the thing done. She could still sometimes hear Louis's mother hissing at her. 'You shouldn't have had a kid in the first place! All you want is to get on!'

She'd told Louis his mother was never to come to their house again. Devastation, for a son of the bourgeoisie.

No more time to think about that. Time to start the analysis of the problem lying enfolded in the dossiers on her desk - and festering out there somewhere on the streets of Cannes.

'Marc, this White Boy business is a real hornet's nest. He seems to have his men all over the place - difficult to know where to start.'

'Yes, it's one of the plagues of the city. He's been involved in everything, pimping, theft. But mainly, of course, it's drugs.'

Cecile pushed her chair back from the desk and stretched out her long legs. She was wearing a pale-coloured fitted jacket and trousers that some-how suggested much more action than was expected in an examining magistrate.

Lenoir was nervous of his new chief, trying to anticipate which way she would jump. Would she opt for the easy life, or start digging like a truffle-hound?

'We want to get him on the drugs charges,' she was saying. 'Anything else and it's difficult to really put him away for a good long time. If we jump on him too quickly, we might not be able to get enough evidence for something serious. We need a lot more. And he's got an associate - what's his name - Caracci, is it? - who's got a record for violence. Known to carry a knife - been seen threatening a witness with it. By someone who would never testify in a courtroom in a thousand years, of course. That's not in Maubourg's report - he told me on the phone this morning.'

Lenoir thought, 'she's digging already. Going outside the reports.' Aloud, he said 'Yes, that's the problem, getting enough solid proof. There's nothing at all to connect him with the mutilations, though a lot of people would feel happier if they could be classified as gangland punishments - it would mean the tourist board wouldn't have to worry. Maubourg's done a lot of work, though.'

'A lot, but not enough,' said Cecile briskly. 'Oh, I don't mean that as criticism - he's clever, Maubourg. But we just need to wait and watch White Boy for a while yet, in my view. This dossier goes back some years, yet there's never been enough evidence to actually bring him to trial. All the prosecutors have been able to do was to refer matters for investigation. Trouble is, he's a nasty customer, isn't he?'

Yes, thought Lenoir, and anyway what they really want, the council and the municipality and all the poor sods who have to make a living fleecing the tourists, what they want is for the police to catch the Mutilator. Good and soon, well in advance of the film festival. Because if they don't do it by then, every television satellite and aerial in the world is going to beam out news from *Cannes, cité de la peur*. And White Boy and his crazy sidekick are pushing and extorting and generally terrifying the wits out of half the populace anyway. Not good for the image, not good.

'So we'd better have them closely followed, White Boy and La Guenon,' said Cecile pleasantly, and it was as if she had read Lenoir's mind. 'I'll ask Maubourg to come in and we'll get a watch put on them. Oh, and there's something else I want to look at again. This death at the Villa Bleue - the English girl, Rosie Cashel, the one whose burial I authorised. Not now, though. There's something I want to finish now.'

The fourth file. The fourth victim, killed a fortnight ago.

Jeanette Auvers, French national. Twenty-six. Waitress, from Poitou. Professional portrait by studio photographer in Cannes. Pretty brown hair, bright turquoise background. Found behind a railway bridge in the mandatory plastic bag. The most horrific mutilations of all, some inflicted before death. Strangulation had occurred after the injuries to the torso. The victim would have been then on the verge of death. The pathologist had added an uncharacteristically merciful note: by then, she would have been almost certainly unconscious through trauma and loss of blood.

There was no trace of drugs, legal or illegal. No convictions. Jeanette had been an ordinary girl from a small provincial town who had wanted the bright lights, but hadn't gone off the rails. She had got a job as a waitress, hoping that when the Film Festival came along, someone would notice her, maybe a director, maybe a star, even a lighting man - anyway, someone would see her and then there would be the stills and the rushes ... she knew all the words. But she was no fool. Meantime, she kept her head, got a job waiting tables, spent her tips on the studio portraits and sent copies home to her mother. She had been murdered three weeks after Barsi's body had been found on the Croisette. Between her thighs, a bloody skinned mess of scraped bone. No sperm.

'The last of the four,' Cecile said, picking up the white folder. 'It's getting more and more savage. But at least I've nearly finished reading the files.'

Lenoir seemed to be hesitating. His eyes were nervous behind the round spectacles. Madame, there is something more ... M. Rigaud mentioned something to me once ...'

So was the prissy little sod about to say something that would help her out?

'Oh, what did he say, Marc?'

'He thought there was a connection.'

Oh God, he was going to go all the way round!

'Connection with what?'

You're going to help me, Marc Lenoir. You're not going to keep any useful titbits from Madame so that she can go her own way to hell and mess up this case and her next posting will be some little country district where putting arsenic in a husband's tea is the crime of the century.

'Come on, tell me.'

She could put some authority in her voice if necessary.

'My predecessor didn't have time to communicate his suspicions. It is your duty to pass them on to me - to act as his executor, in a moral sense.'

That should clinch it. Lenoir thought about the idea, then started to talk again.

'He thought the case of the English girl was connected. But I don't know how. She wasn't one of the Mutilator's victims. And it wasn't ...it wasn't a very welcome idea.'

No, she could see that. A fifth serial-killer murder, and that of a foreigner, and one that would alert the British press.

'Do you have any idea of why he thought there was a connection?'

'I don't think there was any actual evidence. It was just a kind of hunch - but he had a lot of experience.'

'Yes, I suppose he did.'

There was a pause for a few moments. Whether to give any weight to something generated by the sixth sense of an old man who had died in harness?

'I asked her about it - his widow, Madame Rigaud, I mean,' volunteered Lenoir. 'I thought maybe he had mentioned something to her. But she said he hadn't said anything. The Cashel killing was assumed by everyone else but M. Rigaud to be a separate kind of thing altogether, quite different from the other killings. A jealous lover, something like that.'

Marc Lenoir sat down at his desk. He was wearing a red tie with white spots, she noticed. He went on. 'That was the simplest way of looking at it, madame. But she had a lover - and he was never charged. He's a lot older than Rosie Cashel, an English doctor. It was said there wasn't enough evidence against him.'

'Said? By whom?'

'I don't know, madame. Not by Chief Inspector Maubourg.'

There was no doubt about it. He was tipping her off.

Lenoir is a friend, she thought. And then, with her usual caution.

Perhaps.

She picked up the phone on her desk, pressed the numbers.

'Chief Inspector? I'd like to talk to you. No, not here. Meet me at the entrance in half an hour, would you?'

Lenoir looked across at her, but he said nothing. She turned to the computer and tapped in Rosie Cashel's name.

Then she took a set of photographs out of a file and was splaying them across her desk. 'When I started, I never liked looking at these' she observed. 'But I must have seen hundreds now - you do get hardened, you know. You need to make a real effort to take in just what you're looking at. How old was she - eighteen, I think. Yes, that's right.'

Close-ups of marks in the skin of a young neck. Close-ups of a slim oval face with staring protruding eyes.

'At first we thought it was routine,' said Lenoir. 'Maubourg thought it would be cleared up in no time - she had a boyfriend who strangled her in a fit of passion - something like that. At any rate, it's nothing to do with gangland killings - there was no involvement with drugs or sex or anything like that. And there was no evidence of a knife-attack, and no damage inflicted like the mutilation victims. In fact, there didn't seem to be any possible suspects - she didn't have any men-friends, except that doctor, I remember. She was seeing quite a lot of him, according to gossip. He's a good twenty years older, but some young women like that.'

'Ah, yes, Dr. Durrant. Now, did Maubourg really have a good look at him, I wonder?'

'He had an alibi for the time Rosie was killed. He had attended old Arthuis, just across the road from the Villa Bleue. The old man passed away and on the day Rosie Cashel died, Durrant called in to talk with the old man's niece, Monique Arthuis. Durrant was still there when Rosie Cashel's body was found.'

'It was found by the housekeeper, Antoinette Ferrier, wasn't that it?'

'Well, she's not exactly a housekeeper. She used to come in and clean and do some cooking for Rosie Cashel's mother when she stayed there. I believe she still keeps an eye on the place.'

Cecile had jumped up and was already buried deep in the filing cabinet. She wasn't really listening to Lenoir, he sensed. 'Any reason why Monique Arthuis should lie to give Durrant an alibi?' she threw over her shoulder.

Damn, he thought, she's really going to work her guts out. And mine too. But he was faintly amused. This one's got a mind as suspicious as mine, he thought.

'No, none that we could find,' he called out as he subsided into his chair.

'And there was no forensic evidence to connect him with Rosie Cashel's death.'

'Better go through this carefully.' Her voice came muffled, out of the depths of the cabinet. 'I want to open a new dossier on Durrant. I want to know everyone who was involved. And the names and details of everyone who was living near the villa when the girl was killed, no matter how harmless they seem - even the brother, who was in London when she died. I want to make sure everyone's been checked out.'

There didn't seem to be any need for an answer.

'This brother,' said Lenoir. 'He's here in the city now - the police had a tip-off from a taxi driver.'

That got through. She spun round.

'Maubourg can start with him, then.'

Chapter 14

The taxi drew up outside the villa and Charlie paid the driver and pressed a few more notes into the outstretched palm. It wouldn't do any harm, he thought obscurely, to get the driver on his side, just in case there should be any enquiries about his movements. A heavy tip might just earn a little discretion. He walked up the overgrown path of the Villa Bleue.

He had a key in his pocket. Martin had given it to him, after Rosie's death. 'Here, Charlie. You'd better have this now. There's not much in the villa, of course, but it comes to you in the end.' On the last visit, the one where he had identified Rosie's body, he had scarcely noticed his surroundings.

He thrust open the stiff front door, which swung suddenly on its hinges. A scared stray cat fled from the garden as the door banged back against the porch.

Within, the shutters were drawn and the villa lay in darkness. He flicked a switch - the electricity was still connected. He walked over parquet, splintered at the edges, through the empty uncarpeted hall and into a small sitting room where there were one or two battered armchairs that had presumably never been considered worth selling. Beyond this lay the kitchen, where a big green and cream silver-finned fridge, on inspection, seemed to be still in working order. At any rate, it started with a judder when he switched on the plug. It was empty, though. He would have to get in a few supplies from the nearest *supermarché*.

Upstairs, the front bedroom still had a wide old-fashioned double bed, the springs shot to hell. Charlie decided he didn't want to make his headquarters in that room.

At the back of the house was a small bedroom for a maid, with a window which gave out on to the garden and a magnificent view of the sea. A salty marine breeze blew inland, a reminder that even in Cannes the sea was real sea and not just a cinematic backdrop. Out in the bay the Îles de Lérins glimmered in the distance, green and remote from the crowds as the Islands of the Blessed and the distant murmur and washing of the sea drifted up even here.

The room had a blond wood bedstead, a reasonably comfortable and very chaste looking narrow mattress and there was a duvet in a cupboard.

The bathroom washbasin was yellowed and grimy, but the water splashed out of the tap, discoloured at first but running clearer as he washed. He wiped the spotted mirror clear of grime and his face stared back, thin, stubble-cheeked, the grey eyes tired, the black hair flopping lop-sidedly.

It looked a suspicious sort of face, even to himself.

He looked more closely into the mirror, remembering that Imelda, the most utterly unreliable witness a man could fear to have on his side, had been his only source of an alibi when Rosie had been killed. Had they seri-ously suspected him then? He hadn't inherited anything directly by Rosie's death - everything went to Anna as the next of kin - but he might reason-ably expect to get Rosie's share along with his own, in due course. And even in its present state, a villa in Cannes must be worth - what? The equiv-alent of half a million or more.

His brain whirring round and round like a piece of maddened machin-ery, Charlie gloomily contemplated his reflection before pulling off his tie and shirt and falling on the bed in a sort of exhausted relief.

It was evening when he woke in the maid's bedroom, and the sky had a mauve light, in which the worn paintwork of the Villa Bleue seemed less conspicuously dated. Indeed, as Cashel had walked up the path, the deep evening sky and the dusty lavender blue wash of the walls seemed to merge into one another, part of the same world, the same extraordinary skyscape of intense violet-blue.

Charlie didn't know where he was at first; he had only confused mem-ories of tearing up the steps at Waterloo, of a wakefulness and the fear that kept him awake, and then of a collapse like an animal in a den.

Now, he splashed his face with water and made his way downstairs, rub-bing his stubbled cheeks. He needed a shave, had picked up some dispos-able razors and a can of shaving-cream at a pharmacy and had got in some supplies - baguettes, pâté, a bottle of red wine and one of the corkscrews he had noticed thoughtfully hanging adjacent to the wines in the nearest shop, so he had the basics. He'd got a torch too, in case the electricity at the villa gave out - he wasn't sure if the bills had all been paid to date.

On the way to the shops he had passed a *tabac* kiosk. There had been some screaming headlines on a local newspaper: '*Cannes, cité de la peur!*'. 'City of fear' seemed overstating the case, but from what Charlie could make out, the serial killer had been at work. '*Mutilation des victimes*' was easy enough to understand. For a sickening moment, he wondered if it could have anything to do with Rosie's death, but then shut out the thought. Rosie had died quite differently.

He went in to the kitchen, opened out the wine and rinsed a dusty glass under the tap before filling it from the bottle. Then he tore off a hunk of bread and rummaged in a drawer to find a worn wooden-handled knife for the cheese and put the rest of the food away in the huge refrigerator, which was built like a bunker, with a heavy door that clunked solidly shut and a deep throaty purr that had replaced its initial precarious juddering into life.

There was a sound outside. Somehow, it seemed furtive. Charlie stepped out into the hall.

Someone coming up the dusty path, past the dried-up cacti and the overgrown tubs. Shoes scraping gently, shuffling.

A key turning in the lock.

He waited in the hallway. Who else had a key? Martin? No doubt the French police, perhaps the agent who was selling the place?

The light clicked on and flooded the dim passage with yellow. He, Charlie, must appear as a dark outline at the end of the hallway.

'*Qu'est-ce qu'il y à?*' came a woman's voice.

And then, hopeful but frightened:

'*M'sieur le docteur?*'

The figure stumbled against the wall of the hallway.

It was a small round woman, dressed in black, wearing a red nylon head-scarf.

She was plainly terrified and was uttering small shrieks, muted because she was panting with fright.

'*Non, non, madame, n'ayez pas peur!* No, no, please don't be frightened. It's all right. I am the ... the brother of Mademoiselle Cashel ...'

And you, Madame, he realised, will have been asked by Martin to visit the villa at intervals, to tidy up and keep everything in order, so that no overflows or infestations or other calamities befall a future inheritance. Martin, keeper of the family values. He was a good sort. Mustn't knock him. Would he help about the Imelda business? Maybe.

He helped the woman into the sitting room, sat her down in the chair, offered to get her ... to get her what? There was nothing in the kitchen stores at the Villa Bleue.

She was vaguely familiar, now that he could think about it a bit, could cast his mind back over the years to when he'd visited here, stayed in the Villa occasionally, come back here from the beach, his teenage lusts hopelessly fuelled by the women. There had been an occasional presence in the background, carrying piles of wet sheets in an old wickerwork laundry basket - yes, that might have been the younger Madame Ferrier, someone who had been just a shadow ministering occasionally to the needs of the household.

She was calming down, but a piece at a time.

'Yes, madame, you are absolutely right and I should have warned you of my arrival, and I'm sorry to have alarmed you, but you see I did not have your address or telephone number...'

Or even your name, he thought, but did not say it aloud. It might have made her unnecessarily suspicious. Why did not the brother of Mademoiselle Cashel know who was taking care of the villa on behalf of the family?

Subsiding, she began to speak more calmly, and she was now uttering some formal-sounding phrases. Charlie, whose French was not much above the level of basic tourist, suddenly understood that she was offering her condolences.

'Quelle tragédie, m'sieur! Mademoiselle était si charmante!'

Yes, he supposed, Rosie had been charming. He had never thought of that, of the way in which she could create affection in those around her, of her concern for the details of other people's lives, their pleasures and sufferings. I didn't realise it, he thought. How rare it is.

He stumblingly offered Madame a glass of wine, and this time, by pausing effectively as if her name were on the tip of his tongue but just mislaid for the moment, 'Madame ... madame ... excusez-moi ...' impelled her to supply it.

'Ferrier, M'sieur. Madame Ferrier, Antoinette. M. Hollingsworth asks me to see that all is in order here - he is a lawyer, no?'

Yes, Martin would have made some sensible arrangement, but he hadn't told Charlie the woman's name. Now he recollected it clearly: he had heard it from the French police when he had come to identify Rosie.

'Madame Ferrier - wasn't it you who found my sister... You knew her?'

'Not really, not very well, but I used to call in sometimes to do occasional things - washing -' her arms pantomimed washing, scrubbing, - 'that sort of thing, and then I came with some clean things ... and yes, I found her, poor little thing, lying on the path outside this house. I knew death when I saw it, Monsieur Cashel.'

Her eyes were filling with tears. Charlie didn't want to hurt her any more with the memory of what must have been a devastating discovery. He tried to change the subject.

'I don't think you were here, madame, when I used to come here years ago? And I don't think I met you, when I ...'

'When you came to Cannes the last time.'

After Rosie's death, she meant. But he had scarcely made any effort to see anyone, had been in the hands of officialdom, the police, some magistrate, virtually all the time.

Rosie had probably been on first name terms with this woman. Rosie would have learned her name first thing and never forgotten her.

He managed to reassure Madame Ferrier that she had no cause for alarm, that he would be looking after the house for a few days. She still seemed suspicious and he could not blame her - after all, a murder had taken place here, and the killer had never been discovered. He drew out his passport and showed it to her, pointing to his name. Relaxing, she began to ask him how long he would be staying, what he needed.

'Madame Ferrier, could I ask you to do a little shopping and so on for me? If I paid extra, of course. Do you think you could find me some shirts - nothing special?'

She smiled, understanding as he ran a finger round his rumpled collar. She got up and came round to the back of his chair in a maternal sort of way, to look at the size on the shirt label. When she sat down again he thought that now she had a sympathetic look in her round brown eyes. Perhaps she pictured him as grief-stricken.

Thinking of Rosie, he suddenly found that he was.

Chapter 15

Carol Bassett heard the creaking of a chair in the room next door.

Was he going out? Her hand reached for the phone.

The partitions here were so thin; if you knocked against them, they sounded hollow, like being in a cardboard box. She was rummaging about for a biro in the sliding drawer in the top of the secretary's desk, but it didn't contain anything, only some old Treasury tags and dried-out elastic bands.

'Carol - I'm expecting someone. I'll let her in.'

Just as well. She had that will to type out still - he didn't like it done on the word processor. Anyone would think he was really middle-aged, he was so pompous. Bit of grey in his hair. Could be distinguished, just looked old. Couldn't be more than thirty-five, but he usually made such a show of having someone show the clients in. At least he'd started calling her Carol.

The buzzer sounded, squawking, but nobody said anything into the microphone. Footsteps, soft on the new carpet.

She didn't like to open her door before the woman went past, though she was curious. She'd been temping here for three weeks and he didn't seem to have a woman around.

Voices next door.

'I just wanted to ask you ...'

Then too low to catch, but at last the woman, loud enough to hear.

'No, I don't know where - I haven't seen him since. It's all right - I just don't like to think about it too much '

Then murmuring, and suddenly Mr. Hollingsworth's voice, quite aggressive.

'He didn't give it to you? I thought he might have left it with you.'

'No, I haven't got it ...' Almost indignant.

Carol's phone rang. Another firm, wanting to arrange a meeting.

When the client had gone, the temp expected Mr. Hollingsworth to get her to open a file, for the notes he had made during the interview. That was the usual procedure, but she had guessed already that this wasn't a usual client, because Mr. Hollingsworth seemed a bit red-faced. Angry, not embarrassed.

'Shall I open a file?'

She was curious now.

'No - it was just one thing she wanted to ask me about.'

Liar. If anyone had done the asking, it had been him, judging by the sound of their voices. But she wasn't going to let on she had heard the words. Well, of course she must have heard something - it would have been impossible not to - but not what had been said. She wouldn't say anything about the words.

He was quite a big man. Attractive in a way, but wouldn't waste much time, she thought. She could sense his body, bulky beneath the blue suit, hot in anger and warmth. Expensive suit, expensive voice. But his chin always looked bristled by this time in the afternoon, little glints of stubble on the skin. You'd have to shave twice a day before I'd think about it with *you*, boss.

She looked at her watch. Half-past five. Her mac was hanging on the coat-stand just inside the door. Her office was so tiny it was almost impossible not to touch against him if she wanted to go past.

'Can you stay on next week?'

'Yes Mr. Hollingsworth. I haven't got anything lined up.'

'Ring the agency. Tell them I don't need a French-speaking secretary any more.'

But she hadn't said she'd stay on this evening.

Perhaps he realised that.

'Ah, that was the last appointment, wasn't it?'

There was a slight pause.

'Do you want to go for a drink?' he said unexpectedly. 'There's a pub called The Cardinal - '

Yes, she knew it. All red plush inside. Probably called that because it was round the back of Westminster Cathedral, and the clientele looked like it. Bunch of sobersides in dark suits.

She'd been there with Simon, when he picked her up from work. He stood out in The Cardinal like a sore thumb. She could see the men in the bar, men like Martin Hollingsworth, looking at him, thinking 'rough type'.

Yes, but Simon didn't help himself. He looked full of skinhead aggro, even if he wasn't. She was moving on beyond him, somehow.

She didn't have to hang in with this one, though, not any longer than she wanted.

She thought about it.

Chapter 16

There was a slamming against the front door of the villa and a barked command echoing through the hall.

Charlie, alone in the house after Madame Ferrier had left, promising to help him out, didn't have time to get to the door. The lock was smashed open and suddenly the hall was filled with two big men who dragged him outside, his arms pulled painfully behind his back, the elbows thrust upwards in to the small of his spine. Another man was pounding up the stairs and he could hear doors slamming, shouts, footsteps banging up and down the staircase. He had the vague impression that there was a thin black-clad man standing at the bottom of the stairs, shouting orders. He heard the snapping of metal and felt the cold of handcuffs biting his wrists; dragged almost off his feet, he stumbled out into the street and into a waiting black Citroën.

There are two kinds of cops on the Riviera. One kind deals with the daily flotsam of tourism: the stolen credit cards and passports, the undesirable drifters with nothing to steal, the drunken starlets thrown out of semi-respectable hotels. This kind is fairly tolerant and inclined to be philosophical about human nature. They see no point in inflicting much more injury upon the slightly damaged human goods with whom they come into contact, who are mostly petty criminals or fleeced innocents.

Then there's the other kind.

The other kind deals with the endless drug war, has thugs constantly in its sights and outraged citizens perpetually on its back, lives with an underworld of beatings, broken faces and kickbacks, and responds as best it can. Usually with more of the same.

The cops who had Charlie were this kind.

He tried to say something, to ask who they were. An identity card was thrust under his face.

The man who had been directing operations in the villa was sitting next to the driver. He twisted his head back and hissed 'Later!'

The cop sitting next to Charlie on the back seat reinforced this with a powerful slap across the face.

The car tore upwards through the centre of the town, across the super

72

highway that sliced it in half, and headed towards the township of Le Cannet. They passed the shopfronts of any French suburb - Crédit Lyonnais, Le Métropole snack bar. Only a glimpse of the absurd Hollywood-style plaster caryatids on the front of the Cavendish Hotel, their cream paint peeling, their breasts and armpits darkened by the grime of passing traffic, evoked the sleaze and fantasy of Cannes.

There were smart *Résidence* apartment blocks, then cheap high-rises, then dusty oleander bushes on a central reservation and a long stretch of used car lots, *Renault Occasions,* electric pylons marching along the land-scape, and then suddenly the car swerved off the main road and swung into a police station.

This was very different from the place where they taken him after Rosie's body had been found. That was a building on a corner close to the seafront with grey shutters, immaculately clean, more like an ordinary house almost. This was a small concrete box; it could have been in any town anywhere in southern France. Blue uniforms buzzed around the front, but there was a back entrance, and the Citroën swung round the building and pulled up with a jerk. The men who had Charlie rushed him up the steps, past a giant photograph of Chirac and into an tiny office where an elderly air-conditioner unit churned away laboriously. He was cuffed to a chair on one side of a desk covered with a sea of papers, with a computer screen blipping away at one end. There was a painful institutional cleanness about. Through a glass partition Charlie could see a blue-bloused policewoman sweeping the floor.

A big man sat down on the other side of the desk. There was no need for him to give any orders. He was totally in charge in the little concrete box, in absolute control of his territory, like a judge in his courtroom, like a director on his filmset.

Like a torturer in his torture chamber.

Charlie wished he hadn't thought of that.

The man stared at Charlie for a few moments. 'Why did you break into the villa?'

His English was good.

Charlie felt his stomach churning and a sharp knifing pain in his guts. To be honest, he thought to himself, I am shit-scared.

He tried to recollect what he knew of the French police. This wasn't the gendarmerie. *Sécurité?* Responsible only to the Ministry? That or the *police judiciare* - the serious crime squad. And this man's rank - he had a nasty feeling that the more anonymous the appearance, the higher the rank.

He managed a few words, his mouth dry.

'I didn't break in.'

At that point he realised there was a cop standing behind his chair. Realised it forcibly, because the cop pulled on Charlie's handcuffed wrists so that they twisted over a bar on the chair-back. The effect was flaming pain of such intensity that it suggested that wristbones would start cracking any second.

'No - for God's sake! The villa belongs to my family! The key's in my pocket. And my passport - look at it!'

There was a rapid burst of French from the man on the other side of the desk, the grip on the wrists relaxed and the cuffs were taken off.

'Empty your pockets'.

Moving his hands carefully so as not to inflame the ache again, Charlie pulled out the contents of his pockets and tipped them awkwardly on to the desk.

He looked straight across into a face which showed plainly that this was indeed the other kind of cop.

A big man, heavy-jowled, wearing a blue check shirt.

Behind him, pinned up on a noticeboard, Charlie read the words: '*Déclaration des droits de l'homme.*'

'My sister ... my dead half-sister, the one who died - her mother owns the Villa -'

Suddenly, Charlie knew that he had seen this man before. When he had gone to the morgue, to identify Rosie's body. He couldn't remember much of that journey, just that a police car had driven him straight to the morgue, that he had been asked questions by that other, clever man, Maubourg, wasn't that his name?. There had been other people, an interpreter, a doctor, a civilian from the office of the *juge d'instruction*. He couldn't remember any of those faces, all composed into blank masks of formal sympathy, just going into a place like an operating theatre and seeing Rosie, utterly white and lifeless. But he thought this man had been there somewhere in the background, perhaps Maubourg's sidekick.

Now the face leaned forward threateningly.

'You should have informed the police of your presence already.'

This seemed no time to debate the niceties of mutual rights granted to EEC citizens. Charlie said nothing. He hoped his posture indicated abject apologies and kept his mouth shut.

'What are you doing here in Cannes?'

Charlie didn't know what to say. 'Running away' might be the truest answer, running from the whole mess in London.

'I came to .. to clear some things up at the Villa'. The photograph seemed suddenly just too absurd, too tenuous to explain - what had it to do with the Villa, after all?

'What things?'

'Just to see if there were any... any family things left there, before it was sold. We were thinking of selling it. I thought there might be something that had been ... been overlooked.'

He hesitated over the last word, wasn't sure if the other would understand it. But he did.

'You think the French police might have overlooked something, M. Cashel?'

'No, no, I didn't mean that.'

The man didn't bother to ask what Charlie did mean, as if it were beneath his notice. He signalled contemptuously.

There was a rapid bark of French. Charlie was taken away from the desk, his possessions still strewn over it, and led stumbling from the room.

'*Dépannage*' -a calendar on a wall. A corridor, a cell, a grating.

Now he was nothing. A man in a cell. No identity, unless his captors chose to give it back to him, and it was no longer his, it was spread out in scraps of pasteboard and plastic, over the desk of the interrogator, in that stifling office.

He tried to think over the situation. They would surely have to let him go very shortly - once they were satisfied about his identity and that he had a right to be in the villa. But of course they might well get in touch with London - with Martin, whose firm would be on record as the legal representatives of the owners.

Martin! Perhaps Martin could help him here. Charlie didn't know any French lawyers or anyone like that in France. Maybe the police could phone Martin. Find out his story was true.

Then he remembered Imelda, and all the stuff stashed away. No, best keep silent about London, about Martin, about everything there.

The door of the cell opened and a big uniformed gendarme appeared, dragging a thin brown-skinned man by the shoulder. The man was dressed in a long blue robe. The gendarme slung him across the cell, and as an afterthought stepped over and kicked him hard in the ribs a couple of times. The man screamed.

The policeman turned his attention towards Charlie, who felt his stomach churning with physical fear. He tried not to shrink away. The Arab was moaning. Blood trickled out of his mouth and onto the concrete floor.

The gendarme spat in the general direction of the Arab. He beckoned, and Charlie willed his legs to take him a few steps across the floor, was handcuffed again, pushed along a corridor, and finally stumbled back into the little office.

There was a different man at the desk, and now the sea of papers seemed to have been cleared up. Charlie's possessions were in a small pile at the front.

Maubourg's crumpled narrow face was peering at him.

'Sit down, M. Cashel and I hope you will be a little more willing to cooperate that you were with my colleague, Montvallon. We have met before, you know, when you came to make a statement about your sister's identity. Let me remind you: I am from the *police judiciaire* - what you might call the C.I.D. I am Inspecteur-Principal Pierre Maubourg - a Chief Inspector, that would be the closest.'

Charlie managed to muster up some element of self-respect and demanded:

'Why have you brought me here? And you have no right to put me in a cell!'

'On the contrary, Monsieur Cashel, I have every right. I can in fact imprison you for twenty-four hours without even informing anyone in the world of your whereabouts.'

Maubourg paused while this sank in. It was getting hot in the little room. He got up and went out from behind his desk to a water-cooler, its transparent blue sides glistening with chilled condensation. Maubourg pressed a steel nipple and let iced water flow into a paper-twist cup, tipped back his head and poured the water down his throat in one swift gulp. Charlie watched him thirstily, but did not dare to ask for water himself.

Maubourg added as he sat down, 'Besides, there is a new *juge d'instruction* - a new examining magistrate - on the case, the one who released your sister's body for burial.'

'I hope he's up to the job.'

'She, M. Cashel. It is a woman and I assure you she is more than `up to the job.' But your sister was the victim of the most serious crime of all, murder, and you will realise that the matter of her death is still open. We have not closed this case, you know, although I am very well aware that the English newspapers have criticised us for not carrying out a proper investigation.'

Charlie tried to say something to the effect that he did not doubt the efficiency of the French police.

Maubourg cut him short.

'M. Cashel, I am not interested in your opinion. Frankly, I don't give a damn for what you think. But if someone commits murder on my territory, then I do give a damn, as you say, and I don't let it go. If I can find the murderer of Mademoiselle Cashel, then I assure you I will, and compliments or insults are going to have no effect. Now, let us not be naïve, M. Cashel. You, of course, are a suspect. Your alibi was investigated, but it depended on ... ' he leaned sideways and tapped the computer screen, 'on the woman you live with.'

Perhaps he had trouble with the name, an idea which obscurely gave Charlie hope.

'And she, of course,' continued Maubourg, 'cannot be regarded as an unbiased witness.'

Charlie bit his lower lip as his mind followed inexorably along a train of thought.

No, Imelda wasn't an unbiased witness, that was quite true, in fact she was probably useless as a witness of any kind, especially as he had finally walked out on her.

There was even a possibility that he would be locked up right now, only in a British gaol instead of a French one. A thief, a receiver of stolen goods, in England. A murderer in France? Did this man seriously suspect him of having something to do with Rosie's death? If not, why was he being treated in this way?

He tried to concentrate on what Maubourg was saying. It was late afternoon now, and the low rays of sun that slanted through the blinds of the little office were dusty with dancing flecks and motes. The Frenchman seemed to be feeling the heat, though it was still April. He took his jacket off and swung it on the back of his chair, then leaned forward to the computer screen as if now in earnest.

'No, M. Cashel, the rest of your alibi is not so strong, is it? Your sister was killed in the early hours of a Sunday morning. You were at a party till late Saturday night - that was what you said - but when the British police checked they couldn't find anyone who remembered seeing you after eleven o'clock. There is a *Train de Grande Vitesse* that would have got you to the South of France in the early hours of Sunday morning - or you could have crossed over by hovercraft and picked up an express train that would have arrived in Cannes about the same time on Sunday morning. And nobody saw you again, apart from your Miss Imelda Shoesmith, till you went to work on Monday morning.'

He looked down at his notes. 'Your *patron*, he seemed reluctant to help you, M. Cashel. I have it noted down here.'

Yes, sure Ivor had been reluctant to help. And not just reluctant - incapable. They had all been as pissed as rats at that party, Charlie wanted to shout. They wouldn't remember it if I'd stuck coconuts on my balls and danced the Black Bottom after eleven o'sodding clock.

And as for Ivor, my bloody *patron*, he's not going to put in a good word for me, not after Imelda made a laughing-stock of him.

'You stood to inherit a large sum, surely? The Villa Bleue - any property in Cannes is now worth a very considerable amount. Oh, your sister's share would not come to you directly, but after the death of your step-mother-'

Aloud, Charlie said cautiously, 'No! I didn't cross to France that night - I didn't kill my sister, whatever you think, Inspector.'

'Don't tell me you were devoted to her - considering how little you saw of her that would be too much!'

'No, we weren't very close any more - we'd grown apart - but I didn't kill her. I didn't wish her ill. I never wanted any harm to come to her!'

The statement sounded weak, empty. Did it ring true?

Charlie rubbed the palms of his hands over his face and felt sweatier still. Were they going to keep him here until they had rigged up a case against him on this side of the Channel, so that Maubourg could have his clear-up rate all nice and bright and shiny-looking? Was that the way they did things here?

Maubourg was shuffling the documents on the desk. He splayed a handful out with his thumb over the one on top like a conjuror forcing a card on a victim.

'What is this, M. Cashel?'

It was the photograph of the cemetery. Charlie had forgotten all about it, the reason why he had contemplated coming back to Cannes in the first place.

'I don't know ... I have no idea. The photograph was sent to me...'

'Do you know where it is?'

Charlie shook his head.

'No - there was no letter or anything with it.'

'Perhaps it is someone who thinks your sister is buried there?'

'For god's sake, I don't know anything about it. I had the photograph through the post, that's all. I've no idea who sent it.'

'The photograph? Just by itself?'

'Well, the film - the roll of film. I had it developed in London. All the other negatives were blanks.'

'Where was it sent from?'

'From here. There was nothing else in the envelope, but it had a French stamp.'

Maubourg stared at Charlie for a few moments. It was an intimidating stare, direct, challenging. 'If you are a liar' said that stare, 'I'll get you for it in the end. I'll get you.'

He would too, Charlie thought.

The other got up, walked round the room. Charlie felt the prickles standing up on the back of his neck. Maubourg was more alarming when he was just out of sight.

Maubourg's voice continued: 'I know where this cemetery is, M. Cashel. it is two or three kilometres outside Cannes. It was once a cemetery of the local *quartier*. Before this city was so big, before all the tourism and the film stars. It is part of the old Cannes. You have never been there, to the cemetery?'

'Never.'

Maubourg came back round the table, rubbed his jaw, leaned back in his chair and contemplated Charlie in silence.

Then he pushed the pile of documents towards Charlie and poured out a sequence of orders in fast French to a gendarme who stood at the doorway. The man moved aside.

'You are free to go, M. Cashel. For the moment.'

There was no suggestion that he would be taken back to the villa in a police car.

The petrol-laden air of the busy highway outside the police station seemed like the wine of freedom.

He found himself in a remote working class district, seemingly a dormitory town for the army of drivers and pimps and postcard sellers who ministered to the tourist population of Cannes.

Eventually a bus came along.

Madame Ferrier was in the house.

'Oh pardon me, M'sieur. I brought some things for you.'

On the table were a carton of milk, some sliced ham, a blue shirt still in its wrapping. 'Thank you, Madame, that's very nice.'

He sagged into a chair. No point in alarming her by mentioning the police. But there was something she might know about.

Charlie drew the photograph out of his pocket.

'Do you know where this place is, Madame? This cemetery?'

She took the photograph and held it out in her hand at arm's length, as if she were long-sighted.

'Excuse me, M'sieur, I do not have my spectacles. Yes, I know it. It is about two kilometres away. An old place - no one is buried there now. It was all before the tourists came to Cannes, you understand. Just an ordinary cemetery, like in any other town. Did you go there?'

'No, Madame, I have never been there.'

'Then how did you get such a photograph, may I ask you?'

'It was sent to me in the post, Madame. I do not know who sent it.'

She handed the photograph back to him. 'But, M'sieur Cashel...' She was hesitating.

'Yes, Madame, what is it?'

'There are many bad people in Cannes now. I think - it would be...' she was searching for words now ...'very unlucky to have such a photograph sent to you. Of a burial ground, you understand. There are many people here who ...'

She made the absurd cinematic action, melodramatic yet frightening, something from television, yet something from real life, of aiming and firing an imaginary gun with her right hand.

Cashel understood. There was plenty of organised crime on the Riviera - apart from gambling, there were the drugs barons, who would not hesitate to dispose of any inconvenience, such as perhaps an English witness who might have accidentally crossed them in some way. Was that what the picture of the cemetery represented - a death threat?

He looked out of the window and saw the dark shadow at the gate. It had been there since he had got back from the police station.

'Don't worry, Madame' he said. 'You could almost say I've got police protection.'

Chapter 17

'What do you think about her?'

A shower of grey ash fell from the overflowing chrome ashtray. Montvallon leaned sideways and wound the car window down a couple of inches to throw the stub out.

'About her?'

'About Mme Galant, of course. Our new boss.'

'She's all right.'

It sounded abrupt, and Maubourg amended it. 'She works hard.'

He knew Montvallon was looking sideways at him.

'For Christ's sake, don't watch me. If you mean, do I want to fuck her, I bloody well don't. Keep your eyes on the street.'

Montvallon said nothing. Damn it, thought Maubourg, he doesn't mean anything by it.

Does he know?

He caught a glimpse of his own face in the mirror as he turned his head away from Montvallon. The fool throughout the ages. The horned man. The cuckold.

Perhaps they all know in the department. It's the kind of thing they gossip about all the time. Other men's wives, who they're screwing, why doesn't he walk out on her, poor sod's the last to know. Are they laughing at me?

Maybe I should leave her anyway. Her body, white, thin, someone ramming his prick into her, in a room somewhere, anywhere, as soon as she can get out and away.

Somewhere in a quiet street a door is opening and Violetta slips inside. Can't see his face. They'll be running upstairs, can't wait. Maybe they're doing it right now in daytime, the shutters closed.

Have to stop thinking like this. It's madness, this kind of jealousy, where you scratch the itch all the time.

'Montvallon - you got a cigarette?'

Montvallon passed his chief a packet of Camels and a folder of matches.

Maubourg struck a match, spat out a fleck of tobacco. Have to find out the truth, his policeman's mind said to himself. We can't go on with these deceptions, Violetta and I, deceiving ourselves as well as each other. Rachelle will be going away to college in a couple of years; perhaps it won't hurt her as much as I think.

He turned to Montvallon.

'What's the surveillance rota?'

'On Cashel, chief? One tonight. Voisin.'

'Tell Voisin I'll be at home if he needs to make contact. Let's get on with it here.'

'Why are we taking Cashel so seriously? All right, his sister got killed, but he can't have done it - that's why you let him go, no? Everything points to Durrant, the bloke she was having an affair with - it was just a one-off, surely, only we couldn't prove it. She rejects him, he's overcome with jealousy or rage - strangles her. We don't need to use resources following the brother, he's not a priority problem like the Mutilator.'

'It makes it convenient to keep them separate - the Mutilator cases and all the other crime in Cannes. Life is messier than that, Montvallon - and so is death, for that matter.'

'You looking for a connection, then, boss?'

'We need to keep it in mind as a possibility. That's what I'm saying.'

And there was that photograph that had been sent to the Englishman, of the cemetery. He had believed Cashel when he said he had no idea of where it came from or where it was. There was something about it that suggested danger - maybe just the obvious, that it was a gang warning, like a mention of a cement overcoat in Chicago. Watch it, or you'll end up in here, something like that. It was just too much of a coincidence that the Englishman should be mixed up in two separate mysteries in Cannes - one the death of his sister, the other that photograph. There must be some connection between the two.

But how to articulate all this complicated train of thought to Montvallon? To himself, even, it was something more sensed than explained.

The hot leather smell of the interior of the Peugeot, Montvallon's interminable cigarettes.

Ahead stretched the road leading to the Villa Bleue. Some time, Charlie Cashel, released, returned, refreshed, would come walking out of the driveway and set off down the road.

A long road to walk down.

For him and for me, and at the end of it, maybe, the life broken apart.

Must face it. Have to find out.

How? Spying? Surveillance? Bug the phone? Bloody stupid, a policeman who can't even detect his own wife in adultery.

It's so easy, really, to catch someone out in the lies, the deceptions, the excuses. If you want to, that is; Maubourg had done it a hundred times in interrogations. Sweat them, let them feel safe for a moment, then turn the pressure up, know everything about them, get inside their heads ...

Do it to Violetta?

Get it out of your head. Look at the street, stop running a film inside your head.

There was a large poster for the Front National opposite. Maubourg turned to stare at it and Montvallon gestured in its direction. 'He's got a point, boss. Just because there's a few blacks in the World Cup team doesn't mean to say we want the rest.'

Maubourg felt tired, too weary really to counter this monstrous illogic. After all, thirty-odd per cent of the French population apparently agreed with Montvallon.

'As long as you don't let it interfere with your work. Keep it out of the station.'

But was that possible? Wasn't hatred a kind of seeping poisonous vapour that couldn't be sealed off into a separate compartment?

'There's no support.'

He hadn't realised he was speaking aloud.

'Yeah, there is, boss, we can get back-up, plenty of it.'

Montvallon spoke in surprise, and his chief didn't answer. They sat in silence and waited.

Chapter 18

Charlie had elicited from Madame Ferrier instructions on how to get to the cemetery - *'le vieux cimetière'* as apparently it was known. Early the following morning he went out, as Cannes was awakening with its customary champagne hangover, as the croupiers nestled in their crumpled beds and the rich called for room service in the five-star marble palaces along the Croisette, as wallets were checked and splintered fragments of memory painfully reassembled. As the Arab cleaners who kept Cannes from floating away in a Sargasso sea of its own ordure and the stall-keepers who supplied its workers with hot coffee and sliced sausage all went about their tasks in the briefly fresh morning air, and the market in the Rue Forville filled up with flower-stalls full of tulips and heavy sweet hyacinths.

Cashel caught a white-and-blue local bus going out of town and away from the coast. The bus was almost empty. All the traffic was heading into town, or down to the beaches.

He thought that no one was following him. Anyone who did would be conspicuous in the extreme. As conspicuous, he realised, as he was himself.

As Madame Ferrier had instructed, he took the bus to the end of the line, an anonymous square with a few shuttered brick and concrete houses and some stumpy plane trees. Nothing was stirring, except for an old tabby cat who settled itself on a wall near the bus stop. Presumably that would be its snoozing-post for the rest of the day.

There was absolutely nobody about.

He started to walk.

'Take the road out of the square to the right of the bus-stop,' Madame Ferrier had told him. 'Then you have to go about two kilometres down the road. The cemetery might be locked - I don't know. It's so long since I went there. It has ...how do you say...?'

'Railings?' Charlie sketched with his hands in the air.

'Yes, I think so. There is a gate, a little distance from the road.'

The road was empty. For the first half-mile or so it was lined with small modern houses, each with neat white curtains. Charlie plodded on. There was something else he had meant to ask Madame Ferrier, but it had slipped his mind for the moment. He carried on walking. There were trees lining the road on both sides to give shade, but it was facing due east and the rising sun was shining directly into his eyes.

This was a long way from modern Cannes. It was possible to imagine traditional funeral processions making their way out here in the past, a horse-drawn hearse, mourners in black. Charlie sensed that under the tanned and glossy skin of the Riviera lay an older France, simpler, poorer, slower. Buried now. Entombed in concrete. Times had changed: he thought he could hear the distant whine of a moped, that perpetual late twentieth-century background accompaniment to Mediterranean life.

He looked up, shielding his eyes, and saw that off to one side of the road there was a patch of greenery, with an elaborate wrought-iron gate sunk deeply into entwined ivy.

As he turned off the road, he looked behind him. Still nobody.

The gates were nominally locked. That is to say, they were padlocked, but the lock was rusty. He did not need to force it, however, because the railings were broken down near the gate and it was easy enough to climb through, over the tangle of bushes and ivy that had grown up in the gap.

Once inside, Cashel oriented himself. A path led along from the main gate and following it he suddenly saw the view in the picture. A line of cypresses in the background, and here, in the foreground, the white slabs of tombs, sticking up out of the overgrowth.

He pulled the photograph out of his pocket and studied it. Yes, there was the line of trees, and here in front of him a row of tombs leading off the path to the right.

He hesitated, staring at the names still legible in the lichen-covered marble. There was nothing that he recognised, no name that struck upon the chords of memory. 'Marie Lemoine ... 23 ans....le 4 novembre, 1872... Pierre Daniloux... Angélique Daniloux... la famille Corsi...

The innocent names of the past, the dates mostly in the last century. The latest he could see was 1926. Nothing he recognised, yet there was nothing else to do but to chance that something might connect up, somewhere. He began to note down the names on the tombstones, picking out the ones on the slabs that were recognisable in the picture.

He moved on, towards the trees, and heard a scraping sound behind him, as perhaps of an iron gate that had sunk down on its hinges and was being forced open.

86

Spin round, nothing there. Of course not. Imagination playing tricks.

Get to the trees. The sun high now, hot on the back of the neck.

The trees - something moving there? Damn, can't see, shadows too deep.

Again, a sound.

Charlie instinctively began to run. He couldn't help himself, like an animal that has been so alert for danger, with every muscle strained and waiting, that it moves automatically into a flight triggered off by subliminal signals.

Shouts and running feet.

More running.

His lungs bursting, gasping like a hooked fish, his feet pounding along the overgrown pathways, stumbling and slipping, catching in overgrown brambles, yet someone staying there all the time, catching up with him, right behind him at last as he made one final leap and twisted forward like a crazy thing.

Then waves of bursting pain flooding outwards, the sensation of falling, the pain worse as he opened his eyes to a world that had gone lop-sided.

Chapter 19

There were voices over his head.

There was nothing he could do now.

He tried to get up but the pain was too bad to fight.

He sensed he was being partly raised up, partly turned where he lay on the ground. His left eye-lid was lifted and allowed to fall again, which from where his mind had retreated, seemed a relief.

There were two men standing over him and he felt himself being lifted up bodily. He stopped struggling. Now more movement, more lifting.

'M. Cashel, you should take more care. We try to guard our tourists but we cannot anticipate that they will wander round in such solitary spots - what do you say 'off the beaten track', is it not?'

His head was still a furnace of pain but he recognised the voice, though he opened his eyes reluctantly, wincing at the bright light.

Inspector Maubourg. They were in a car; Cashel was half sitting, half-lying, in the back; Maubourg was twisting round from the front seat to talk to him. Cashel sensed, rather than turning his head to see, a big and powerful form next to him, which smelt of Gauloises and a leather jacket, so there was at least one more French policeman in the car. The car started to move off in the direction of Cannes.

'My men were obliged to stop you when you did not answer us.'

'They were following me? It was your men who hit me?'

'Montvallon has rather - what do you say - a heavy hand, is it? You did-n't stop when he called after you and he doesn't like that. But M. Cashel, what did you expect? You are here for no very good reason, in the city where your sister was murdered. You are in my territory - what I believe my counterpart in Britain would call my manor, is that not so? Naturally, I want to know what you are doing. Don't be naïve. But it may be very for-tunate for you that the police were here - after all, your sister was the vic-tim of a killer and there is a possibility that you yourself may be the target for a murderer.'

'But why? Why should someone want to... want to kill me?' Charlie was still feeling waves of agony through his head. He was never again going to believe those scenes where the hero gets hit on the jaw, shakes his head and leaps back instantly into the fray. Being hit is hell, he told himself, and it doesn't go away. You get hurt and you stay hurt.

'It could be that someone resents your family owning the Villa Bleue - or it could be that they think you know something about your sister's murder. The killer of your sister is still at liberty, still free to kill once more.'

Charlie shifted, winced, reached in his pocket and found a handkerchief. Blowing his nose seemed to reactivate a fresh attack of red-hot needles stabbing through the top of his skull, but it did seem to clear his vision. Maubourg had his head thrust over into the back of the car and Charlie was suddenly aware of the intelligence in those restless eyes.

'So there are some good reasons to fear for your safety, M. Cashel. But if there is another reason, apart from casual theft, then you must have some ideas. No man comes close to a murder without having some notions about it. You came back to Cannes for some reason connected with your sister's death. You went to that cemetery. Surely it is a place of no interest now - there are a few local people who have relatives buried there, but otherwise no one ever goes there. Your sister's body was taken to London, was it not? I remember distinctly, because the magistrate and I had to agree there was no reason to keep her body in France for further investigations. What interest do you have in this cemetery?'

'It's the place in the photograph. Madame Ferrier - the cleaner at the Villa - she recognised it and told me how to get there.'

'Ah, yes, the famous photograph that was in your pocket.'

There was a pause. The car had slid back through the town. Then the driver braked. They were outside the Villa Bleue.

'Get out, M. Cashel, book a flight as soon as you can, get back to England.'

Charlie remembered what Madame Ferrier had said - that the photograph might have been intended to be a kind of threat, a symbol of what would happen to him if he came to Cannes.

'You think the photograph is a warning?' he asked Maubourg.

The detective rubbed his hand across his face wearily. 'If someone is after you, M. Cashel, I don't have the men to protect you. I have too many drug dealers, too many missing people ... I tell you this to convince you there are dangerous people around. Don't get mixed up in anything - don't try to solve anything, like some idiot English Boy Scout. Just get off my territory - get back home.'

Charlie got out of the car, lurched up the path of the Villa Bleue like a drunk making for home.

There was a rapid conversation inside the Peugeot as they watched the Englishman turn his key in the lock and disappear into the interior of the house.

'Put him on a flight, boss?'

There was a pause.

'No, if he won't go of his own accord, let him be, for the moment. He's a stubborn one - either that, or there's something worse waiting for him at home in England. There are some things that take patience, you know that? You can't solve everything by kicking shit out of Arabs, Montvallon.'

Chapter 20

Charlie got some painkillers from the local pharmacy, swilled them down with whisky, fell into a deep sleep and woke to see dusk descending. He still had a savage ache in his head but the miniaturized inquisition torturers had departed from his skull.

He washed in cold water, peering in the mirror at a long cut and graze over his forehead. There was some disinfectant in the bathroom cabinet and he dabbed at the cut wincing as the stinging liquid trickled into the gash.

Downstairs, he made some coffee, got out some ham, bread and olives and sat down at the bare wooden table in the kitchen. There was some hard thinking to be done and however little he felt like it, it had to be done now. He had a life to fight for - a life outside prison bars, whether in France or England.

Maubourg, first. He had recognised the cemetery when he had seen the photograph at the police station. Charlie could visualise the heap of possessions taken from his jacket - passport, wallet, credit cards, keyring - and amongst them the shiny colours of the photograph, lying face upwards on Maubourg's desk. But he had said nothing about the name of the place - Charlie had found out where the cemetery was from Madame Ferrier.

And Maubourg could make him leave the country right now, if he really wanted to. All he had to do was to take him to the airport and put him on the next flight. By far the simplest way of dealing with a damned nuisance of an Englishman causing trouble on his patch.

So why hadn't he done so?

Because, whatever Maubourg said, he was after something? He - or this new magistrate - wanted an arrest.

So Maubourg needed more evidence.

So he was going to let Charlie run loose till he got it.

'Have to get there first' said Charlie, to his thick head. 'Where?' said the head. 'Get where?'

Suddenly, something floated up through the mists. He had forgotten to ask Madame Ferrier something. Now, perversely, in spite of the blow to the head, he remembered what it had been. Perhaps the jolt had set something off.

He woke up and realised he'd fallen into a deep, heavy sleep. When Madame Ferrier arrived, he was sitting at the kitchen table waiting for an ancient coffee percolator to boil.

They sat at the small table in the kitchen. Madame Ferrier had come in with bread, milk, cleaning stuff. She was very solicitous about his head, advised him to go to hospital, that he must have an X-ray (the word was oddly recognisable), and insisted on making him some lemon tea when he absolutely refused to go, though he didn't do this very convincingly. Shaking his head, he discovered, still brought on a wave of agony. But he managed to ask the question that had come into his head just before he fell asleep.

'Who was it, madame?'

'Who do you mean, M'sieur?' countered Madame Ferrier.

'When I arrived here, you said you thought I was somebody else. I think you said 'the doctor' - was that right?'

Madame Ferrier suddenly looked uncomfortable. Her face seemed even more concerned and anxious.

'I thought it must have been a doctor who came to look after Anna - my stepmother - when she was ill. But then I realised that was not very likely - it must have been years since she was here. So it was probably someone else - someone you had seen here more recently.'

Madame Ferrier moved uneasily on her chair.

'Non, M'sieur, I assure you - it was nothing. Just a mistake on my part.'

There was something about her manner which seemed almost pitying. Was it something which also said 'don't dig any deeper: this will cause you pain?'

Cashel had never listened to inner voices.

'Please tell me, Madame. Who did you think it was?'

She put her cup down on the bare little table. There was a pause.

'M'sieur, I thought it was ... Doctor Durrant.'

She pronounced the name carefully, giving the 'rrr's' their full, Provençal rolling sounds. Charlie was not to be certain that it was an English name till later, when he saw the nameplate beside an entryphone.

'An English doctor?'

'Yes, he is living nearby. He lives a little way along. Just a little way.'

There was something in the way she repeated the last phrase that made Charlie understand.

Madame Ferrier was indignant now. 'He was attending the old man, Monsieur Arthuis, who lived in the house opposite. Dr. Durrant used to come once or twice a week to see Monsieur Arthuis, just ordinary visits, no one thought anything of it. But then he started to visit more and more often, and we all noticed it - the niece, the gardener. Dr. Durrant would call at Monsieur Arthuis' house for a few minutes and then he would come across the road here to the Villa Bleue, as if Mademoiselle Rosie were a magnet for him, as if he could not stay on the other side of the street from her, even. It was truly shocking, M'sieur, the way he behaved, in my opinion. Your sister was only a girl, after all. But he - ah, I have no trust there at all. He has not at all the proper manner for a doctor. And no discretion - he came here to this house at any time, night or day ... that was why, when I saw you, your shadow in the hall, I thought it must be him.'

'He has a key, then?'

'I understand he was to send it back. To Mademoiselle's family. I don't know if he did that.'

'Where does he live, Madame?'

She became agitated. 'Oh, no, please M'sieur...'

'It's all right, I shan't make any trouble. Too late for that. But ...' he thought of an excuse ... 'there are some documents she may have entrusted to him.. family papers ... I want to ask him about.'

This seemed to work, presumably reassuring her that Charlie was not about to stampede round in the role of possessive male relative enraged at his sister's seduction, and beat out the good doctor's brains with his bare fists. In any case, in his present condition, Charlie doubted if he could beat out the brains of a sea anemone. He didn't know the French for sea anemone, so could not convey this thought, but the general state of affairs must have been pretty obvious to Madame Ferrier.

'Family papers? Family business is important, Monsieur Cashel, that is quite right. Well, I suppose you could find out quite easily where Doctor Durrant lives, in any case,' she said. 'He lives in the Hôtel Fleurie - along the coast a little way. We all thought he would move after ... after the death of Mademoiselle. But he stayed. Monsieur Arthuis' niece, who inherited his house, she thought Dr. Durrant would surely not remain in his apartment nearby. But he did - like a dog that hangs around the place where its owner used to live! A grown man, almost an old man, imagine!'

Chapter 21

The Hôtel Fleurie was anonymous, its only character derived from wrought iron balconies overlooking the street, which was ten minutes walk away from the Villa Bleue. It was not a hotel in the usual sense of the word, Charlie realised, more a *Résidence*, a block of furnished apartments, the kind that might be taken on temporary short-term lets, for the summer season.

There was a buzzer and a nameplate. Dr. R.D. Durrant.

The buzzer worked.

'*Qui est là?*'

The voice distorted, the accent rendered unrecognisable by the squawkbox.

How did one say these things? 'You were my sister's lover. Someone killed her.'

'My name is Charles Cashel.'

He thought the squawk-box had blown a fuse. There was no sound for a few moments. Then:

'I'll be down in a minute.'

How does one pass the time, whilst waiting for one's dead sister's lover to descend? Charlie kicked and scuffed at the gravel, saw curtains and blinds tipping suspiciously upwards and sideways. For the first time, he became aware of this area of Cannes not just as a perch for passing tourists but as a real place, where people lived behind their curtains and conducted their lives and muddles and got mixed up in what their neighbours did. The town that he had always taken as a pleasure ground, as a filmset, had a three-dimensional life after all, a life that could trap its inhabitants as effectively as any place on earth. Pain, snooping, gossip - all these ingredients of ordinary life were inescapably here in Cannes as elsewhere.

He listened to the sound of descending footsteps. If there were a lift, Dr. Durrant preferred to keep fit. Either that, or he was delaying the moment.

A tall, thin man, much older than Charlie had imagined, wearing an expensive cashmere pullover. His hair greying at the temples, immaculately trimmed, nothing so naff as tinted, just too well cut. An ageing playboy, not very successful at disguising the passage of time. And yet he looked lean and fit, ranging easily along the street. Perhaps that was what had attracted her, to a man twice her age.

Charlie thought of this man with Rosie, and tried to disown a kind of protective jealousy, totally unexpected, that was suddenly hitting him worse than the blow over the head.

They went to a bar. Durrant ordered the drinks, first asking Charlie's preference with politeness. Charlie didn't care, asked for a beer. The glasses were set down on the little round marble table with a scraping chink. Durrant had thick wrists and powerful forearms, a strong exercised body. He spoke first.

'Why did you come here?'

The voice was pleasant, that light voice that comes from the upper chest, the well-mannered vowels of the southern Englishman. But he had wasted no time whatsoever.

'What do you do here?' countered Charlie, and he did have a real curiosity about it. The man seemed a paradox. 'I mean, there must be plenty of doctors here already.'

'I have a medical specialty. I treat sporting injuries - tennis sprains and so forth. I have a good practice with young players.'

Charlie said 'So it lets you pick up kids like my sister?'

'No!' said Durrant, forcefully. And then, 'If you come here making accusations like this I'll sue you! It's a very serious offence to blacken a doctor's reputation, you know. Is that all you've come to do - be abusive?'

Charlie took the picture out of his pocket and set it down on the table. It was getting a bit tatty now. The contrast between this expensive bar, with its marble-topped tables and designer steel décor, and that homely café in Victoria where he had first seen the photograph suddenly made Charlie absurdly homesick for London.

'Somebody sent me this. Is it anything to do with Rosie?'

Durrant gazed impassively at the photograph. His face had long lines, but possessed that well-turned tan that comes to sporting types in a good climate. He spoke carefully.

'I've never seen this picture before. I believe it is a cemetery somewhere near here - I may have driven past it at some time, I suppose. But why bring this photograph to me?'

'I think it has something to do with Rosie's death.'

'Rosie's death.'

He repeated it after Charlie.

As he repeated Rosie's name, Durrant's outer appearance seemed to crumple. The well-groomed man-about-town vanished. To his amazement, Charlie saw Durrant putting his head in his hands. He looked old now: not a youthful and well-preserved forty, tanned, exercised, but a middle-aged man nearing fifty. Charlie thought he recognised grief. Grief is ageing.

Durrant seemed unable to speak.

Charlie said nothing for a few minutes, then found himself launching into a tirade.

'You and Rosie were lovers, was that it? She was only eighteen years of age - didn't you think about what you were doing to her life? Good god, you must be at least twenty years older than she... than she was.'

Charlie listened to the sound of his own words. It's all wrong, he thought. I'm behaving like a pompous forty-year old fool, and this middle-aged man is the idiot in love. He felt like a naïve nitwit, the Englishman out of his depth, the innocent abroad. Yet he could not stop the fierce protective spurts of feeling that overtook him when he thought about Rosie.

Durrant stood up.

'I don't have to listen to you, Cashel. You had no place in her life anyway. What claim did you have on her? I don't know what the hell that photograph is about, but I had nothing to do with Rosie's death. I told the police everything I knew that might help them get her killer - if I knew who did it I'd chop the bastard to pieces with my own hands. Anyway, what has this to do with the photograph? There's no connection at all, is there?'

No, not on the face of it. Only that it had been sent to Charlie from the town where his sister had been murdered - and where the only people with whom he had even the remotest links were those connected with her.

Durrant threw some money down on the table and walked out. The canvas awning flapped in the breeze as the frosted glass door swung shut behind him.

Charlie gave him a few minutes. As he followed him out of the door, looking down the long tree-lined street, Charlie saw Durrant turning the corner at the end. The doctor didn't seem to be returning to his flat. He was making in the opposite direction.

Chapter 22

The fat man in the white suit was wheezing as he walked across the bar to the chrome table and lowered himself into a leather armchair behind it. His jowls were black with stubble but his face was a bleached pale colour, the folds of flesh falling like small soft pillows over the stiff collar at his neck.

'Shut the blinds' he said angrily. A ray of sunlight had slanted through the window opposite to strike on his cheek. He took it like a blow, an insult.

A man moved rapidly in the dim depths of the room and pulled down the cords; the blinds sealed up into solid shields against the light. White Boy was allergic to sunshine: it brought out rashes that mottled the vast moon-like expanse of flesh that was White Boy's face.

'We had to warn him once already, said the red mouth beneath the jowls. White Boy had absurdly small and dainty lips. 'He's undermining our business.'

'Shall I finish him, boss?'

Caracci, otherwise called La Guenon, or the female monkey, as he was known for reasons of sexual insult, was leaning forward opposite White Boy. A thin bristle was growing through La Guenon's shaved scalp. His real name was Jean Caracci. He hated *les cons*, he hated *les arabes*. He said these things frequently. No one knew anything else about him.

'No, no, - he can still be useful to us, if he learns his lesson. And compensation. No, not revenge - the best compensation, Caracci, is money, though I know you don't think so. As for the Englishman - well, leave him for the moment, anyway. Watch him - where he goes, work out what he's been told. Then we'll know who to go for.'

La Guenon leaned forward, his heavy-booted feet planted wide apart.

'He's been talking a lot already, boss - the Englishman, I mean. Couldn't get near him at the cemetery for coppers - Maubourg practically had his finger up his arse.'

Caracci wore an old ex-British Army paratrooper's jacket, not clean.

White Boy tipped his weight away, more comfortably to one side of the chair. His fat thighs bulged under the suiting that covered them. It was still only late spring, but already White Boy felt the heat of summer approaching; he changed his suits two or three times a day in the height of the season. Had to: the cloth around his thighs and over his back became drenched with perspiration after a couple of hours. The air conditioning never seemed cold enough for him.

'All the same, we'll have to make sure no one else talks to the Englishman.'

White Boy said this quietly, leaned forward and smiled.

There was a pause.

'We'll have to issue some warning.'

La Guenon stared back hopefully.

'Wipe your mouth!' added White Boy, disgustedly. 'And I still want the girl. Either she's got it or she knows where it is. I'm entitled to compensation, you know.'

He leaned forward and began smiling at his own forthcoming joke.

'I've got a business to run, after all!'

Chapter 23

The Arthuis house across the road from the Villa Bleue seemed unoccupied; in fact it was for sale. There was a noticeboard outside bearing the name of an agent in central Cannes.

The house was larger and in a much better state than the Villa Bleue, and Charlie did not think that it would take long to be sold. He walked past, up and down. A big white house, the paint fresh and clean, with elegant pale grey shutters; the gardens, much grander than the scrubby little strawberry-patch at the Villa Bleue, would have the mandatory view of the bay from the top of the hill. Green branches that would soon burst into brilliant flower trailed over the shutters and the lintel of the doorway. There was a gardener clipping the edges of the lawn; no doubt he was retained in order to make sure the grounds would appear in good shape to prospective purchasers. And from the front of the house, there would be an excellent view of the somewhat overgrown environs of the Villa Bleue and its peeling paint, though the two houses did not face each other directly.

The curtain had definitely twitched, Charlie decided. He walked across the road and gazed idly up at the house opposite, at the windows on the first floor. Bait for the curious.

Sure enough, there came again that tell-tale flick of the white edge of the curtain.

The doorbell sounded deep inside the house. The gardener gave him an openly curious glance, but then turned his head away. The house, after all, was for sale: strangers calling casually at the door were only to be expected. 'But,' Charlie asked himself, 'do you really look like the type who would casually purchase a property on the French Riviera?' He had to confess to himself that he did not, and tried to wear the relaxed air of a crumpled and eccentric millionaire.

'*Excusez-moi, Madame*, the house is for sale?'

He rehearsed the line.

She would know that he wasn't telling the truth, of course, if she had really been doing her stuff as neighbourhood watchdog, for she would have seen him going in and out of the Villa Bleue. But he was gambling on one fact - that her curiosity would be greater than her caution. And the gamble paid off. When she opened the door, he could practically see her whiskers quivering.

If Charlie didn't look the type to be buying a few million pounds worth of house, Monique Arthuis didn't look the type to be selling it.

She was a short, square-faced woman, with a beige powdery complexion and a knitted suit. A dry sweetish smell as of stale cake emanated from her. She did not invite him in, but spoke very forcefully and repeated it so that there should be no misunderstanding. All arrangements to do with the sale were to be made through the agents.

He asked her if she spoke English. She did, rather stiffly. No, he could not see the house. 'All arrangements concerning the sale...' She added, rather rudely 'Anyway, monsieur, you are a complete stranger - I have no idea who you are.'

Charlie thought she might have every idea, but they both continued to keep up the fiction that she never peeked through the twitching curtains.

He took a risk.

'I am acquainted with Dr. Durrant, Madame. Dr. Robin Durrant. Perhaps you know him.'

'Non, scarcely at all, M'sieur. That is to say ... in his professional capacity only. He attended my uncle in his last illness.'

There was a long pause.

'I do not know Dr. Durrant well, Madame - I have an elderly relative myself who is thinking of moving to the area. Would you recommend this doctor as a medical man? Where could I find him?'

She sniffed. The question had been risky - she might have learned from some local grapevine that Charlie had seen Durrant already.

But evidently, she was not suspicious of the question. It was not difficult to read her thoughts - they were reflected in the conflicting expressions that flitted across her features. Charlie was a stranger, some restraint should be exercised, but she could not resist. The lure of imparting scandal was too strong.

'Not so long ago there was only one place where you could always find Dr. Durrant. The Villa Bleue, across the road. I am surprised you haven't heard about it.'

'No, I know the Villa Bleue, but he comes there no longer, madame?'

'No, not since the woman there died. Not the old lady - the young one. Couldn't leave her alone - disgusting for a doctor, such conduct. However, I must mind my own affairs, M'sieur - I am not one to be always watching everything - oh no!'

'Does Dr. Durrant have many patients here?'

'Oh, no, why should they go to him? Sometimes he has an English tourist who cannot speak French and turns up here, or he has to interpret at the hospital if there has been an accident. My uncle, of course, was a foolish old man in many ways - I think he was the only French patient of Dr. Durrant. Still, at least the English are white like us. France is full of blacks now. It isn't safe at all, not anywhere. That young girl was found murdered quite recently! Such things in Cannes! You have to blame them on the foreigners. Anyway, Dr. Durrant attended my uncle, Monsieur Arthuis, till he died.'

Evidently, from her manner, the woman expected Charlie to be somehow *au fait* with these facts which she was revealing. He did not betray his ignorance.

'Ah, yes, your uncle...'

'Yes, Monsieur, my uncle insisted on having Dr. Durrant, even at the end! He liked to practise his English with the doctor, that's what he said. What on earth was the point of practising English - he would never go to England again! He would never go anywhere again and that was the truth! But Dr. Durrant used to come along this street to see him almost every day - at least, he used to say he was going to see him, but I didn't believe it for a moment - well, he probably called in, but really, he was going to see that girl at the Villa Bleue - the young Englishwoman, the one who was killed!'

Here, she shuddered. 'Oh, that was horrible, Monsieur, I don't stay in this house alone. No, I have a friend here - we are always within call of each other.'

If Monique Arthuis was cautious of strange men, that didn't seem to impede her willingness to go on talking away to a complete stranger, now that she had the bit between her teeth.

'Imagine, the police haven't got the man who killed the girl. He might still be around, you know. Oh yes, it was just across the road. No distance at all. So it was a good excuse for the doctor, you see, that he was making professional visits. It's no wonder Uncle Antoine died of a heart attack - between the doctor who never stayed more than a minute or two and that terrible drug addict of a housekeeper... I'm sorry to say it but those English people ... well ... they ..'

'Your uncle's housekeeper was British?'

'Didn't I say so? And a drug addict as well! There was a real colony of them here. I have to say, Monsieur... Monsieur...'

'Cashel'.

That stopped her in her tracks.

She stared voraciously, doubtless scanning him for emotions to report to her friends with the next bulletin of gossip.

'Then you are ...'

There seemed nothing more to say. She stammered into unreal apologies and he sensed that she was glad she had spoken her mind about the dead English girl - glad that she had not known then that she was speaking to her brother and so been obliged to restrain herself. Her formal expressions of regret dwindled into murmurings, and finally, her curiosity evidently still ravenous from the way her eyes were fixed on his face, Monique Arthuis forced herself to pull the door shut.

As he walked away from the door, a brisk middle-aged woman in a suit, the material far too thick and heavy for the time of year, strode round from the back. She gave him a curious, long look and then produced a key from a pocket, opened the front door and slipped inside the house.

The friend, presumably.

Chapter 24

'It's empty, the villa? It's for sale?'

Charlie didn't care any longer if he appeared a total idiot, considering that there were notices plastered all over the gateway. He might as well play the mere English innocent, who had naturally fallen into conversation with the gardener after Mademoiselle Arthuis had refused to let him in the house, had kept him standing on the doorstep.

They conversed, Charlie in stumbling French, the gardener with the broad strong accent of the region.

'Evidently, Monsieur, the villa is for sale.' He was probably not a forth-coming type in normal circumstances, a spry man with a wrinkled acorn-brown face and a rather military little moustache, standing practically under the À Vendre notice.

But he was glad of a break, stood up and rested his arms on his hips.

'How long has it been for sale?'

'Oh, a few weeks, I think it is.' He scratched his head. 'The old man, he died and his niece, she does not want to stay here. She only moved in a week or so ago - she is here to clear the house out, that's all.'

'Yes, yes.'

This was low-grade gossip. Charlie had heard it in the pâtisserie where he had stopped to buy some rolls. 'Yes, Madame, I'm staying at the Villa Bleue'... 'Ah, Monsieur, the price of houses round here now, you wouldn't believe ...' Old man Arthuis was dead and his niece would sell the house ... the woman behind the counter had made that gesture of rubbing the thumb and forefinger together, so that metaphorical cash registers rang joyously in the air. Plainly, the niece was not especially liked around here.

Again, Charlie got the sense of a little community surviving in these shops and flats, the beleaguered stubborn ordinary life that clings on beneath a town given over to tourism and the surreal industry of film. There were people here who sold bread and knew their neighbours' busi-ness, who patiently weeded the gardens of the rich all year round, who lived here month in and month out whatever the season.

'The house must be worth quite a bit,' he offered to the gardener as a gambit.

'Oh, yes, Monsieur. The niece, she will do very well. But to speak truth, I do not care very much for the lady, Mademoiselle Arthuis. The house-keeper, now, she was a very nice person to work for ... always polite, very considerate... and yet when you come to think of it, she was a bad one. Ah, it's funny, isn't it, M'sieur, the honest people are not always the most pleas-ant!'

'What was the problem with the housekeeper? I heard there was some-thing...'

'Something indeed!'

He produced a crumpled packet of Gauloises, offered it courteously and when Charlie did not accept fumbled out a flattened cigarette, then lit it with an ancient lighter produced from somewhere in the depths of his voluminous blue overalls.

'Drugs, M'sieur. Even here, in this house.'

'What did she do?'

'They said she'd taken some from the old man. I don't know what - some sort of tablets she could sell. It's usually heroin - of course, that's when there are the dealers involved.'

Charlie's heart sank. He had enough of women inclined to criminality with Imelda.

'She is an addict?'

'Oh, I never saw any signs of it, M'sieur. She always seemed normal enough with me. But what is normal, in this city? The croupiers in the casi-nos, are they normal? The vedettes - the film stars - are they? No, nothing is normal in Cannes any more - we have no normal life left, you might say. This is a city in a film, not a real place. But it was the way she got the stuff that shook people.'

He became more confidential now, dropping his voice.

'But I shouldn't say these things! The niece, she resents having to pay me for the work I do here anyway! Her friend - Mademoiselle Rolland, I feel sorry for that one! Don't know why she stays with her - unless she has to. Although, frankly, I think there is more to it than money - those two women are ... well, I don't have to say it, do I? It's even fashionable now! Oh, it's a tolerant place this, Cannes - a good place for them to come to. No, I don't think I can say any more ... perhaps I said too much ...'

It was blatant, but by now Charlie was well and truly hooked. A hundred franc note somehow found its way from his palm into some discreet flap in the overalls.

'You were saying about the housekeeper ...'

'Well, she took the drugs from the room where he lay dead. She went in there when his dead body was lying there and took some things from his bedside table! Can you imagine? That woman must have the heart of a murderess. There was a terrible scandal ...'

'But how ...'

'How did they find out, seeing that there was no one else in the house! That you may well ask! It was the niece. She noticed that some tablets that should have been given to the old man were missing. After the old man died, the niece moved in as fast as she could - checking up on her inheritance, no doubt. The housekeeper was packing her things. And she didn't get anything from his will, although she'd looked after him for two years or more - and the niece had hardly been near him all that time. But they found the drugs in the housekeeper's bag. And she got clean away with it! You know, the police didn't even charge her. Too soft on foreigners, that's my opinion. Anyway, everyone knew about it. It was common gossip, you might say. Everyone round here knew. But she didn't have the decency to go home, the housekeeper! Shameless!'

'You mean she's still in the area?'

'Oh, yes, on the other side of town, living in some terrible place, full of Algerians. In the Rue Caillebotte, I think, or thereabouts.'

'What is her name - the housekeeper?'

But his memory had suddenly failed him and was revived only by the happy discovery of another hundred franc note magically transferred to the palm of his hand.

'It's a British name - perhaps you know it. At least, they said she was British, though the name is like the American president. Vashington. Miss Vashington.'

Chapter 25

Outside the Hôtel Fleurie a long black Peugeot slid discreetly into the kerb. The windows were of tinted glass and the occupant of the back seat was a blurred large white shape, slumped indolently into the leather upholstery. The car was carefully parked so that it was in the shade of the plane trees along the street. All this had been achieved at a leisurely pace, but then the front passenger door opened and with a very quick movement a bullet-headed man clad in army fatigues slipped out, stretched his legs in a long stride or two and rang one of the neat row of doorbells at the entrance to the apartments, and slid back into the car.

There was a screech in the entryphone as the bell was answered, and the watchers in the car made no move to respond to the urgent questions that emerged from the grille above the bell. But they had no need to do so: the entryphone fell silent, and curtains in the apartment above were jerked sideways as a face looked nervously out to see what was in the street below.

'He's looking out the window for us, boss,' said the skinhead to the shape in the back. 'Must have a guilty conscience.'

There was no answer, but the figure at the back of the car wheezed a little, which might have suggested some mirth.

There was still someone looking out of the upstairs window as an arm emerged from a rear window of the Peugeot and a hand beckoned downwards almost idly. This hand was plump and its rings flashed in the sunshine; it described an arc leading back to the car in a leisurely way.

As if jerked by marionette strings, the figure at the window started to move back into the room, its shoulders stooped as if it knew it was embarked on a hopeless journey, that the hand waving imperiously from the car was implacable.

Dr. Robin Durrant emerged on the pavement. He hovered for a moment on the doorstep, looked desperately back as if seeking safety inside the entrance hall, then reluctantly stepped out and into the dusty warm spring day. He had only three or four paces to go to get to the car, yet he seemed on an eternal journey, moving slowly, slowly as he dared. But at last the slow-motion steps brought him up to the car and then suddenly the frames speeded up and there were a series of rapid flickering movements as the car door opened and the skinhead's hand shot out and gripped the doctor's upper arm, pulling him down and off balance so that he almost fell into the Peugeot.

Inside, there was a blind down across the glass partition between the front and back seats. Durrant could not see, only sense, a large presence in the back of the car. Scents reached him, something of lavender and hide from the back of the car, a powerful stench of sweat from the man beside him, who was wearing an old khaki sweater tied round his waist. Sweat, and something else, Durrant thought, something he didn't want to think about.

'The boss told me to ask you a couple of things,' said the heavy slow mouth.

Durrant said nothing. He shrank back against the seat.

'He doesn't want to say anything himself,' the voice went on, and then it laughed. 'Not yet. So I've got to say things for him. He made me learn them off by heart. I'm stupid, you see. Stupid in some ways, like. Not with everything.'

A tattooed fist shot out and grabbed Durrant's lower jaw, and it was holding the entire stretch of the jawbone in its span, so that it could wrench and twist the mandibles.

'Don't want to dislocate your jaw,' said the skinhead. 'So just tell me while you've got the chance. Otherwise you might lose your tongue as well. Then you'd have to write down what the boss wants to know.'

Durrant gave a harsh murmur in his throat. It was taken as some kind of assent and the grip of the huge fist relaxed.

'Now what he wants to know is this,' continued the voice. 'Where's his compensation? You spoiled a good little business here, so he wants something instead. Course, you could go back to your old ways, seeing that innocent little English bitch isn't around to reform you no longer. But it's too late for the boss - there's no going back on the deal. You offered him something special to make up for the business he lost and that's what he wants, no messing about, no excuses.'

'I haven't got it', said the doctor, in a whisper. 'For God's sake - it's somewhere I can't get at it now.'

'So where is it? That's what I have to get an answer to, and the reason the boss picked me is that I'm very, very good at getting answers, and if you don't tell me what the boss wants to hear I'm very good at teaching lessons. We could make a nice little example out of you. Keep everyone else in line that way. So you tell me where it is, if you haven't got it. And don't shit yourself in the car.'

There was a long pause. Then Durrant started to speak. 'It's the girl. I heard it had gone to the girl. That's what he was going to do with it, anyway.'

The shaved head jerked backwards, looking for orders, and there was a signal from the rear of the car. Then Caracci was holding Durrant's left wrist up somewhere near the small of his back and there was a cracking sound. 'What girl? Where?' Durrant's lips were moving, babbling now.

In response to a signal opened the car door and pushed Durrant out. He was sliding to his knees on the pavement, scrambling to get to his feet. Inside the Peugeot a voice was murmuring something from the back seat. 'I think we should teach him a lesson anyway. Not right now. Later on. Being slack, it's bad for business.'

Caracci watched Durrant staggering to his feet. 'We'll be back, then, boss?'

'We'll be back. Let him think he's escaped for now.'

Chapter 26

A narrow alley, leading steeply upwards, with small children playing on the littered pavements: a gritty little breeze drifting through it. Now, in spring, it was still bearable - in the height of summer, it would be hellishly hot.

Arab script above the shopfronts. Floating white writing on a grass-green board, the long slender minaret of a mosque. Shops selling spices, ladies' fingers, couscous, tahina. Platters of yellow-golden bread piled high on barrows. Smells of coffee and cardamum drifting across the street. Rapid movements of young men walking in robes, in jeans, surrounding him, jostling him defensively. Looks of hostility: 'who are you? - what do you mean to us?'

A group sitting on a pavement outside another mosque, talking intently, silent when he approached.

Do they know a foreign woman, a Miss Vashington?

'*connais pas.*'

Hostility increasing.

Sudden realisation on his part.

'It's nothing to do with the police - nothing official. I'd just like to talk to her.'

Still hostile stares. But then one of the men shrugged and jerked his head over his shoulder. '*Numéro vingt-six.*'

A matter between a stranger and an Englishwoman, that was all, the shrug implied. Nothing to do with him.

Twenty-six was a tall, peeling house with shiny curtains pulled across the windows and tacked over the doorway. A man opened the door in answer to the knock: middle-aged, heavily built, moustached. Again the suspicion.

This time Charlie said immediately that he was nothing to do with the police. That he was looking for Miss Vashington.

The house was very bare and very clean. A long corridor with old brown lino that gleamed and flaked. Doors opening off it, the paint peeling. A voice was calling out in long, swinging, sentences of Arabic that hung like silken strands in the air.

A door in the corridor opened and the woman behind it peered at him with the suspicion to which he had become customary, yet he sensed that this was of a different order. It was not the general nervousness of people driven to exist on the outside of a world, but that of a woman who was frightened of something in particular. Or of someone, for whom she was watching.

'Mahmoud, I don't want to see anyone. Make him go away.'

The door was closing.

Very quickly, so that she could hear the name before the battered panels of flimsy pine slammed against him, he said:

'I'm Charles Cashel.'

The door stopped swinging on its arc.

There was a long pause.

The room was like the rest of the house, bare and scrubbed-looking. There was a bed with a cheap orange and blue cover, a small rug made of some hand-knotted tufts of wool, thin curtains drawn across the window. One or two other pieces of furniture: a small table, a couple of upright chairs. It was the poorest room he had ever been in, so poor it made him feel ashamed.

She was standing upright in the middle of the room, staring straight at him. The curtains at the windows were not quite closed: a streak of light fell over her face. She was thin, with long hair pulled back and grey eyes beneath deep arches, would have been pretty, even beautiful, but for the deep lines around her mouth and the yellowish tinge to her skin. The eyes looked almost hooded, so thin and deep were the hollows of her face. She was younger, though, than he had thought, perhaps in her late twenties.

'Miss Washington?'

It was a relief to use the open pronunciation of the name.

Some instinct made him say, simply, with no preliminaries:

'Tell me what happened at the Villa Bleue.'

Chapter 27

Cecile Galant steps into the chilled air-conditioned atmosphere with a shudder of her black-clad shoulders. In a side room, she dons protective clothing - disposable overalls, surgical-style cap pulled over her dark blonde hair, space-age galoshes over the glossy black leather shoes that have trodden briskly in the mundane and ordinary paths outside.

Like some medieval ritual, she thinks to herself, some purification by which all traces of the contaminating outer world are hidden before the participant undergoes -

Undergoes what? A metamorphosis, a transition? Yes, a spiritual ordeal of a kind, undoubtedly. Although she has endured it many times before.

Clad now entirely in white, she steps into a white room. Tiles, cabinets - no living human world this, but a scene from an alien planet.

She raises one hand and signals, and after a series of clicks a drawer slides open and presents her with a long offering lying on a steel shelf.

Mme Galant stares down for a few moments. She is aware that eyes are watching her through a viewing panel.

She looks steadily at the bluish-white naked body, the penis, the coarse grey pubic hair, and then to the torn mass that was presumably once a face, lying directly under her gaze. Really, she thinks, one can only tell it was a face because of its position on top of the neck. If one were presented with a picture of it, it could be anything - some abstract work, almost, an expanse of clotted and uneven browns and reds with white strips of musculature exposed here and there, around the mouth, for example, and scrapings of white bone on the cheeks. Have the eyes been scooped out? She bends a little closer, for the benefit of the unseen viewers.

This, she has found, is the best way to look at these things, mentally as if they were mere pictures, compositions of dark blackish circles trimmed with ruffles that were once eyelids - no, that's getting too close!

She lifts a dead hand from its neat position, meekly lying at the side of the body. Well-kept, clean nails.

Cecile walks round to the head. The hair is neatly trimmed, iron grey.

The heavy odours of formaldehyde and disinfectant are permeating through the air-conditioning.

It is quite difficult to breathe calmly when looking at a dead body in a morgue, at least, if you do not do so every day for a living. The ribs suddenly feel cramped, the throat, dry and bitter, is threatened with spurts of bile.

Take Cecile, for example. Cecile's lungs always seem to want to gasp of their own accord, to take in great breaths of air, but this place is airless, of course, because fresh air would, like Cecile's own clothes, her hair, her skin, be contaminating. Some traces, some fibres or hairs, some pollen borne from that outside world where there is actually a springtime and flowers and trees, some spores of living creatures, might reach this mass of torn and bloody flesh, and then under microscopic examination reveal minute impediments to investigation, tiny pieces of false evidence that might eventually be weighed in the judicial balance. So every precaution must be taken to keep the dead flesh unpolluted.

She makes a signal and turns away, not pausing to see the steel shelf slide silently back into its place in the row upon row of numbered pigeon-holes that line the wall behind her.

In the disrobing room, she tears off her mask and breathes more easily. Her outer garments go into a bin to be discarded, and she is ready to leave this special ritual passage, revealed as she stands in her customary dark suit, a professional in her mid-thirties, ready to rejoin the normal world of dirt and dust, the world of minute hairs and atoms of contamination.

She has touched nothing, she was wearing gloves in any case, yet she goes to a sink, nudges the taps into operation with her elbow, and washes her hands carefully for several minutes.

Cecile Galant moves into the world outside the morgue.

She steps into the back of an official Peugeot; the chauffeur has the engine running, moves away without asking for orders. He has them already.

The woman he works for is automatically one of the most powerful people in the South of France. Cecile can order the arrest and imprisonment of anyone she suspects of involvement in serious crime, she instructs the police in their duties, she can call on expert witnesses of any kind. There was, in fact, no need for her to visit the morgue and see the body of the murder victim, for she could carry out the entire investigation in her office, summoning pathology reports, dental records, and anything else she deems necessary. But she has found that it is important to demonstrate that she can actually stand up to proximity with death. The people whom she instructs are mostly male, and although there are quite a lot of women prosecutors, lawyers and *juges d'instruction*, some of the policemen and scientists are still not entirely easy with them...

So Cecile always makes a point of looking at the *corpus*. Anyway, this one hadn't been so bad. The face was cut about - cut off, would be more precise a description - but not the body. There had been murders here in Cannes where women had been slashed and ripped apart.

But it was an unusual death in some ways.

On her mobile phone, she makes a call which is answered by a police operator.

'Chief Inspector Maubourg? Cecile Galant here. I'd like to see you - could you come to my office? The body found on the Croisette.'

It took Maubourg half an hour. By the time he arrived, Cecile's car had reached her office building and she had combed her hair, checked her face in the mirror and seated herself at her desk, which faced the door.

Chapter 28

An array of chairs stood on the other side of her desk, all of them more or less uncomfortable. Maubourg took the one in the centre.

There was a brief pause. The woman opposite him was composed, calm. Not bad for a woman who's just looked at a corpse with no face, he thought. Some of his men were worse affected. Her eyes, long and brown, were steady.

She didn't say anything. He felt himself beginning to grow awkward, as her silence persisted. Was it a technique?

In response, he decided to play her at her own game. He studied her; it was the first time he had really had the opportunity to observe the woman who would now be in overall charge of the investigation and all its procedures and legal ramifications. Their previous meeting had been the shortest of discussions, a formal five-minute briefing, most of which she had spent holding a dossier. Now she had been subjected to stress, to direct contact with death and brutality, instead of sheltering safely within the magistrates' office like her predecessors.

'What is the face of a woman supposed to look like when she's running an investigation into the most vicious killings we've ever had on the Riviera?' he asked himself. 'Like a saint or a haunted spirit or a power-freak? What does she feel like underneath?'

The woman opposite gave him no clues.

'The body found by the dustcart this morning on the Croisette. The prosecutor has turned the case over to me to direct further investigation.'

He hardly needed telling - he wouldn't be here otherwise, but the way she was careful to spell out their roles meant she was a stickler for formality and official procedures.

Calm voice, too. Nicely pitched. Would carry well, estimated Maubourg. He had once been interested in amateur theatricals in his youth and joined a theatre group. He still liked to recognise good voices. Cecile Galant's came from somewhere low down, in the region of the solar plexus, like a trained voice, very controlled.

One of the most important things about a *juge d'instruction*, he had always thought, was the determination to carry a case through, not to let it hang in mid-air, unresolved, for rumours to darken and thicken the truth, for evidence and memories to grow stale. Especially in a murder case, where scandal and speculation muddied the waters, where gossip sometimes named names and destroyed reputations before the law did.

This woman wouldn't lose her nerve, he thought.

Perhaps she was waiting for him to respond to her opening statement. Well, it always made a good beginning when you knew who the deceased was.

'There's been no doubt about his identity. An English doctor, resident in Cannes for - ' he glanced at his notes - 'for eight years. Name is Robin Durrant. His wallet was intact - contained about a thousand francs - and he was carrying various papers identifying him, including an international driving licence.'

'What I saw was not exactly recognisable.'

Yes, she thought, it was always important to see for oneself, no matter how appalling the sight. Who had identified the body, and, in this case, how? Those were the first questions that would be asked in mounting the defence of any accused.

Maubourg took her meaning instantly.

'There's no doubt that it was Durrant. The concierge of his apartment block and his former secretary both said that he had a long scar on the right wrist, exactly like the body in the morgue. We showed them photographs of it.'

'Have you brought them in to identify the body?'

'Not yet - we can do, but everything else fits - age, condition. Durrant was a very fit man for his age.'

'You said `former secretary'?'

'Yes, he has seen private patients by appointment only for the last two years. Before that, he had a surgery near the Cannes Beach Sporting Club. He specialised in tennis injuries and so on. That was where the secretary came in, but he must have made enough money to be able to give up the practice and just take the occasional patient.'

'So he could have fought his attacker?'

'Yes, but he didn't. The first blow was struck from behind, according to the pathology report. A powerful blow to the base of the skull, inflicted with a heavy weapon. The mutilation occurred after death, probably some time later, when the victim was supine, so the blood would have sunk down from the facial vessels. There wouldn't have been as much blood around as we might think. No spurts of arterial blood, for example, nor pouring veins. No heartbeat to pump the stuff around.'

'Then it won't necessarily help to look for major traces at the site of the killing.'

'No - and anyway, where would we start to look?'

Cecile turned a page in the dossier.

'The deceased was naked... the skin and hair were very clean; he was fastidious, nothing out of the ordinary, soap, shaving astringent, nothing that he couldn't have picked up anywhere... except a few animal hairs sticking to the blood.'

'Probably a cat or a dog - that's quite normal. Funny how many people mixed up with violent crime turn out to be pet-lovers.'

She smiled - a crack in the armour at least. 'Inspector, I've been reviewing a number of unsolved murder cases in the dossiers here. Now, the odd thing is this: Durrant was the lover of another murder victim, the English girl, Cashel. But she was killed in a completely different way, strangled with her scarf. No blow to the head, no mutilations. But Durrant fits into a different pattern altogether. This is one of several similar murders with facial mutilation, is it not? And in none of them was there, as I recollect, any attempt to hide the identity of the deceased, so that was not the purpose of the damage inflicted to the facial areas.'

He outlined the other cases, but only in so far as he needed to get across his own ideas. She would have read the files, of that he was certain.

She said, 'There have now been five mutilation killings in the last six months. That's a new type of crime for Cannes, isn't it - this is one of the safest cities on the Riviera. There's a lot of wealth here, a lot of famous people - they attract crime, of course, but usually soft drugs pushing or robbery, that sort of thing. But I don't need to tell you that, of course, you know the town far better than I do.'

He didn't say anything, which was at least tactful considering she had told him something he must know already, she thought. But she sensed that he was not good at dealing with the political repercussions of crime, the fear of stomach-churning stories in the press, which must afflict the powers-that-be here. He was an honest man, the kind of man who can't see the scheming and manipulation, the strings that have to be pulled to get things done.

'The sexual mutilations are the characteristic pattern of a serial killer - the kind who is a pathological maniac,' said Cecile. 'They appear in just about every country in the world - Peter Sutcliffe in Britain, the Monster of Florence, Ted Bundy in the States. No reason why Cannes should be immune.'

Maubourg somehow felt forced on to the defensive, though God alone knew why - he had no special reason for identifying with Cannes. He himself was from Toulon.

'No,' he agreed. 'Though we haven't had any warning signals. No earlier lead-up crimes involved with episodes of extreme cruelty to children or animals, for example, to help us trace the killer - I believe those are usually found in cases of sadistic murder of this type. But there is one very unusual factor, and that is that this killer attacks both men and women. Usually, it's just females.'

Cecile leaned forward, her chin in her hand. She looked less in control now, less lacquered, somehow. More like a very serious student.

'In the case of the Monster of Florence, the victims were couples,' she said, 'but he mutilated the women only. Oh, there was an exception - he attacked two German boys, where he could have been mistaken about the sex.'

'And in this case we have two men and three women.'

'You can classify them by sex,' said Cecile thoughtfully. 'Or you can shake the kaleidoscope and arrange a different pattern. Supposing we look at the social backgrounds. What sort of people were they?'

'What sort? Well, two of the victims - one man and one woman - were from the fringe of the criminal world. One of the dead men, the one with traces of narcotics in his bloodstream, had slipped some information to a gendarme - I can't pass on the officer's name, you know how it is with the gendarmerie. Last thing they want is to appear in our files.'

She nodded. The enmity between the two police forces, the gendarmerie and the *police judiciaire*, needed no spelling out. Any friendliness from one side to the other would certainly be very covert.

'And the other victims?' Cecile pushed images of dead faces - what had been left of their faces - somewhere into the back of her mind.

'Couldn't find a pattern. The first man was a taxi-driver. There was some suspicion he'd been involved in small-scale arms smuggling, but not since he'd held a taxi licence. Then, one of the women was a prostitute, so she was on the verge of the criminal world - they usually have some connections with pimps and pushers. We looked into that, but didn't find anything that would give us a clue to her murder. Her pimp was the obvious suspect. He was the usual brutal specimen who used to beat her up regularly, but at the time of the murder, he had an unbreakable alibi. He'd actually been involved in a street fight and got himself arrested, so he was safely locked up in a police cell when - what was her name?'

'Véronique Dupuis,' supplied Cecile smoothly, as if she knew he would be testing her. Did he imagine there was even a flicker of contempt as she said it? Sort of 'grow up, man, I know my job'?

'Véronique Dupuis, thank you. Anyway, when she was killed she had some minor criminal associations. Except that in the end nothing is ever minor in this part of the world - the little fishes have bigger ones close behind them, and then there are the real sharks lurking in the background. Anyway, the second woman was a waitress and the third was a tourist; nothing connected with crime of any kind known about them. The tourist was Australian - the other victims were all French - except now for Dr. Durrant.'

'So, they vary in social background, in nationality, presumably in standard of education.'

Maubourg had to admit to himself that he hadn't really looked at things like this. Yes, it was possible to group the victims in different ways, to make different kinds of links between them - and previous analyses had only classified them according to sex. But he doubted very much that it would lead anywhere.

'Yes, that's true enough. The Australian was a teacher, so she and Durrant were university-educated professionals. The others didn't have much education, in fact, I doubt if Véronique was really literate. But in any case didn't Denis Nilsen, that London serial killer, didn't he mutilate male victims?'

'Yes, but it was a sexual motive. Is there any evidence these men in our dossier were homosexuals? Or part of the gay community?'

'No, apparently not. The taxi driver had a wife - and an ex-wife as well, back in Corsica. He came to Cannes about four years ago, after he'd got divorced, and remarried.'

Cecile was getting some photographs out. She must have already taken them out of the file, have had them ready. The previous victims of the Cannes Mutilator, as he was known to the press, and around the police stations of the city simply as the Mutilator. Not the horrific pictures from the scene-of-crime report, but taken before they met those terrible deaths that brought their photographs here to fan out across an official desk like some parody of a card game. The Australian woman's picture was evidently taken from her passport, a full-face mugshot. The others varied, from a professional studio portrait of a young woman with pretty brown hair to a police-custody shot of a middle-aged man and another official passport-sized photo with a taxi driver's license application attached.

Cecile picked up the studio photograph. The woman smiled out from a bright blue studio background that matched her eyes. 'Glamour photos?'

'That's the waitress? You mean she might have come here as a film extra, wanting to catch a director's eye, that sort of thing?'

The Riviera was full of such hopefuls, drifting along from town to town, doing a little waitressing here, maybe a little sleeping around there, usually nothing very serious. They sometimes went to model agencies and got themselves 'portfolios.' That was the euphemism, anyway.

'We checked the photographic studio out. No porn, nothing even top-less. Mostly family stuff - weddings, and so on. They remembered this girl. Jeanette Auvers from Poitou. It was taken on her twentieth birthday. She wanted a nice photo to send home to mum and dad.'

'Looks a nice kid. And then, Inspector, when it came to the murders, the women weren't all treated in the same way.'

'Two had their... sorry, their genitals cut up, and the third didn't. Odd thing is, the one he only got the face off was the prostitute and the other two - the ones where he slashed the...'

'The labia and the vagina.'

He went on, sounding easier, grateful to her for saying it for him. 'I don't know a lot about it, but I did some psychology courses and as I recall the usual reason for those frenzied sexual mutilations is that the guy has some deep-seated hatred of women. But there's not a consistent pattern here.

Could be that in the case of Véronique Dupuis he just didn't have time to do it. If he works on the face first, maybe he got interrupted.'

There was a pause as Cecile considered.

'There is another possibility, Inspector. Shake the facts another way. Véronique's drug habit - there were injection marks, but they were old ones. She hadn't taken anything recently, had she? There was no trace of drugs in the body.'

'Yes, I remember that. The needle punctures were healing up. Nothing fresh.'

'Do you think she was trying to quit?'

'Could be.'

'In which case, although she was a woman, she might have been seen in the same category as the gun-runner turned taxi driver or the man who was suspected of being a police informer. Not exactly an informer - but a defector, if you like. A reformed addict is pretty dangerous to the pushers still out there - like a reformed smoker, they're the most crusading of all! Or like a born-again Christian. What if Véronique Dupuis had seen the light and was trying to get off the habit, and was willing to do the dirty on her supplier?'

'So where does that take us?' But Maubourg already knew even as he listened to Cecile.

'The ones where he cuts the face but doesn't mutilate the genital area - maybe those are punishments. Or warnings. Anyway, they're business, if you like. Carried out in the line of work, for his boss, perhaps. But the others, where he does his own thing - those are pure pleasure. He's killed five times - three times the victims might have been selected with a rational purpose, and the other two, the waitress and the Australian - '

'Those were for his own pleasure. His boss let him off the leash.'

But it was all too theoretical, he knew. These were spider-webs as fine as gossamer spun out of mere possibilities.

'Don't stop there, Inspector. Take it one stage further.'

He wanted to say 'But every step may be further away from the truth.'

She went on, following her train of thought.

'How does Durrant fit into this pattern? Not as a sexual victim, apparently. So he was killed for a different motive. And the reason for the other deaths like his - if it was for revenge or retribution - he had betrayed someone. Or he had tried to quit something. Any trace of drugs?'

'They haven't done the path tests yet. But it certainly didn't look like it, not of hard drugs, anyway. There were no needle-marks, he was in good physical shape. Maybe a little designer cocaine now and again, but I'd say he was a man who took good care of himself. That sort doesn't usually take to drugs. Too vain.'

He liked her answering laugh.

Chapter 29

In an office perched high above a London street, Martin Hollingsworth waited till Carol had gone out for her lunch. In a few minutes she would bring back her sandwiches and mineral water to eat at her terminal, but he had a short period of grace while she dashed out to the delicatessen-cum-snack-bar nearby. He was hungry himself, but it would have to wait. Normally, he always gave himself a three-course special at the French-style bistro down the road. They were everywhere now, these little places, and all with the same authentic French trick of making the menu seem half the price it would turn out to be when you got the bill. Still, Martin felt he owed it to himself to eat decently, and anyway he rarely paid for a meal himself: it was usually on clients' expenses.

He tipped back in his chair; the walls of his own room were a blank, with nothing but his qualifying certificates and a calendar. The little cubby hole of a reception office outside had two expensive chairs and a low table: a few glossy magazines, and a portrait of Queen Elizabeth I, a poster from the National Portrait Gallery. There was nothing cheap about Martin's office, and nothing personal. The temps added nothing to it. He preferred temps: they could be got rid of if there was any difficulty. Sometimes they had ideas of permanency and tried creating their own little kingdoms: one brought a pot plant, some left old pairs of indoor shoes, another had even tacked up a picture of Leonardo di Caprio, but as soon as any of them started making the place her own, Martin said he no longer needed her, and threw out any little relics of her reign before he got the next girl.

He wondered how long it would be before Carol started getting confident enough to try setting down these little markers of a permanent presence. So far, she had been remarkably anonymous, though he had taken her out for a drink from time to time. Nothing more: he just wanted to find out some things from her, if he could. Like whether she had heard any of the conversations about the business in Cannes - he had spoken a bit too loudly last time.

Of course, he couldn't ask Carol Bassett directly what she had heard, but it was better to get to know her a little so he could keep some sort of check on her, find out a few things about her in case he ever needed to know. Ever needed to find her in a hurry. Anyway, she couldn't understand French, so the calls to Cannes didn't matter.

But she didn't seem to have any curiosity about the office at all. That was exactly what he wanted. Martin was in business on his own and that was what suited him. He had a clerk who drafted leases and conveyances for him, but he handled most of the work himself: contracts with employees, rentals, insurance - the business generated by the flotsam and jetsam that washed round Victoria station, looking for jobs, for pawnbrokers, for cheap flats and rented houses in quiet anonymous streets in South London where no one would enquire much what went on. Mr. Hollingsworth did not think it his business to enquire either.

But Martin didn't like this seedy side of the legal business, even though he didn't handle legal aid or court work. He wanted a solid practice, something with conveyancing and trusts. Needed money, though, to buy into something like that. Needed a lot of money.

Sometimes he, as Charlie had recently done, thought of childhood, and of the house by the sea where he had gone to stay sometimes with Rosie and Charlie, always an older and wiser cousin, always counselling prudence to a family who seemed to him to be increasingly feckless. Martin was related to Charlie's mother, and when she died and Charlie's father remarried, he disliked the second wife on several grounds: not just that she took the place of his own aunt, but that she was a big tanned woman, wearing low-cut dresses and laughing at his embarrassment. And refusing to sell that place in the South of France, that ridiculous Villa Bleue, the whole thing as outdated as some fifties movie star's holiday home.

Anyway, Martin reflected now, it had been lucky for him, that Cannes business, in the end. Dragged out there to see to clearing up the legalities after Rosie's death - but it had ended very luckily for Martin.

He looked out of the window and saw Carol emerging from the front door and rushing along the windy street. He'd keep her on for several more weeks, and then keep tabs on her. Mostly, she keyed in at a terminal from a dictaphone, the trailing wires coiled about her neck, only occasionally being summoned to deal with him directly.

She had good legs, a short skirt that showed her thighs. She did arouse him, there was no doubt, he felt it now, thinking about putting his hand up between her legs, under that short black skirt.

Martin abruptly reminded himself that he must take no risks of discovery, even if they seemed remote. Sex always involved risks - though that was what got him excited sometimes.

Everyone else was now safely out of the building, he thought. The other secretaries gone to do their hurried lunchtime shopping, the two partners in the travel firm above had gone to an important lunch with a big company (he had heard them talking on the stairs) and Martin's clerk was at an auction.

There was a call Martin wanted to keep private.

Very private indeed.

He dialled the long string of numbers.

He said, when the phone was answered, without any preliminary, 'Where has he got to?'

There was a brief burst of sound at the other end.

'Too close,' Martin said.

He spoke serviceable French, although he disliked speaking it.

'Have you seen it?' was his next question and this time the answer, short and tinny, barked out of the phone.

There was a clatter of high-heeled shoes on the stairs.

He repeated in English, 'Too close' as he put the phone down.

'I'm back, Mr. Hollingsworth!' called a voice from the next room. 'They only had Brie and rocket salad left. And no granary.'

Martin made sympathetic sounds.

Always so thoughtful, Mr. Hollingsworth.

Chapter 30

Daniel Galant stepped across the parquet of their small apartment. He moved carefully, carrying the supper dishes. Cecile was loading the dishwasher.

Daniel was her second husband and she not only loved him, she was grateful for him.

He worked for a computer firm based in Grasse, and did most of his programming at home. He had short, stiff yellow hair that stuck up in a Tin-Tin quiff, and eyes of a rather light blue, set in a young face. Daniel was in fact eight years younger than Cecile.

Daniel's firm created computer games, of a specialised kind - shoot-out and quest programmes, and a multi-player horse racing game that was designed to appeal to betting types who wanted to please their offspring with expensive electronic toys. Daniel was working on this one at the moment, creating in-built odds.

Cecile's first husband had wanted a very conventional partnership, the traditional French bourgeois alliance, making a kind of corporation of family and possessions. It had taken them five painful years of marriage and one child before they had both discovered that this wouldn't suit either of them as a partnership for life.

Louis was a notary specialising in property deals. He hadn't wanted her to take risks, had tried to dissuade her from getting involved in dangerous prosecutions. That is, investigations that might be dangerous for her own health, like those into suspected drug-running. Or into semi-political matters, like the Le Pen enthusiasts who tried to run immigrants out of town under claim of popular support.

'Your family comes first!' he had insisted.

But she couldn't accept that, much as she wanted to.

'I can't change' she had said, helplessly, looking down the long road of the future and seeing herself and Louis always at odds, always fighting over this. 'It's better we live apart.'

But it had been a terrible blow to his pride. And she had suffered from a desperate loneliness, which had made her even more ambitious, because apart from her child there had been nothing in her life but work, till Daniel came along, training lawyers on a computer course.

She was amazed at how relaxed life was with him, how easy he was about her job and her work. Though Daniel thought her work might be dangerous sometimes. 'You don't have to go out so much yourself,' he said. 'You can send people to do it for you. Stay in and read their reports.'

But there was always something they didn't, or couldn't put in the report: the precise degree of guilt on someone's face, the extent of fear in which someone had been placed. Staying indoors and coordinating everything - yes that was the traditional role, working the case until it could either be handed over to the prosecution or a suspect could be eliminated. Anyway, Cannes was a lot safer than Marseilles, where the gang-killings occurred. If you could stay out of the clutches of the Mutilator, of course.

Whatever the risks, Louis and their child were at a safe distance now, in the Haute Provence hinterland, where they always went for family holidays, swimming in the calm turquoise waters of the mountain lakes or boating along the Verdon River, and she was here in Cannes, taking risks, with a man who earned his very living from risk-systems. I'm a fool in some ways, she thought. I want my child protected, but I want to take risks myself.

'I'll phone Florence after we've had our coffee,' she called to Daniel. 'She'll just be going to bed then.'

Suddenly she felt a wave of physical longing for the child, to hold her small muscled body close and smell her soft fine hair. Such a powerful urge, she thought. Is this what the female animal feels, when the young are taken away? I desperately want my child; I have to fight myself and say that she's better off away from me at the moment.

And safer, her brain insisted on adding, though she tried to push fear deep down into the undertow of her mind.

The dishwasher began its steady swishing and they poured themselves their usual evening drinks, Cecile taking a small cognac and Daniel some Danish concoction with bitter aromatic herbs that he said cleared his brain after the contorted torments to which he had subjected it during the day.

'Maubourg wants to go for them now - for the White Boy gang,' said Cecile.

'Do you think there's enough evidence?'

'No - the worst outcome would be that they get off, laughing at us. And there's not much movement in the other thing I want to crack - the murder of the English girl. I'm having Cashel followed.'

'He's the one whose sister was killed?'

'Yes, his sister, Rosie.'

Cecile paused. 'And she was an innocent - a real innocent. The type whose death makes me angry. Because she wasn't involved with the drug scene at all, as far as we could find out - no drugs in her body, no record of association with addicts. God, she was just a nice kid of nineteen staying in the family house. Didn't run with the film crowd. The only doubtful mark against her is that she was seeing a lot of a man who was old enough to be her father - but Madame Ferrier, the woman who took care of the Villa Bleue, thought that was a pretty one-sided affair - that Rosie wasn't so keen. 'The doctor is a middle-aged man,' she said to me.'

'Meaning?' Daniel liked to have things stated clearly, out loud. He didn't like obscurities, dark hints or tenebrous remarks. The clarity, the daylight, which he let in on any scene was one of the things Cecile loved about him.

'Meaning, I think, that he was besotted, willing to make a fool of himself. Not the last man who's fallen for a girl half his age - less, I think. He must be forty or so. Anyway he was Rosie Cashel's only known male associate - sexually, that is ... so maybe it wasn't a sexual motive.'

Daniel was looking sceptical. She was doubtful herself.

'Why do you say that?' he challenged.

'Well, a man of that age ...'

'Do you think he's less likely to kill for passion than a younger man? There are cases in the papers every day - there was a man of seventy who killed his mistress because she was seeing another man, only the other day. No, I think it's quite possible you can't eliminate a sexual motive, because after all, in some ways it's worse for an older man if he's rejected. What chance has he got at his age of competing with someone whose whole life is before him? I don't think you could entirely rule out the doctor.'

'Perhaps. Anyway, I still feel it wasn't a gang killing. She was strangled, and that's not their usual style. Not White Boy's, and he's the only show in town when it comes to organised crime. He's like the Krays in London, he's mopped up all the smaller fry. White Boy sees revenge as an economy, you see - not just a murder, but a warning to everyone else. 'Pour encourager les autres.'

'But these victims, 'Les Mutilés de Cannes' as the papers call them - didn't this start long after White Boy got operating? He's been trying to make

128

this city his private fief for several years, and the first mutilation killing was only about six months ago.'

'I put that to Maubourg. He's got a theory. White Boy's got a new hench-man, a new executioner, if you like. Called Caracci. He came over from Corsica about six months ago. Just before the first mutilation.'

'But surely Durrant was harmless enough? How could he have been involved with White Boy?'

'He must have given away - or intended to give - information that White Boy wanted kept quiet, or else he maybe just wanted to stop working for him, like Véronique Dupuis. White Boy wouldn't have that - it's a power thing with him, as well as business, I think. Any way, Durrant was seen talk-ing to Cashel recently - one of Maubourg's men was following him. Maybe someone else saw them - someone who told White Boy. He's got people everywhere in Cannes.'

Cecile got up as she spoke, going into the kitchen to emerge with a tray of smoky transparent coffee cups and a percolator that had just come to fruition. It seemed odd not to have to step over some forgotten plastic telephone or toy grocer's shop. She carried on talking as she sat opposite Daniel and poured the coffee out, then added a little cream and swirled it reflectively round the rich brown depths. During her first marriage, she had scarcely touched caffeine at home: Louis had forbidden coffee, claiming it was bad for the nerves. Daniel lived on it.

'Do you think we could get Florence a *Paradis des Oiseaux* for the bal-cony?'

'A what?'

'One of those bird-tables - with all sorts of little perches and nesting-boxes. That's what they're called - I saw one in a shop window.'

'Yes, why not? Kids need creatures round them.'

Daniel paused and drank his coffee.

'When the police talked to Cashel,' he asked, 'did he say why he had come to Cannes again? Was it about business - something to do with the Villa?'

'No, it was odd. He claimed it was because of a photograph. Someone had sent him a picture of a cemetery. The old cemetery here.'

'How strange.'

'Yes - and as a matter of fact, it wasn't even a photograph of the place itself. It was a photograph of a painting of the cemetery. A modern oil painting, it looked like to me.'

'So it was the cemetery, but at two removes, so as to speak. A photograph of a picture of the place. Complicated!'

'Yes, but Cashel said there was no apparent connection between his sister and the cemetery - he went out there and Maubourg followed him, just to keep an eye on him.'

'But how had Cashel got hold of the photograph in the first place?'

'The film had been sent to him. In an envelope postmarked Cannes.'

'And who do you think sent it?'

'Now, that's the question Maubourg and I have been asking ourselves. Apparently Susanna Washington, the housekeeper across the road, did know Rosie - so Maubourg says. He questioned Susanna about some pills that were found in her suitcase soon after the old man, Arthuis, died. But she says she didn't send the film - and didn't even know Cashel's address in London. And why should send it, anyway? there is no evidence that there was any connection between her and Charles Cashel in the past.'

Cecile had one eye on the clock. In a few minutes, she would ring Florence, and tell her a story over the phone. What would it be tonight. About the noisy little dragon?

'What about Durrant?' asked Daniel.

'Again, what motive could he have had in sending the film?'

'The fact remains that someone in Cannes was interested enough to send it to Cashel in London. And either they knew Cashel's address already or could get hold of it easily. Doesn't that narrow down the field a bit?'

'Not really. Charles Cashel was Rosie's nearest relative, after her mother in Australia. His address was on file in a lot of places - with the undertakers, for instance, with the municipal council for local tax purposes connected with the Villa - it would have been very easy for anyone to get hold of. But presumably they did so because they wanted to rouse his suspicions about his sister's death - they wanted him to come out here and start looking round.'

'But if White Boy somehow became involved - d'you think it's dangerous?'

'Yes, to be honest, I do. For Cashel - for everybody involved.'

With Daniel, Cecile could be open about something she'd never felt able to admit to Louis.

'It is dangerous. Frankly, darling, I'm scared.'

Chapter 31

They were sitting in a little café with gilt chairs and a crumpled tablecloth, eating Lebanese food; she had chosen from the menu for both of them, and Charlie ate greenish-black, mint-flavoured packets of vine leaves and tiny spicy kebabs with rice. The food was leaving him hungry, but it had seemed easier to go to a restaurant than to talk in her room. She had not wanted to go out at all at first, but eventually had agreed. 'Not far, though. I want to stay nearby.'

By then he had got over the initial surprise of her Scottish accent - she had been described as English, but to the French, he supposed, all British voices were 'English'. Yes, she was from Glasgow, had those sharp sounds and reverberations; he felt an undercurrent of toughness as she spoke, like an underwater cable scraping along rocks. Or was that his imagination? Was that what prison had done to her? Her face was strikingly pale but perhaps she had lived like an Arab woman since her release, perhaps she never went out of that heavily-curtained house save on rare occasions such as this.

There had been little choice of where to eat. All the restaurants in the area served Middle Eastern food.

'How long have you been living here?'

'Since I came out of...'

'It's all right - I know about it.'

'Oh, yes, I'm sure you do - the whole bloody town knows - everyone expected me to go back crawling to Glasgow with my tail between my legs. But I'm staying here. Brazen, aren't I? But I didn't do it - thieving those damned tablets, I mean. And if I just turn tail and go home - that'll be a kind of admission, don't you see?'

He did see.

'Not that my parents wouldn't take me in if I wanted to go home. They're Presbyterians, but the forgiving kind. Forgiveness is their speciality. They'd make a whole production of it.'

'If you're innocent, you don't need forgiveness.'

'Well, good for you, Mr. Charlie Cashel. You see the point.'

'Why are you staying here..'

'With the Arabs, you mean? They're good to me. A damned sight better than those stuck-up bastards on the other side of town. The Brits living in the expensive places - they wouldn't want to know. Even the ones who were friendly to me before I went in. They'd drive me out if I tried to move back there, even if I had the money. Which I don't. No, I can't afford to live anywhere else - and I earn a little by teaching English to some of the Arabs.'

'But how did you come to be here in the first place?'

He felt a kind of urgent curiosity about her, the inside of her life. But better to answer her question first. He sensed that she was the kind of woman who wanted the cards on the table.

'The police took me to the police station and put me in the cells for a couple of days, after they found the drugs,' she said, 'but they never charged me. I think Maubourg might have suspected they'd been planted on me, to tell you the truth. It was all just a little too inconvenient. And the way the niece had sacked me made a bad impression. That companion of hers - Mademoiselle Rolland - I think she was sorry about it. They said she came to the police station to enquire about me once, but they wouldn't let her see me. Anyway, to get back to the point, there was an Arab woman called Leila in the cell with me. She had a miscarriage - the cops had given her a thumping, and she lost her baby.'

Charlie said 'Surely they don't beat women up!'

She looked at him for a moment, and he remembered the fear he'd felt when Maubourg had him thrown into a cell for a few hours.

He was silent.

She continued to talk, pleating the edge of the tablecloth with her restless fingers.

'They'd put us in the same cell, so I looked after her. When I came out, well, there was nowhere to go, so Leila and Mahmoud offered me a room.'

He offered her a plate of some little pieces of spiced meat. She took them and ate hungrily.

There was some music now, a woman with a silken handkerchief trailing from her hand singing something with long, soft, wailing notes.

'I earn enough to pay for my room and some food,' she said, 'but not enough to eat in a place like this.'

'You had a hard time.'

She laughed and brushed her fair hair back with one hand. 'Nothing

133

compared to being in prison. That's how I can stick it out, you see. It toughened me, so I can stand it all. This life here, I mean. It seems good to me. Anything does, after a cell. But you wouldn't know.'

There was a flick of contempt in her voice. He supposed this was how it felt, when life had swallowed you up and spat you out, and you came to the surface of the filthy water and saw all the nice clean people still on dry land, leading their nice clean unbruised lives. But he had a taste of it: he recalled the gendarmerie where Maubourg had questioned him, the sense of being buried alive in a hole where he could scream his head off with no-one paying any more attention than they would to a pig on its way to the slaughterhouse.

She went on talking. 'I haven't spoken English for a long time. It feels funny. Anyway, Leila and Mahmoud helped me. She got me this dress - I hardly had any clothes, even, when I came out.'

She touched the shoulder of her dress. It was a pale yellow colour with washed-out flowers all over it, and an unfashionable high neckline. He imagined how Imelda would have laughed at it.

'Didn't you have some things at the villa? You'd lived there, hadn't you?'

'Yes, I was the old man's housekeeper. I had a couple of suitcases - had them all packed when that niece of his came along and claimed I'd taken the drugs from his bedside table! They took my cases off to the police station and I never got them back.'

'Why should they take them away?'

'Didn't someone tell you? I should have thought you would have got a blow-by-blow account of it all. They claimed to have found the drugs in one of my cases - the stuff that was missing from the old man's room.'

'And they charged you with stealing them?'

She looked at him fiercely. 'And I denied it absolutely then and I deny it now. That niece of his, she hardly came near him when he was alive. So he died with only me there - and I wasn't actually *there*, if you see what I mean. I just heard a crash from his room and found him lying there in bed - he'd stopped breathing and I couldn't feel a pulse. So I ran downstairs and phoned Doctor Durrant. Of course, the old man had a bad heart - he'd had a heart attack the year before I came. Anyway, the doctor came and said he was dead.'

'You said that you could tell me something about Durrant.'

'Oh, yes. Well, when he came that night, I went into the old man's room with him. I was standing out of the way, near the door, while Durrant got out his stethoscope and banged on his chest and looked in his eyes and all that. I went back to my room.'

There was a pause. The singer wailed gently on, fluttering her handkerchief gracefully from jewelled fingers. She was a stout woman, in her fifties probably, but some of the diners, all men, were watching her with a rapt expression, as if lost in some dream-world of longing and adoration.

Cashel and Susanna Washington looked at each other.

He said, 'There was an inquest on the old man?'

'Oh yes, all according to French law - he had died suddenly, so they had a post-mortem and a *juge d'instruction* investigated the death. But he died from a massive coronary - there was no doubt about that.'

'The doctor came out a minute or so later - just after I had gone back to my room. I was just shutting my door - he was walking along the corridor, closing his case. And then he called out and said he would telephone the niece.'

'So what was the story about your suitcases?'

'It was the next day. I was packing up.'

He was startled. 'Wasn't that rather soon after the old man's death?'

'The niece came round the day after he died. I asked her for the wages that were owing to me and do you know what she did?'

No, but he could believe almost anything of that unpleasant woman. Susanna continued, 'She said that Dr. Durrant told her the old man had died at about eleven o'clock at night. So she would pay me up to midnight! She didn't even pay me for a day longer than she had to.'

'So you left?'

'No - I was about to. I never made it.'

'What do you mean?'

'I went to my room and packed everything and phoned the airport. There was a plane for Heathrow leaving that afternoon. But then a policeman arrived ... quite a high ranking one, not one of the thugs. Maubourg, that was his name. It had been a case of sudden death, you see, and they had to investigate it. The post-mortem came later. Anyway, Maubourg told me I was to stay, in case he needed me as a witness to the old man's last hours. The niece didn't like it, but he was pretty sharp with her. Said it was a judicial investigation of a death. So she couldn't throw me out. But then came ... then came the business of the suitcases.'

Her voice was hesitant now. Her eyes suddenly seemed very deep-set and her face looked haggard. She was fingering a little necklet chain, rolling it between her fingers.

'Would you order some arrack?'

He ordered arrack for her and a vodka for himself. She poured water into her glass and watched the swirling oily clouds as they formed in the liquid. The smell of aniseed, with its strange sickly cleanness, drifted across as she raised the glass towards him and nodded a sketchy gesture of acknowledgement.

'Thanks. I don't often touch it. I suppose it's living with Muslims - you just get out of the habit of drinking alcohol.'

'Isn't it a deprivation - for a Scot not to touch whisky!'

'Well, my parents were Presbyterians, as a matter of fact. I was brought up quite strictly. Didn't go wild afterwards, when I left home, either. It all seems a bit strange if you've been indoors for a while - the outside world, I mean, if you can call this the outside world.'

'We could talk again later, if you like.'

'No, no time like the present. I know I can't stay here for ever - it was a bolthole, but some time I've got to get out of it. Only I need some help.'

She looked at him in a long, speculative, way.

'Maybe you could help me, Charlie Cashel, though you look a bit of an innocent yourself. Anyway, I've got to start somewhere. So let's start at the point where I left the Arthuis house. Well, I had put my suitcases in the hall. I was just on the point of leaving - I'd packed everything and I was going to 'phone a taxi. But then there was a knock at the door and it was the Inspector. Maubourg.'

'I saw him - when my sister died.' He was not going to mention his subsequent encounters with Maubourg. He didn't want to alarm her.

'Well, you know what he's like, then. Shrewd as hell. Anyway I had packed two cases and put them in the hall ready for when I left. One had some warm winter clothes, and the other had my summer dresses and toilet things in. They were both locked, but I unpacked my night things and my toilet bag and I left that suitcase unlocked. I didn't know how long the police would want me to stay.'

There was a long pause. She had her hand over her face for a few moments. He waved to a waiter and asked for coffee. 'Mademoiselle would like some too? Yes ... How do you like your coffee?'

'They'll make it with cardamum here.'

The coffee was brought in a long-handled brass can. It was black and sweet, streaming out clear over a sludge of fine dregs.

She took a sip and breathed in the steamy scent above her thimble-sized cup.

Then she started speaking quickly, as though to hurry through the memory.

'I went to lie down in my room. Maubourg had gone. I was pretty fed up with everything at that point. The mean bitch of a niece - the police making me stay there. I heard her pick up the phone and then she was speaking to someone else, - well, not speaking, whispering - I couldn't have heard what she was saying anyway. I thought it was all to do with arranging the funeral and maybe she was whispering about the will because she didn't want me to know anything. I didn't pay much attention.

'It happened about a quarter of an hour later. There was a banging at the front door and I heard her opening it and telling someone to come in. Even then, when I heard people barging about downstairs, I didn't understand. But then I went out on to the landing and looked down into the hall ... and there was my suitcase lying open and all my things pulled about ... and Maubourg was looking up at me. He'd come back. With another policeman, a man in uniform.'

She stopped.

Charlie said, 'That's all right. I don't need to know any more,' and wondered to himself why he needed to know any of it. But the same thought did not seem to have occurred to Susanna Washington.

She said, 'They found some sleeping tablets in my suitcase - some that had been prescribed for the old man. He couldn't sleep, you see. They were very strong sleeping tablets. He had been operated on for a trapped nerve in his back but the operation wasn't successful. I knew he was taking them, but I didn't even know what drug it was. Anyway, they found them in the lid of one of my cases. The lining had been slit open and the bottles of pills - that's what they were, little bottles - pushed inside.'

'But they didn't charge you?'

She laughed. 'I suppose there's some justice in the world! It was Maubourg. He recommended that I should be released without charge. My fingerprints weren't on the bottles.'

'Was that reason enough to let you go?'

'You sound as if you think I'm guilty.'

She was in danger of reacting defensively. He sensed it.

'No - no, just surprised that they didn't press on with a prosecution.'

'Well, it's not the police who decide here - it's a *juge d'instruction* who goes through the evidence against the accused. But of course a lot depends on how honest the police are in the first place.'

'And Maubourg's honest?'

'In comparison - with some of the others, anyway, and what's more important, he doesn't automatically hate all foreigners. He's not a racist. He protected this area against some Front National skinheads last year - put a police cordon round it. Oh, it's all relative, as they say. Some of them are real bastards. But the thing was, there were no fingerprints at all on the bottles - not mine, not anyone else's. And there should have been. The old man's should have been on them, at any rate.'

'So did Maubourg think they were planted in your suitcase?'

She turned indignant. 'They *were* bloody planted!'

'I'm sorry.'

There was a long pause, during which her anger seemed to subside. Then she said, 'I'm sorry too. I'd forgotten that what happened to your sister was terrible - so much more terrible than any of my problems. Maubourg asked me about that, too - whether I'd seen anything that might help find the murderer. The Arthuis house overlooks the front of the Villa Bleue, but my room was at the back and I hadn't seen anything. And when Rosie was actually murdered, I was already here. Old Arthuis had died just before your sister was killed, and that bitch of a niece moved in, with her girlfriend. I'm pretty sure that's the relationship, though that generation never admits to it - Monique Arthuis always calls the Rolland woman her companion. Anyway, they were in residence when poor wee Rosie died.'

'Did you know my sister?'

'We talked a few times, but we never got to be friends - I was too busy looking after old Arthuis and she seemed - well she seemed to be spending most of her time with Durrant.'

'You don't like him, judging from the way you mention his name!'

'I don't trust the bastard, but that's pure instinct, as I told Maubourg! I think they're still investigating it officially, by the way - your sister's death. There was something in the newspaper a few weeks ago - the local council was calling for a new *juge d'instruction*. That's the person really in charge of the investigation in a case of this kind. The prosecution just hands the whole file over to an examining magistrate, I think we usually translate it, but they're professionals, not like British magistrates. They're in charge of the whole thing - they give orders to the police and when they say, 'jump', everyone jumps! Anyway, the *juge d'instruction* in your sister's case was an old chap, a bit past it, I'd reckon, and there's some bright new spark going to take over the dossier.'

'Do you think that's why they haven't got the murderer?'

'I don't know, to be honest. I think Maubourg's done all he can. Look, I think if you don't mind I want to go home now. I'm tired of all this.'

On the way back, he asked her if Dr. Durrant had come frequently to the old man's villa.

'Oh, yes. He liked to stop and talk. They would sit out in the garden, drinking beer or lemonade, talking for hours. Dr. Durrant must have heard his entire life story.'

'You don't think much of Durrant?'

'I didn't like him, but I was sorry for him.'

This last seemed to come reluctantly from her.

Charlie was startled.

'Why, sorry? Surely there was no reason for that?'

'Your sister, you mean? Oh - I shouldn't have said that. But it wasn't like you think it was. Not at all. Oh damn it - I'm not going to say anything more.'

'Tell me.'

'He was a very weak man, Durrant, and I think he felt... he felt your sister was probably his last chance... he was so much older than she was. I didn't like him, but I could see what he felt for her.'

He was struck by her detached and cool way of looking at things. She seemed a good judge of people - better than he was, probably much better than poor Rosie had been.

'Did you know Rosie?'

'Yes - she was lovely. Her nature, as well - trusting, you know? But she was a strong character too, in her way, with all her life ahead of her. Durrant didn't seem to have much to offer her. God, that was terrible, her death. Oh, I'm sorry, perhaps you don't want to talk about Rosie.'

'As a matter of fact, it's a relief in a way to hear someone speaking of her. Have you got any idea at all of who might have killed her? '

'No, I can't imagine anyone hurting her. Not unless Durrant might have gone off his head for some reason - and there would have to be some terrible reason for him to attack her, I'm sure of it.'

They had walked along the Rue Caillebotte. The mosque doors were open; inside, he could see carpets and lights. The call to prayer drifted down the street. 'Funny, now I've got used to it, I think it's beautiful,' she said.

On the doorstep she turned to him. 'I'm sorry about your sister but there's nothing I can say to help. Thanks for the meal but don't come and see me again. There's no more to tell you.' She seemed to have made her mind up about something, and he knew that he wanted to see her again, not just because of Rosie.

'Wait!' he said. 'Wait!' There was something he had forgotten.

'Did you send me a photograph?'

She stared at him for a moment, as if in puzzlement. 'No, of course not!' she said.

'You didn't post it to me in London?'

'Post you a photograph? Why should I?'

She looked blankly at him for a moment. Then she shut the door.

A black car slid along the south end of the Rue Caillebotte as Cashel made his way northwards.

A small boy sitting in the street looked up and gazed at the car as if in recognition. He spat deliberately in its direction as it glided past.

Chapter 32

Maubourg banged on the door of the Villa Bleue. There was the sound of footsteps inside the passageway, and the door was opened by Charlie Cashel, rubbing a stubbly chin.

Wordlessly, the Englishman held the door open.

Maubourg entered. There was a car at the gates with two leather-jacketed men inside it.

'You coming in alone, Inspector? Don't want to bring your heavies with you?'

'You are courageous today, M. Cashel,' observed Maubourg pleasantly. 'No, I'll come in alone. But there is something I want to ask you about.'

They went into the shaded kitchen. It was about ten o'clock in the morning and already, even in March, the sunshine was getting a southern heat in it. By midday, the temperature in here might be quite unpleasant if the Englishman did not have the air-conditioning switched on, reflected Maubourg.

He did not waste time.

'You went to see Mademoiselle Washington yesterday.'

It was a statement and not a question.

The Englishman was tense, jumpy.

'What if I did?'

'Monsieur Cashel. Please try to understand this is a murder enquiry. No - not just about the death of your sister. There is something else I must investigate. Something that may be connected with the murder of your sister. Please do not try to be - as you say - to be to clever with me.'

They were seated on the awkward upright chairs. Cashel said, 'I want a cup of coffee anyway. Do you want one, Inspector?'

Maubourg nodded and waited while the filter coffee and hot milk were poured into two big, steel breakfast bowls which the Englishman took down from a cupboard.

'Good invention, this,' said Cashel, as he held his bowl by the wooden handles, and drank deeply. Then, abruptly, he said, 'What has happened?'

'Another death. Yesterday morning. The body was found by our rubbish collectors early in the morning.'

For some reason, the face of Susanna Washington leapt into Charlie's mind and he was filled with fear. Oh God, he was saying to himself, don't let it be her. Please don't let it be her.

Outwardly, he was saying, 'Who was it?'

Maubourg said simply, 'Come with me, M Cashel.'

It was a short drive.

As they went into the building, Charlie suddenly remembered a school holiday, an exchange with a French boarding school, unheated, bare, with its own particular smell, a special kind of institutional cleanliness pervading the building. It had been the smell of Eau-de-Javel, the universal disinfectant in France.

Maubourg gave him no warning. There was a sudden clanging of doors, then he was rushed down a long white-tiled corridor that reminded him still of that school in Paris, and as they emerged through a door at the far end he realised abruptly that childhood nightmares had been left far behind. This was the place where horrors come true.

The room was entirely white-tiled. One wall was lined with numbered metal lockers.

The tiled floor had channels and drains. There was a steel table in the middle of it.

When he had identified Rosie, they had made things easy for him, treated him carefully, respectfully, giving him plenty of time. She had been lying beneath a sheet, which had been drawn gently back.

Now Maubourg brusquely signalled to an attendant, showed him a pass, gave him a number.

The attendant moved slowly along the metal rows.

The drawer slid open. Charlie had a sensation of falling into a void.

The body was naked.

There was no face.

Maubourg was staring down, seemingly peering into the bloody depths.

The chest was grizzled, the legs had ropes of blue veins knotting along the fat, white flesh.

The hollows of eye-sockets and the mouth were visible, caked with blood and edged with gleams of white bone. The nose, lips and cheeks had been sliced off, as in some old illustration of Turkish atrocities. At the edges of the massive wounds, the hanging shreds of skin were hard and shrivelled. Stumps of teeth gleamed through the fleshless cheeks.

Charlie flung himself out through double doors that closed shut behind him like an airlock and vomited on to the tiles.

Maubourg followed him out.

'You met him, didn't you?'

'Who the hell is it?'

But he knew, before he heard the answer.

'Durrant.'

'What did they do to his face?'

'A fairly expert carving job, but not to conceal his identity; they'd left his wallet intact. In any case, with DNA analysis, we can tell more in some ways from the tiniest scraping of cells that we could from the entire facial appearance. No, the identification might have been delayed a little - that is all. But I think the mutilation is the mark of a gangland murder, M. Cashel, of a gang that deals in drugs and extortion. They specialise in tracking down any weak elements, shall we say. This man was probably an informer and his killing, this brutality, is meant to deter others. And it will succeed - it is horrible, is it not? The newspapers will make the most of it, believe you me. 'Faceless body found on the Croisette!' Poor fellow, it's a sordid way to end up - after a blameless life attending to tennis injuries!'

'You didn't need to bring me here, you bastard, you knew who he was all along!'

There was no reply from Maubourg. They got into the car in silence. Charlie found that his hands were shaking.

As they neared the villa, the car radio suddenly squawked and Maubourg stopped the car at the end of the street.

'I'll drop you here.'

As Charlie got to the gates of the Villa Bleue, a long black Peugeot slid along the street. Going up the stairs to the bathroom he turned, opposite a window on the landing, to catch a glimpse of the car disappearing into the distance. He stopped on the stair.

A long, shiny black car, slipping out of the edge of his vision, gliding just out of sight, with a maddening familiarity, lurking at the very edge of his consciousness and memory, so it seemed.

Then memory sprang back, just for a split-second, but long enough to know where he had seen the car before. At the end of the Rue Caillebotte.

Charlie slipped downstairs again, phoned the number of a local taxi firm, drummed impatiently on the telephone table while he waited for them to answer the phone. Suddenly he felt released from apathy, from a kind of hopelessness that had overtaken him with Imelda. He was doing something, taking control of a situation, though he didn't know how Susanna Washington would react. She might tell him to go to hell.

Chapter 33

Susanna answered the door herself, this time, but drew back as soon as she saw Charlie's face.

'There's nothing more I can say,' she said.

Charlie pushed past her into the shabby hallway and slammed the door shut. Then he moved down and into her room and said urgently,

'Grab a few clothes - whatever you need. You can't stay here.'

'What the hell are you on about?' she said angrily.

But he was already looking out of the window, watching a dark shape sliding along the street.

'Christ, there's no time. I don't know what they want but they're here all right. Is there a way out at the back?'

He grabbed her hand and dragged her down the passageway. There was a stone-flagged kitchen, with an old gas stove and a sink in one corner. The house seemed empty.

There came the sound of hammer blows on the flimsy front door.

A faceless mass of blood.

Charlie could still visualise the man's body.

He pulled Susanna along and through another door.

They were out in a yard, through a gap in a fence and then running down an alleyway. Susanna was gasping out exclamations and questions, but Charlie did not stop. He somehow kept going, dragging the girl along, until they came out on another street that must lie parallel with the Rue Caillebotte, and here he saw that they were close to the edge of town. There were a few small shops and a garage, and then beyond lay countryside, steep and hilly, with scrubby arid plantations and pines.

They slowed down. He mopped his face with his handkerchief, tried to smooth down his hair, tried to breathe normally like a man who had not just fled for half a mile as if all the hounds in hell were after him.

She pulled her arm away from him.

'What the hell are you playing at?'

Yet there was a frightened edge to her voice, half-guessing that there was something fearful almost at their heels.

'We have to get as far out as we can - can we get out of the city this way?'

There was a straight and dusty road, lined with poplars, ahead of them, leading into the distance. No cover, damned little shelter, he thought. He was almost sure he could hear the revving of an engine near at hand, as if a car were nosing along through a side street. They'd know by now the birds were flown - whoever 'they' might be. All their pursuers needed was to cruise around, nudging that big black nose of the Peugeot along till they saw their quarry ...

The bus came along suddenly, turning out of a side street, so that he nearly missed it, almost failed to take in that they were a few yards from a sign that said, 'Arrêt'.

Even then, he wasn't sure it would stop.

But it did, an old rattletrap, a country coach with worn paintwork and ESTEREL on the front.

He didn't understand what the driver was saying for a moment or two, and she took over. 'Esterel isn't a town - it's a region. There are plenty of little fishing villages along the road. I think he'll go as far as Fréjus - we'll get off somewhere on the way.'

There were some rapid bursts of French and she turned back to Charlie. 'Have you got any money?'

He scraped the change out of his pockets and handed it to her, desperately hoping it would be enough, that it wasn't one of those buses where you have to book the tickets in advance, that the driver would sell them tickets, that he would let two sweaty and bedraggled tourists on his bus ... and at the same time found that he was watching out for something creeping up at the back of the bus, for a long black shiny bonnet sliding out of a side street ... praying that the driver would get on with it, that he wouldn't haggle over the fares ... and then suddenly they were sitting down in deep seats of worn fuzzy upholstery and the coach was belting along the empty road so that the poplars sped jaggedly past as flashing bars of black and white. Looking back, he could see a cloud of dust in the middle of the road. What it represented, whether their own tracks in the country dust or the Peugeot speeding after them, he could not tell.

They were turning out of town. An endless stream of traffic was making north, but the bus swung off to the left before they hit the motorway.

'It's the old road along the coast,' said Susanna. 'Used to be called the Corniche d'Or'.

It was a strange landscape of purple-red rocks and dark blue sea. Inland, broken and rocky hills rose on the right of the Corniche, with scrubby gorse growing out of the barren wastes.

'That's the real Provence,' said Susanna. 'Where the living was hard. Still is, for some. Not like the coast, with all the tourists. Sometimes, when I had a day off, I used to come up here.'

She paused, as if remembering. Then she went on briskly. 'Now tell me, what the hell's going on?'

He told her, as much as he could. He didn't want to terrify her, but somehow he had to break through any incredulity and convince her of the danger. She caught his seriousness and watched him gravely as he talked, his grey eyes intense, sweeping his black hair from his forehead in his earnestness.

He hadn't figured it out straight away. He'd been tired, confused. The implications of what Maubourg had told him hadn't sunk in, but now he explained it in full to the girl.

He remembered what Maubourg had said. 'The mutilation was meant to deter others.'

To deter others who might give information to Charlie Cashel, who had come snooping into the circumstances of his sister's death?

'Listen' he said, 'I was talking to Durrant and I've been talking to you. And I think both times they saw me. And you know what happened to Durrant? They killed him.'

Chapter 34

The bus had reached a small fishing port, with a couple of restaurants and cafés along the waterside. The walls of the buildings were painted winsomely in blues and pinks, looking almost washed-out beside the brilliant deep blue of the water and the dark harsh porphyry of the landscape. The bus lurched on, out of the little scattering of buildings.

'We're nearly at St. Raphael,' said the girl. 'I bought tickets as far as there. That was as far as the money would take us.'

Charlie felt, not for the first time, that he was living in a strange dream. The extraordinary landscape, the recollection of a name glimpsed only casually on the label of a bottle - surely St. Raphael wasn't a real place?

But it was, and they were getting off the bus at a palm lined esplanade, near a fountain and a children's carousel with red and gold trappings.

There was a small café-bar in a side street; it had tables outside and an awning flapping in the breeze but they went into the bar inside, a dark and stuffy interior, where Charlie told her as much as he knew. That their pursuers were somehow connected with those who had killed Rosie, he had no doubt now.

There was little enough to go on. He produced the photograph again, just as he had in that little Italian place in Victoria in what seemed another lifetime. It was crumpled now, but the colours shone out in the darkness of the bar in St. Raphael, as they had on that clammy grey day in London.

She stared at it.

'Do you know the place?' he asked.

'No, but I know the picture,' she answered. 'It used to hang in old Arthuis' bedroom.'

It suddenly dawned on Charlie. All this time, he had been trying to identify the place in the picture - but was that what really what mattered?

His thoughts seemed to be shifting like a kaleidoscope, showing him a new pattern, a new perspective.

Suppose it wasn't the subject of the picture that mattered. Suppose that was immaterial - it might have been anything.

Because the important thing wasn't the subject of the painting at all.

The important thing was the picture itself.

'Oh God, I've been so stupid!' he said.

Susanna Washington stared at him.

'You look like a man who's just had a revelation! Something apocalyptic, no less!'

Even through his racing thoughts, he liked her forceful Scottish accent.

'Look, the thing is that it's the painting that matters! Would you expect to use Van Gogh's painting of sunflowers to identify a species? It's not a botanical illustration, after all. Or to learn about agriculture from a picture of haystacks by Monet? I thought it was important to know which cemetery it was, that there was something there in that particular place, maybe even some special grave or tombstone. But that's not the point at all! The point is the painting itself - and the artist who painted it!'

Susanna suddenly sat back in her chair. 'And you think maybe it's a famous artist. You reckon it's a valuable painting - and of course that's the reason why someone would have bothered to photograph it.'

'Yes, and that's why there's only the one photograph.' He recalled the negatives, the rest of the film blank. It wasn't that the photo of the picture had been selected from a whole set of pictures. Only one frame had been taken. 'If they were photographing a place - on a visit to the country, say - they'd surely have taken more than one shot. But they just took the one that they wanted...'

'Perhaps they didn't have time to take any more?' suggested Susanna.

'Could be,' he replied. 'But do you know anything about the picture?'

'He was very attached to it, I can tell you that. He told me once or twice...' her voice trailed off.

'You said it hung in his bedroom? Try and remember everything about it!'

She closed her eyes and concentrated.

'Let's see, what was the room like? Well, there was a great old-fashioned wardrobe, in some wood like ebony, I think, and one of those tallboys with a pair of silver-backed men's hair-brushes on the top ... and an oriental rug ... and at the side of the bed - that's it!'

She stopped suddenly and opened her grey-blue eyes: large eyes, Charlie thought, remarkable eyes.

'The painting was always hanging on the wall facing the end of the bed - so that he could see it. And when I went in ... when they accused me of stealing the drugs from that table beside his bed ... the very bed where he had died ... I ran into the room and looked at the table.. and the drugs were gone. I didn't look for anything else, but I can see it now. I stared at that bedside table where the drug-bottles had been ... and then I turned my head ...'

She turned her head as if re-creating the scene in her mind.

'That's it! It's gone!'

So vivid was her reliving of that moment at the side of the old man's dead body that Charlie felt a shudder.

'What was gone? The picture?'

'Yes, but it didn't register! Because I was only thinking about the drugs - about what they'd accused me of. Nothing had been mentioned about the picture. But I can see it now - there's a grey space on the wall, where the wallpaper hadn't faded - it was almost white everywhere else. And a hook - yes, that picture has gone!'

Chapter 35

It had been hard to leave Charlie. She was in no doubt about that - but in no doubt, either, that she could not be pulled around after him any longer. He had rushed her out of the house in the Rue Caillebotte, and somehow they had ended up in St. Raphael, because he had some urge to protect her.

Come on, be honest, she told herself. And because you trusted him. Some innocent Englishman who has no idea of what his little sister might have got involved in, who is wet behind the ears when it comes to the real life of this part of the world - the drugs, the organised crime, the sex joints where it's all served up like meat on a slab.

But it would have not been possible to go on like that, running with him, having her hand held, being under his protection as if she had been some helpless creature in peril. And early that morning, in the hard light of day, it had been difficult to truly think that she and Charlie were in real danger; there had been no sign of their pursuers since they had reached the Esterel. No, she had not been frightened when she had slipped out of the room over the little café in St. Raphael. But it had been difficult, in some ways.

Oh yes, she had to admit it to herself, leaving him had been hard. His body, long and naked, sprawled out across the bed, dappled with springy hair, his arms reaching out for her even in his sleep. It had been a long time since she had slept with a man - she had almost forgotten the pleasure of it, the feel of his rough skin and hair against her body. 'A good fuck!' she thought to herself, giggling with pleasure, like a teenager. It was the first time she'd laughed out loud for a long while.

But she was in a bit of a spot, running out like that. She didn't even have any money of her own with her - he had dragged her out of the house just as she was, in the old cotton dress. She hadn't even had time to grab her bag when she had left the house in the Arab quarter. When she slipped down the staircase and out into the street in St. Raphael, she realised that she didn't have a sou in her pocket. She had to hitch a life back to Cannes.

She'd been lucky - a woman driver had stopped almost right away, a well-dressed blonde in her thirties who talked in a slow creamy voice about the bar in St. Raphael she had been negotiating to buy. 'I told the guy, in case you think I don't look like I can handle it, I'm already running one in Cannes. Who says a woman can't manage a night-club? - you just have to handle things right. Get control, if you see what I mean. Good staff.' She laughed, as if at some private joke.

'Where are you from - you English?'

Susanna felt some obscure resurgence of nationalism. She was tired of constantly being taken for English, of never saying anything because she would just get a blank stare. 'No, I'm Scottish'.

Écossaise.

The word seemed to register with the blonde woman. 'Oh, fantastic. *La Reine d'Écosse.* I saw a play about her once - the one who had her head chopped off - now she didn't handle the situation very well, did she? You know what they say about the Scots, though - they're honest. They have that reputation with money, eh?'

The woman turned quickly to look at Susanna.

'And, you don't mind my saying so - you look as if you might need some work. Not in the bar, of course - frankly, you don't seem that type. But I might just need an honest Scot - someone to do - well, sort of office work. If you need a job, come and see me. My name's Sandra. Just Sandra will do - we don't bother with surnames!'

The stranger had a small shiny leather handbag in pimpernel red, from which, when they stopped at a set of traffic lights, she fished out a deckle-edged pink card with gilt lettering. 'La Boîte Rouge - Bar-Disco.' There was a curvy-lettered address. The address and the phone number beneath it were in Le Cannet.

Sandra dropped Susanna on the way into Cannes, not far from the Villa Bleue, with a wave of her fingernails, which had little gilt suns dotted on their long, curving, scarlet shields by some expensive manicurist.

But Susanna didn't go into the Villa. Instead, she waited, and crossed over to the other side of the road, watching in the shadow of a tall clipped hedge, watching the front door of the Arthuis house, whence she had been taken away shamed and in disgrace, the housekeeper-turned-thief.

She didn't have long to wait and soon she walked briskly up the path and banged on the door.

There was the sound of shuffling footsteps from somewhere inside, of middle-aged feet dragging over a thick carpet.

She saw Mademoiselle Rolland set off, bag in hand, probably to do some shopping in the Renault. The woman's shoulders were bowed, her small pink face wrinkling in anxiety as she got into the car. Monique Arthuis' companion, thought Susanna to herself, presumably her lover, and wondered if the two women slept together, if they still felt anything for each other. Presumably it was like an old, companiable marriage. But you could never rule out sex - look at Durrant, capable of ridiculous, humiliating passion for a teenager. Still, the two women seemed to lead tranquil enough lives.

It wasn't difficult to get inside - all that had been necessary was to follow the postman on his round, to press the bell and to shout something about a parcel through her cupped hand. The distortions of a voice calling through a thick panel of wood had done the rest. The front door of the house with grey shutters swung open.

The thin mouth, with traces of pink lipstick embedded in the wrinkles of the lips, opened in a gasp.

Susanna had the door open and was inside, slamming it shut after her.

'What do you want?' said Monique Arthuis angrily. 'I don't want to talk to you - you're the scum of the earth!'

But Susanna was already beyond her and opening the door of the sitting room. It looked unfamiliar: the Persian carpet had gone and bleached linen covers had been thrown over the backs of the chairs. There was a low glass-topped coffee table in the style of thirty years previously, a heavy brown rug thrown on a long sagging couch, as if to make a day bed. All was tidy and immaculate, as dull and drab as the woman herself. These possessions had not been here when Susanna and Mr. Arthuis had been in residence; clearly, they had been imported for the temporary convenience of Monique herself, while she emptied the place of the valuable and beautiful objects that old Arthuis had collected over his lifetime. All gone now, it seemed.

Except for one thing. Blazing away on the wall, filling the dull living-space with its luminous presence, defying all the stultified beige and brown conventions which Monique had imported, was an oil painting.

'I suppose that belongs to you now?' asked Susanna, staring across the room. There was no need to say what object she had in mind. Only one possession in Monique's entire drab existence could ever have merited such urgency.

'I'm not going to tell you anything! Get out of here - you're a thief and a drug addict - and a whore for the Arabs!' The woman's ugly mouth was frightened, yet self-righteous. Her thin lips opened wide over stained teeth.

Susanna anticipated what was going to happen and slammed a hand over that open mouth, before it had time to formulate a cry. She grabbed the woman with one arm. Still with a hand over Monique's mouth, she held on to her as she tried to get out of the living room and back into the hall. Susanna was half disgusted at the unpleasant acrid smell that arose from the plump unmuscled body, half disgusted at herself. God, what was she doing, grabbing hold of a woman of sixty like this, clamping one hand over her mouth?

She tried to put you in jail, she told herself. This poor old harmless respectable creature did her damnedest to get you convicted on a drugs charge. If Maubourg had been a bit less honest - if he had been willing to press things a bit further - then she, Susanna, might still be in a cell right now.

'Oh, I'm not going to hurt you!' she said, impatiently. 'But there are things you've got to tell me. There's no point in screaming - I saw the other woman going out a few minutes ago.'

Monique was gaping for breath, but subsided as Susanna said into her ear, the coarse grey hair brushing unpleasantly across the younger woman's lips, 'I'm not going to do you any harm - I came here because you accused me of stealing the drugs! You planted those drugs in my suitcase, didn't you? But why, I want to know why? What did I ever do to you?'

The old woman was sagging now. She subsided on to the couch, Susanna letting her grip relax as the awkward body slid down on to the fat cushions.

'I knew what you were from the moment I first saw you.' The wrinkled mouth was hissing venomously. 'Call yourself a housekeeper! Oh, I could see what was going on. You were trying to worm your way in - no doubt you thought you were in for a legacy. Well, perhaps you were. But I thought if I could get you ... get you deported - driven out of the country for ever ... then you wouldn't be here to claim anything under the will.'

She laughed. 'As it was, he hadn't left you any money anyway! So I needn't have bothered to try and get rid of you.'

'Did you take the picture? Take it from his room? It wasn't there just after he died - I'm certain of that.'

'No, no!' Monique said, with a sharp little laugh. 'Why should I? I've inherited everything after all. It belongs to me anyway. Why would I steal my own property? It's a valuable picture - an original. It belongs to me!'

'Valuable?'

'So Antoine always said. He said it was a Leclant.'

Susanna looked up at the picture. The brilliant blues of the sea beyond the red-brown earth, the geometric white shapes of the tombstones, were so brilliant that, seen at such close quarters, they seemed to make her eyes dazzle. She had heard of Leclant, of course - the artist who had worked in Provence in the thirties, and whose merest sketches now commanded six-figure prices. But she knew little about painting. Could this really be an original Leclant?

The frame was faded and over-elaborate, worn gilt in a florid style. There was a bit of string sticking out from the back, less than an inch, probably where it projected from a knot.

An impulse seemed to make her reach out and lift the picture down from the wall.

'What are you doing - you thief!' squawked Monique, grabbing at her arm. Susanna fended her off.

'There's something very strange about this painting' said Susanna. 'I'd be careful, if I were you. There are some people after me - and I think they're after this as well.'

Monique seemed to believe this with a readiness that half-astonished Susanna. The woman's mouth dropped open in a gasp.

Susanna couldn't repress a feeling of pleasure at Monique's obvious terror, but turned her attention to the canvas, gleaming with thick brushstrokes in oil; there didn't seem to be a signature. She had a look at the back, in case there was a label there.

The string on the back of the frame was quite new and looked rather amateurish. It seemed not the usual kind, and Susanna realised that it was ordinary household string, not professional framer's cord. There was nothing on the perfectly ordinary brown paper that covered the back of the picture - no label with an artist's name or gallery.

'The police - I'll call the police,' Monique was muttering.

'No, I don't think that would be a good idea. Inspector Maubourg didn't do what you wanted last time, did he? He didn't charge me with stealing the drugs. If you try to get me arrested again, he might get suspicious of your motives.'

'They'll believe anything of you! Living with foreigners the way you do.'

But Monique seemed reluctant to actually make a move to the telephone; her protests appeared to splutter away.

Susanna turned the picture over in her hands again. What was so significant about it? She didn't know much about Leclant, but tried to recollect what she had heard. Surely there had been something about a picture of his coming up at auction in Paris - an American millionaire collector who had been bidding over the telephone as the price of the Leclant which was being auctioned was rising by a thousand pounds a second. Worth a lot of money, then.

'If it's a valuable picture, isn't it dangerous to keep it here?'

'So what if it is - I can do what I like with it! I want to have it hanging on my wall. Why shouldn't I - do you think I have no culture? I like art!'

This was proclaimed in utter defiance of all the evidence in the room around them, which included the only other object remaining on the walls, a calendar with a photograph of snow-covered Alps and a washed-out sky.

Susanna reached out to put the picture back on the hook

Afterwards, she was never sure what prompted her to say:

'Who put the new string on the back?'

Now why had she said that?

'What a daft question. If you must know, it was the doctor. Doctor Durrant.'

Chapter 36

As she passed along the Rue d'Antibes, where long-legged women, their skin a smooth golden tan even this early in the year, clicked along in expensive high-heeled shoes, Susanna caught a glimpse of herself, mirrored in the shopfronts. Her straight, heavy, honey-coloured hair hung limply down to her shoulders and her dress, long-sleeved with pale pink and white stripes, looked poor and washed-out, second hand, which was exactly what it was. And she longed to be again safely back in the Rue Caillebotte, where her appearance would cause no surprise, evoke no comparisons or comments.

It would be a long walk - about three kilometres, she judged - she was used by now to assessing distances in kilometres, food by the gramme and the kilo.

She would have liked to be able to go and have a cup of coffee on the way, in some little café. She found herself looking longingly through the window of one such place, at the customers sitting contentedly around, as a television blared away above the bar.

And suddenly she was inside and looking up, impelled into the café by what she had seen from the pavement outside, listening to the commentary droning away.

On the screen, there was a dilapidated building in a familiar street. The camera panned slowly up the walls. All the windows had been smashed. Across to the front door - or where it should have been, there being instead a splintered mass of wood. There was an ambulance waiting ready, a shot of a mosque and a minaret. The house had a terrible familiarity about it, the curtains flapping in the shattered windows were recognisable, though Susanna's brain didn't want to do it, to make the connection, to perform the act of recognition.

She tried to concentrate on the reporter's voice that droned over the images of destruction. There were murmurs from a couple of the customers - horror from some, but a pitiless laugh from a bespectacled old man who sat near the door. The others turned to stare at him, which took their attention off Susanna.

The commentary continued remorselessly. 'The attack on an Arab property in the Rue Caillebotte is believed by some to have been started by right-wing extremists ... the house was attacked last night by masked men with axes and crowbars. The Arab family occupying it were threatened but most of them managed to make good their escape through a rear entrance.'

Shot of the door at the back. There were great gashing wounds in the wood, deep gouges. Susanna imagined Leila and the children fleeing desperately as the pickaxes crashed against the planks.

The commentary continued. 'One man was taken to hospital suffering from injuries ... police are investigating the crime.'

A neighbour now, interviewed. A frightened brown face. Yes, there had been threats and in the early hours of this morning she had heard a hammering on the door to her own ... they were terrified of the Front National, which had now taken to attacking Arab families ...' Susanna felt herself swaying as she saw the faces on the screen.

A school photograph of the children. Yussouf aged eight and Said aged six and the baby of the family. Aged three-and-a-half years.

The children of Leila and Mahmoud.

The whole family attacked in the house where, if it had not been for Charlie Cashel, Susanna herself would have been asleep and unknowing in the early hours of this morning.

Chapter 37

In the police station where Cashel had suffered his brief experience of imprisonment in the cells, Maubourg watched the television monitor in the information room. He leaned forward to watch the scene of destruction, the smashed glass, the splintered wood.

'That's where the woman was staying, chief. The one who used to be the housekeeper for old Arthuis. We traced her there easily enough - she gave it as her address when she registered as a foreigner. Wasn't hiding when she went there - just wanted somewhere to keep her head down for a bit. And somewhere cheap!'

'French bureaucracy - thank God for it!' said one of his colleagues and they all laughed.

'But they haven't said whether anything was seen of her after the attack,' continued Montvallon.

'Did you check with the gendarmerie?'

'Yeah.'

It had been the local gendarmes who went to the Rue Caillebotte in response to the emergency call from the neighbour.

Maubourg scraped his teeth with his thumb nail, thinking, as he always thought when he found himself occupied with this familiar habit, 'Damn, that's disgusting.'

'They're blaming it on the Front National. The commentators, the squad - everyone. On the anti-Arab movement. The politicians are screaming for action - the right says it's all a put-up job! It'd get them all off our backs if we threw a couple of the local thugs into jail.'

'Let them run. It's easier to see rats when they come out of the sewers - besides, I want to see the prosecutor. He'll probably be interviewed next.'

'Oh fuck Maupuis - damned squeamish college boy! He may be the leading light of the judicial whizz-kids but he's too inexperienced to know a damned thing about policing. Him and his sacred rights of humanity!'

'Maupuis is a clever bastard, though - he can master the details of a case overnight. Anyway, the one who really counts is the examining magistrate. The prosecutor can't do anything unless he decides there's a case to go to court. Or she, since Galant will take it on. And she's not easily deceived - not even by policemen.'

'What a suspicious old cynic you are, boss! A nasty mind you have!'

'Very nasty! Anyway, the Cashel girl's murder's been passed to Galant. Seems the Mairie and the Chamber of Commerce got a bit worried that the murder of a foreigner might be bad for the reputation of the town, if it weren't cleared up. She's already dealing with the big one - the Mutilator.'

Montvallon was listening from the other side of the room. 'Well, Rosie Cashel will be a morsel on a side plate in comparison,' he said. 'But I don't know why they've insisted on Galant.'

'She's got a hell of a reputation from Marseilles. Cleared out the waterfront,' said the man behind the desk.

'It could be that,' answered Maubourg. 'But I don't know if those political types really understand what she did there. No - they may have a different reason in mind.'

'Such as?'

'They might think because she's a woman they can bring more pressure to bear on her. But I tell you this - she's a bloody tough nut to crack!'

Maubourg grinned and walked out of the information room.

The leather-jacketed officer turned to the man behind the desk.

'Oh, Christ,' he said. 'Bloody thugs, and he wants to let them run.'

The man at the desk looked up thoughtfully. The television monitor had now moved on to some other story - it looked like a famine. Wraith-like figures stumbled across the screen in a cloud of dust.

'Maybe he's got his reasons,' he said.

'His wife still screwing around? Maybe that's why he's blowing it.'

'If she is, he doesn't know. And don't talk about it, Montvallon. Nobody knows, except Longlant saw her with a bloke that one time. Anyway, it's none of your fucking business.'

'No, it's not, unfortunately.' Montvallon grinned. 'She's a beauty, that one. *Bien foutue, on dirait.*'

'Shut your mouth, Montvallon.'

Chapter 38

Charlie woke with a start. He was lying wrapped in a blanket on a bed that occupied most of a very small room.

There was a cool dawn light coming through the shutters of a window opposite the bed. The barred rays had that distinctive early morning feel of a country where you know the day is going to get warm, and that this brief half-hour is a respite between the complete dissipation of darkness and the first breezes that would come with the evening, after the long day was closing.

Charlie rolled over in the bed. The previous evening he had drunk a lot of local red wine, but his head was clear. They had eaten here in the little café below, where they had taken refuge as soon as they arrived in St. Raphael. After his stroke of genius in realising the importance of identifying the painting and not its subject, after Susanna had recalled the disappearance of that same picture from the bedroom of her dead employer, they had stayed at the table and talked ... about themselves, he realised now. About Imelda and about what Glasgow meant to Susanna and a thousand other things, because one subject had seemed to lead naturally to another. And the coffees which they had originally ordered led into aperitifs with some stinging local herby liqueur, and then the simple menu had arrived, and somehow they found they had talked themselves hungry. They were, to their surprise, ravenous, and fell on the little bowls of black, cracked olives dressed in lemon and garlic that preceded the meal, and then devoured crayfish with aïoli, fruit and sweet round cheeses rolled in pine nuts, till at last they found themselves with plates that had been wiped clean by some sort of coarse local bread, and, full circle, with cups of coffee once more, accompanied by tiny golden glasses into which the proprietor had splashed cognac from a squat bottle with a torn label.

And then, it had seemed entirely natural, it had been inevitable, that it was dark outside and that enquiries as to a hotel for the night from the owner of the café had led to a small room upstairs, which the proprietor rented out during the tourist season, and which it so happened was available now, so that there was no need to go further afield. And by then, of course, there was no question of going further afield, as they pulled their clothes off in the dark little room and fell naked on the huge double bed, into a long night of exploration and excitement and violent, unexpected, passion and pleasure.

Till he had slept, not long before dawn. And woke now to find she had gone.

He was surprised at the powerful sense of loss. Stupid, he thought. Stupid to think there was anything more to it than a single night of pleasure for two lonely people, two people driven by different circumstances away from their normal lives and plunged into a situation where they had been driven close to the limits by fear and stress, so that all reactions were unnaturally tense and heightened. He had tried to do something to save Susanna from the nightmarish things that seemed to be closing in, but she was determined to remain un-saved. In which case, the best thing that Charlie Cashel could do was to look out for himself and set about saving his own hide.

He got out of bed, looked ruefully at his crumpled face in the mirror, splashed it with cold water from the tap over the tiny washbasin, and began to forget the scent and feel of Susanna's body.

And yet, as he took milky breakfast coffee in the little café downstairs, Charlie found that he was unconsciously alert for any trace of her. When the phone behind the bar rang a couple of times, he was listening out in case it was for him. As he paid the bill ('Yes, the lady had to leave very early this morning') he even asked if there had been any messages for him, but of course there were none.

Yet it was at this moment, as he was putting the change in his pocket, that the proprietor casually switched on the radio. It was still difficult for him to follow a news broadcast in French, but there were some things that were impossible to miss. The words 'Cannes' and 'Rue Caillebotte' for instance. And then he felt his stomach sinking into some terrible pit as he stared at the commentator standing before the ruined house, and understood the words for attack and violence.

He tried to ask the proprietor for more information. The man shrugged his shoulders. 'Les arabes,' he said, 'les arabes', as though there were no need of any more details such as names or motives.

He tried to comfort himself by working out possible journey times and thinking that she couldn't have got back to the house in the Rue

Caillebotte before the attack had taken place, and yet he was uncertain of the time she had left and anyway he didn't know how she was travelling or even whether she had any money on her.

There wasn't anything he could think of doing except going back to Cannes.

'Think it out,' said Charlie to himself, stepping out into the morning sunshine. 'Think it out'.

About all he knew of Rosie's life in the Villa Bleue was that she had a lover, Doctor Robin Durrant. Susanna Washington, who had witnessed some strange behaviour on the part of Durrant, had been the target of an attack - of that he had no doubt.

There were two threads running through all the events that had happened, and he clung on to both of them. One was the painting, the photograph which had brought him here, the whereabouts of which he didn't know. The other was Durrant.

Chapter 39

La Boîte Rouge had a long, narrow bar that stretched far back from the street front into mirrored depths with swags of red plush. All the way along glittered arrays of facetted bottles and steel bar stools. At night heavy rock boomed out into the narrow alleyway, and the punters looking for sex and highs drifted up from the smart front of the town down in the bay below, deeper and deeper into the warm noisy depths of the nightclub.

There were always a few thick-shouldered bouncers on the door, and a couple more lurking in the inner depths who could pass any trouble that developed inside out to their comrades at the entrance. Comrades in a special sense because quite a few of the employees here were from the former Soviet Union; many were citizens of breakaway Central Asian states who had no intentions of embracing the restrictions of Islam. They were cheap to employ, good with their fists, but unreliable, Sandra explained to Susanna.

'They are always getting drunk and fighting amongst themselves. The Chechens and so on, they have no self-discipline. All they want to do is make a lot of money here and then they think they can just go back and run things when they want. They don't understand that there's a loyalty you have to give.'

Sandra herself understood that very well. Dinin commanded her loyalty: Susanna was not sure how much gratitude and fear combined in Sandra.

Dinin was certainly a different proposition from the rough blouson-clad gangs of Kazhakstans and Georgians who hung around. When Susanna had first seen him, her immediate thought was that he was stunted, but after a while she realised that his shoulders were so broad that he was almost an inverted triangle. It took some time to notice this because he invariably wore suits in dove grey that were a miracle of Italian tailoring, skilfully cut to minimise the heavy pyramid-shaped structure of Dinin's frame. His hair was black; the top of his head was like a crow's wing, so sleek and glossy.

Susanna thought at first that Dinin owned the Boîte Rouge, but after a while she understood that even Dinin had his place in a pecking order which stretched a long way up, up into realms which could not be touched.

Asking questions, however, was the last thing she intended to do. She

164

had found herself, shocked and penniless, walking away from images of rubble and smashed door fames, with nothing in her pocket but the card that Sandra had thrust into her hand after depositing her on the Croisette.

By the time she got to the Bar Rouge, Susanna was exhausted. She had not eaten for twenty-four hours, had drunk water from fountains and washed in public lavatories. She looked like, and in fact was, a tramp.

They nearly threw her out, but she produced Sandra's card, the only possession in her pocket. While the barman retired to a phone at the end of an expanse of shining glassy surface, the few customers there at midday looked her up and down and away. Mostly away. She could see for herself in the mirrored reflection behind the bar a waif-like face framed with lank, dusty locks, a stained blue sweater. With a shock, Susanna realised she was looking at her own reflection.

The barman was looking at her, talking into the phone. He came back down the bar for a moment. 'Sandra wants to know where you got her card.'

'She gave me a lift from St. Raphael.'

He was talking into the 'phone, peering at her as if he were describing her to an unseen questioner.

He came back towards her.

'Sandra says she'll be down in a few minutes.'

He turned away to rub at something with a cloth, then turned back.

'You don't look like the type who usually comes in here.'

Susanna laughed.

'In fact, I'd put the punters off! Isn't that what you're thinking?'

'What I'm thinking is that you could do with something to eat.'

As he cut some rolls open, sliced at a ham, put a handful of black olives beside the bread, filled a cup with coffee, Susanna found her body taking over - the juices started to flow in her mouth, something in her jaw demanded to chomp and chew, her stomach was desperate to get the food down inside her.

'You look as though you were starving!'

He sliced some more ham, put the wonderfully succulent, glistening pink pieces on to her plate. She thrust them into her mouth.

He poured himself a cup of coffee, raised it in her direction as he took a sip.

'Here's seeing you. Don't know when anyone's come in here just to eat before! You want her to give you a job?'

Susanna, her mouth stuffed with ham, nodded her head.

He produced a comb from his pocket, waved it in the direction of a sign saying 'Dames/Reines'.

'Go and wash up.'

She took the comb gratefully. In the little washroom which had a purple ceiling scattered with silver stars she washed her face, scrubbing off the grime that had accumulated as she stood at the side of the road, and damped and combed her hair.

Back in the bar, he took the comb from her and slid it back into his pocket. 'You look like more of a human being.'

'Thanks. Oh - by the way,' she stuck out her hand, 'Mathilde.'

He took her hand with a laugh. 'Bernard. But if your real name's Mathilde, just call me Julius Caesar! Still, what's it matter? Who says my real name's Bernard?'

He was a good-looking man, fair-haired, in his thirties, she judged, and possessed of the professional barman's dexterity in juggling with things: glasses, bottles and probably drunks.

'Thanks, Bernard.'

'Though I'd like to know what she's got in mind for you,' he continued, 'presumably not the usual role,' when Sandra entered at the far end of the room.

Sandra was wearing a silky lilac dress with her blonde hair clipped back in a shiny nineteen-thirties style. She looked Susanna up and down, but said nothing. Bernard tactfully moved away to the end of the bar.

'Ah, so it's the Scottish girl from St.Raphael! Well, I didn't really expect to see you again. What's your name - Mathilde, eh? Well, never mind, it will do. You won't want to have an attractive name here.'

Susanna couldn't find any other way of saying what she wanted.

'Will you give me a job?' she blurted out.

Sandra laughed. 'You, in a place like this? But I did say I could use someone like you, didn't I? No questions asked. Well, let's see - you need something, I can see that. Hard times, darling? And you're not the type to do the obvious thing - anyway, you wouldn't make any money at it, I can sense that straightaway. Have you ever worked in a bar before? - no, I guess you haven't. Well, don't despair. Maybe there is something you could do for us - like I said in the car, there's a job I need someone to help me with, someone I can trust. I do trust you somehow - I always judge people instinctively, and my instinct about you is that you are an honest woman - honest to the point of being boring, if you must know. And worse than honest - frankly, darling, you look as if you need a bath.'

Chapter 40

Maubourg stared at Cecile Galant across the long polished table. She's a good-looking woman, he thought. Her hips were swinging as she walked into the room; expensive-looking shoes.

They were talking in a large room, panelled with dark woods and filled with overstuffed chairs. Portraits of worthies hung around the walls, one or two bewigged characters needing cleaning, white jabots of lace at their throat gone brown with age, the majority rendered in the flat daubs of uninspired twentieth-century likenesses.

It was a chamber in the municipal offices, a place for long, dreary commercial discussions, meetings of pompous old men, or for plump burghers who desired to fulminate on the moral probity of their fellow citizens. It was a room that went unnoticed except on the rare occasions it was used for such uninteresting gatherings, notable only for torpor. There was a special table for the press, but the press never attended, knowing by experience that their columns would be better filled by chasing ambulances or mingling with the crazy, suntanned crowds down on the beach. The room was one of those places, found in any den of bureaucracy, that is always overlooked.

He presumed that this was precisely why Cecile had chosen it.

When Maubourg had walked into her office, she hadn't wasted any time.

'Ah, I believe I know what you want to talk about.'

'Well, matters arising from the death ...'

'Of Mademoiselle Cashel. Exactly so, but I have a meeting in five minutes' time, so I wonder, Inspector, if you would be so good as to walk along with me - we can talk on the way. It's on the fifth floor.'

He was taken aback by her directness, the way she took charge without preliminaries. Also by the oddity of this conspiratorial behaviour. He thought for a moment that perhaps she was interested in him sexually, and realised that he was interested in her, sensing her body under the dark suit. He could scent some faint trace of expensive cosmetics, though she didn't seem to wear much make-up, she was more the athletic type, as she walked past him to the door, which she opened without waiting for any attentions from him.

He followed her into the lift without comment. On the second floor, she opened the door of this long, empty conference room on the second floor, a room which he had been confident would be unoccupied, and entered abruptly, pulling the door shut.

'Do you know this room, Inspector?'

'No, never been in here before!'

'Precisely. Neither have most of our colleagues - yours or mine. That means that very few people are interested in its existence.'

Maubourg looked at the woman, then slowly around the room, scanning the ceiling with long pendant light-fittings, the great sweep of polished mahogany desk top. A boring, innocent room. He understood Galant's meaning. Innocent of bugs. What had she said? `Very few people are interested in its existence.' A place where no one would bother to plant a listening device - unlike the offices of the *juges d'instruction* or their secretarial department, for example. He wondered if she trusted her clerk, Lenoir.

'White Boy has a long arm,' he acknowledged.

'Listen, there are plenty of people with fingers in this particular pie, Chief Inspector. The English girl's death - that's just the least of it, in a way. There's a lot at stake, but we must make some sort of a move before long. The Front are agitating - they're putting it all down to the Arabs, the Maghrebis. According to the Front, they're responsible for most of the crime along the coast - and the Fascists are putting out more and more propaganda, and they're getting support. They've taken over the municipal government in Toulouse already. This might be the nineteen-thirties rather than the nineteen-nineties. If we're going to keep the right-wing from carrying out racist attacks here in Cannes, we've got to get them under control - but that means not giving them any cause for propaganda. In other words, we have to deal with them and with crime as a whole - you know what I mean.'

There was a pause. We're on the same side, this woman and I, thought Maubourg. But there aren't that many of us.

Cecile Galant was speaking again as she moved towards the door and he followed her.

'There's something I thought we might do, about the Cashel case. Durrant was treated in the same way as other victims of the Mutilator. So there's a connection between Rosie Cashel and the Mutilalator killings and the link is Durrant. So we need to look at him - really look, at every detail. Is anything known about Durrant's patients? Did he specialise in any special aspects of medicine?'

'We made a few enquiries. Nothing unusual - he wasn't a legacy-hunter, if that's what you mean, preying on sick and elderly patients. If anything, his patients were younger than average - a lot of sporting types.'

'I don't remember that in the dossier.'

'I don't think it was thought worth entering. Just one of my men gossiping with a pharmacist.'

'Everything should be noted in the dossier.'

She must trust Lenoir, then, thought Maubourg. He has access to all the information there.

Cecile was speaking again.

'Anyway, the pharmacist gives me an idea. Did you visit Durrant yourself? How did he keep his records?'

'Oh, in the old-fashioned way, as far as I remember. Load of files. Like our records.'

'Yes,' she said abstractedly, 'we need to do something to get that up to date.'

'I've been asking for new equipment, but the problem is the manpower to put all the back files into a computerised system.'

'I'll bear it in mind.' Her voice suddenly became alert again, as if she were a terrier that had turned aside from its digging for a moment. 'But back to Durrant. Did he make up his own prescriptions?'

'No, we looked into that straight away. He didn't have a dispensary.'

'So his prescriptions were made up by pharmacists, and they'll have more up-to-date systems, won't they? Based on computer programmes?'

'Yes, that's how all the dispensaries keep their records now. Makes it easy for us to check. As a matter of fact, I think the drug companies can supply them with programmes that do the job.'

'I want copies of all the pharmaceutical databases in the area - from all the pharmacies where they might have made up prescriptions for Durrant's patients. I can get someone to work out how to analyse them. And some he may have dispensed himself - so I want a check on his own records, though he may have covered his tracks. But he should have some legitimate records, anyway.'

'I'll need an official order. That's confidential personal information. And some help with copying the data.'

'I'll give you a *commission rogatoire* - that'll give you the authority. And get you some advice on the computing operations. Plus, I've got to take on the Cashel case,' she said, changing the subject. 'That's been made very clear. There's a connection with the mutilation murders, obviously, now that Rosie Cashel's grey-haired lover has been found with his face slashed about.'

'The press went for '*Les Mutilés*' in a big way,' he said. ''The Mutilator strikes again.' 'Will Psycho attack during the festival?' That's what the municipality, the Chamber of Commerce and so on - that's what they're interested in.'

Ah, thought Cecile. You've understood that.

There was a bitterness in his voice as he carried on. 'But when the Australian teacher was killed, and Durrant - now, that's going to make international headlines. That might really frighten them off the fleshpots!'

'Don't be so vehement about it. It has its flipside. We can have whatever facilities we need. That's official.'

She turned to move towards the door, then stopped. 'One more thing, Chief Inspector. You took Charles Cashel to the morgue.'

The tone in her voice had suddenly become sharp, accusing.

'I thought he needed a fright.'

Damn the woman, he thought, why do I find myself having to explain my actions?

'I can imagine what you thought, but that is not at issue. You took him in to view Durrant's body - without wearing protective clothing.'

'But we didn't touch anything at all.' He cursed himself. Now he sounded like a schoolboy, pleading, whining.

'That is not the point. There is the possibility of contamination of the evidence. If it were to come to a trial, then Cashel's lawyer could claim that any traces from his client that had been found on the body - any hairs, or traces of skin particles - had been acquired in the morgue.'

'Has anything been found on the body?'

'No'. She conceded the point reluctantly. 'No, there is nothing in the pathology report. We are dealing with professionals, not some bungling amateur who leaves his mark all over the body. And if we get the Mutilator of Cannes into court, everything will have to stand up to the most intensive kind of public scrutiny you've ever imagined. Every word, every scrap of evidence, is going to be turned over by the press. I have to think about that, you know. But it is a point of principle, Chief Inspector. A principle of our working methods.'

'Yes, Madame.'

The servant had been ticked-off and put in his place.

As Cecile vanished into the lift, he gazed after her with resentment. What the hell did she know about it, cloistered in the magistrate's office? But then he remembered. Old Rigaud, the *juge d'instruction* whose tenure had just finished, whom Cecile Galant had replaced, had never bothered himself with the actual corpses. He sat in his office looking at photographs and reports, working from the dossier, from pieces of paper, from live witnesses washed and spruced up and brought to his office. Galant's reputation had preceded her, and part of it was her toughness. It had become legendary that she always insisted on viewing the body herself. 'Even the floaters from the docks' the voice over the phone had said, in its emphatic Marseilles accent. 'Oh, Galant, she's got guts. I wish you joy of her in Cannes!'

Chapter 41

'I just wanted to have a quick word with you - as you're new here. Put you in the picture, so to speak.'

The voice at the other end of the phone had already identified itself briskly, 'Commissaire Marchand here.'

Cecile had not spoken to him before, but she knew who he was. A very high-ranking policeman - Maubourg's boss, in fact.

'Have you familiarised yourself with the file on the mutilation cases? I'm sorry to ask you this so soon after you've taken up your appointment, but there is a matter we must discuss.'

'I'm studying it at the moment, M. le Commissaire.'

The voice at the other end seemed to become rather more hesitant. It had begun confidently, self-importantly.

'Of course, you will understand that Cannes has a certain public image - it's not like Marseilles, for example.'

Where anything goes, thought Cecile, so a few faceless corpses wouldn't matter. Really, this man is hardly the embodiment of tact.

It was possible Marchand realised that what he had said was not an entirely appropriate welcoming remark to a new *juge d'instruction*, and he seemed to falter for a moment. Cecile said nothing and waited for the voice to recover its authority. It rapidly did so.

'It's vital for the public presentation of this city to get these gangland killings sorted out and the whole matter over as soon as possible. It's appalling publicity.'

There was a long pause. Cecile wondered if she were too angry to speak, or too cautious. Then, as if irritated by her lack of response, he began again, and this time there was no doubt, it had turned into a tirade.

'Of course, clearing it up is in the interests of all concerned, including the police resources, and the public are anxious about the delay. In fact, I think we should hold a press conference on the matter in the near future, to reassure them that the case is being vigorously pursued. We need to do that soon, very soon, if we are to maintain public confidence and the Chamber of Commerce's continued support for the Municipal Council. You understand me, Madame. It must be resolved quickly.'

Before the film festival, he means, thought Cecile, cynically. Pompous ass. Still, it's his job - and he's probably got a fat bunch of politicians and the whole Chamber of Commerce breathing down his neck.

'Yes, M. Marchand, I take your point. But I'm not at all sure that these were all gangland killings.'

She could hear his breath drawn in and then his voice came, rapid and irritated.

'But surely there is proven involvement - the victims were associated with the underworld and the same weapon appears to have been used in each case. That is made clear in the scientific reports.'

'Yes, but there were two victims - the waitress and the Australian tourist - who had no connection with any known criminals.'

The voice at the other end overrode this glibly.

'But who is to say they were not involved in some criminality? There is no reason to suppose they were little saints, those two women. Some casual prostitution, handbag theft, maybe, credit cards...'

'We found no evidence of anything like that in the cases of these two.'

'That does not prove they were innocent of everything.'

Cecile began to feel defeated. This was the easiest course, and it was being offered to her. Accept that all the victims had meddled in crime and brought their own deaths upon themselves. Agree that all the deaths were the work of gangsters, men who were not going to terrorise law-abiding citizens, who were going to leave the innocent public unscathed, and were merely dealing out their own form of justice to those who had been dabbling on the wrong side of the law. No cause for alarm - in fact, if these people had been involved in drugs or sex or stealing - well, it served them right, really, didn't it? Hadn't people in London rejoiced that the Kray brothers had murdered a whole lot of lesser criminals, like snakes killing off scorpions?

She struggled on.

'But M. le Commissaire, those two women had more than facial mutilations!'

She knew he would get the underlying meaning: there may be a sex-killer at large, preying on women who were complete strangers.

But that, of course, would conflict with the presentation of the mutilations as the work of an organised gang, targeting a criminal element. It might even start a panic on the streets of Cannes to acknowledge there was a sexual psychopath attacking women at random.

'They can still be the victims of a hired killer!' His voice sounded triumphant, as if he had scored the point.

'M. Marchand, men like that are surely too dangerous for a boss - even someone like a big Mafia or Camorra boss - to control. They kill for their own gratification. There's a lot of well-established documentation on such cases.'

'That is psychological theory and mere speculation, and we should be irresponsible in presenting it to the public.'

There was a pause. He seemed to be waiting for Cecile to make another comment, but she said nothing and after a few moments he went on, 'In any case, the important thing is to get this solved quickly. And in that connection there is something ... something rather sensitive which I wanted to mention to you.'

'This is a cleared line. They check it regularly.'

'No, I didn't mean sensitive in that sense. Personal, perhaps, would have been a better word. It's about Chief Inspector Maubourg. I imagine you haven't had much opportunity to get to know him, as yet.'

'No, that's true. We've talked professionally a few times, that's all.' What the hell was he getting at?

'Then you don't know that we believe he has been under some strain lately.'

'No, I didn't know that.'

And who is 'we' in this context, she wondered. Senior police ranks?

'Yes, as a matter of fact - it's his private life. There's a rumour his wife is having an affair. Oh, I know what you will say - this isn't America - in France, a man's private life is his own! We're not hypocrites here, certainly. But it's his reaction that matters - and the stress may affect his work. You see what I mean?'

'Yes, but what can we do about it? It's a matter for his concern only.'

'Well, taken in conjunction with the failure to get this case moving ...'

'No, I deny that! This matter has been very carefully handled. On reading through the dossier, I find it has been constantly updated!'

'Then let us say the failure to bring it to a prosecution ... I am not convinced that Maubourg is the best officer to be in charge of the police aspect of the case. The fact is, I am seriously considering replacing him. But I wanted to know your reactions. The dossier is, after all, under your control.'

Cecile was startled into being direct. She had no intention of losing Maubourg; he was a clever man. But this was dangerous ground.

'Take a man off the case because of some gossip about his wife?'

'And to ensure there are no procedural laxities,' said Marchand, smoothly. Had he heard about Cashel's visit to the morgue? It still didn't seem enough to provoke such a reaction. There must be more, Cecile told herself.

And there was.

'You see, there may be more publicity for Chief Inspector Maubourg than would be normal, even in a high-profile case such as this. There is a conflict arising at his daughter's school which will probably appear in the press - there is a Muslim girl who is trying to wear the headscarf and the school authorities have forbidden it.'

'But there must be hundreds of children at that school! Why single out the Maubourg girl?'

'We gather from her teachers -' now what did this euphemism conceal? wondered Cecile. A discontented deputy head, perhaps, someone whose career was blocked and thought they might find a way round it by doing small favours to those in authority?

'We gather from her teachers that Rachelle Maubourg supports the right of Muslim women to wear headscarves in accordance with their religious beliefs, and is likely to join any demonstration of support outside the school.'

'But isn't she just a child! How can it matter what her views are?'

'She is sixteen. In any case, the point is that someone is bound to ask what her father thinks of the matter.'

'So?'

'Chief Inspector Maubourg's views may not be generally supportive of French culture.'

French culture? As in Cannes during the festival? Come on, be serious, man. A parade of women in G-strings up and down your streets in front of the world's cameras?

'You mean he may say he is in favour of the girl's right to wear a headscarf to school?'

'Precisely'.

There was a long pause.

No, thought Cecile, I will not be a part of this.

She spoke carefully.

'Commissaire, Maubourg is a very intelligent policeman with an excellent record and he has worked on this case from the start. I should be very sorry to see him replaced now.'

Say something more, Cecile told herself. Something that will take things a stage further. Go on the attack, take it into the enemy's camp.

'And I should regard the need for another police officer to familiarise himself with the details of the case as an unnecessary waste of resources, requiring official comment.'

Had she said enough?

'Very well, Mme Galant. We shall leave matters where they stand at present. But I do hope you will bear in mind that Chief Inspector Maubourg's state of mind may not be entirely to be relied upon at present.'

'Thank you, Commissaire.'

Cecile put the phone down with relief as her clerk came in. 'The Arthuis woman is here to see you.'

'Right. Just give me a few moments.'

She set about composing herself.

Chapter 42

Susanna's task at the Boîte Rouge was not difficult, but required her presence at unusual times.

She was required to count money.

Every morning towards dawn, as the club closed, the previous night's takings were brought into Sandra's private quarters and the piles of notes and coins set out on a silver-topped table. Then Susanna was brought in, and sat down on a little upright chair.

Every movement of Susanna's fingers as she flicked through the money was reflected either in the gleaming table-top or in the mirrored panelling that lined the walls. The first time Susanna counted the takings, Sandra sat and watched and maintained an unnerving absolute silence during the proceedings. A calculator was provided, but Susanna did not use it. She had the uneasy feeling that the money would be counted several times, that she was just one step in the process of getting it along a series of gutters and channels till at last it was flushed out into a broad flowing river that syphoned off the takings of a hundred bars like the Boîte Rouge - and flowed out with them as the Rhône flowed into the sea, washing with it all the dirt and misery it had collected along the way, and then flooding far out to feed the gaping mouths of great deepwater fish with rich and rotten garbage.

Outside the door, when the money was being counted, there were always two men; Susanna was never told their names, and never asked.

When the take had been counted, Sandra entered the amount carefully in a notebook, which was then locked in a safe.

The cash itself was transferred to metal boxes. Then there would come the sound of a car pulling up in the street outside and Dinin would take the boxes out. The engine did not stop running. The car door slammed.

Then the money vanished somewhere into the growing dawn.

There were amounts that arrived at other times, sometimes during the day, sometimes at night. Once or twice Susanna was woken up at night. 'Mathilde, would you come to my room, please.' And there would be a heap of money on the silver table. Sometimes the notes would be crisp and rustling, at other times so dirty and crumpled they were soft as worn linen, and Susanna went to wash her hands afterwards to scrub the grease off her fingers.

After the first few days, Sandra sometimes went to St. Raphael about the new club there, and Susanna sat in the room alone to count the money; she was shown how to note it down in the little book and place the book and the cash-boxes in a self-locking safe, which contained nothing else.

Otherwise, she was free to come and go as she pleased, but she chose not to come and go, and no-one at the Boîte Rouge remarked on this. There was a careful incuriosity there; it was in its way, she thought, like joining the French Foreign Legion. No-one wanted to know her past; no-one would enquire her real name. She was given a room, which was clean and had a door that locked, and could have as many baths as she pleased. Her meals were taken with Bernard or occasionally with Sandra, and sometimes in the evenings she helped Sandra with her hair or clothes. Out of sheer boredom she went down sometimes and helped Bernard in the bar, but this was never a success and she was nervous of the customers, so that Bernard told her she was putting them off.

'For God's sake, they want someone behind a bar who smiles and laughs a bit!'

How long this existence lasted, Susanna could never afterwards be certain. She thought it was only about ten days, but fear, she discovered, was disorienting and in any case at the Boite Rouge night was turned into day as part of normality.

Sandra often had a small colour television set on in the background as she lounged around her room and they were idly watching the news as usual when a face loomed large, covering the small screen.

Susanna stopped puffing styling gel round Sandra's head.

'What is it - does that policeman interest you? Well, well, my little Mathilde - worried about the police, are we? I thought there might be something about you - I can smell it, you know! Our little Mathilde is on the run! Is that it? Come on, tell me, Mathilde, what have you done?'

Sandra was laughing, but Susanna watched the television like a rabbit fixated by a stoat.

'Yes, I think there is a real danger if this rally goes ahead,' Maubourg was saying. The camera cut to a gang of screaming youths dressed in black with swastikas on their sleeves, then back to Maubourg's calm, serious face. 'My advice is that we should not take the risk of allowing the National Front to march through the streets of Cannes. It will inevitably lead to racial violence - these are fascists, we must understand that. You know, we are convinced that they were responsible for the attack in Cannes a couple of months ago, when a family of five Algerians narrowly escaped from injury in a violent attack on their home.'

Susanna was concentrating so hard on what was being shown on the screen next, a re-hash of old news, rapid images of the Rue Caillebotte, of the smashed and broken home where once she had lived, that she did not at first hear Sandra's voice breaking in over the television commentary.

'He's an idiot, that policeman', said Sandra casually. 'Doesn't have the slightest idea of what happened. That attack had nothing to do with the Front - nothing to do with politics at all - Dinin told me. There was a boss in Cannes who wanted to get hold of someone. The Arabs were in the way, that was all.'

'To get someone?'

Susanna's voice was low and carefully calm. It sounded unnatural to her own ears. But Sandra did not appear to notice anything. She idly sprayed at a strand of hair, teased it out, sprayed again.

'Yeah, I don't know who. Just someone who hadn't done what they were told, I suppose. Who cares about a few Algerians, that's what Dinin said.'

'Did they ... did they get them in the end? Whoever they were after?'

'Funny, I don't think so. Dinin said they got away. The guy in Cannes won't stop trying, though.'

Suddenly, Sandra fell silent. She seemed to be thinking her own thoughts. Susanna did not dare to ask any more questions and perhaps attract attention to her undue curiosity. For all her casual attitude, Sandra was a sharp observer. More than once, Susanna-Mathilde had felt herself watched.

Perhaps she had said too much already.

Two nights later, as they were having an omelette and a glass of champagne (there was nothing unusual in this: Sandra always drank champagne), Susanna was aware that she was being studied. Sandra was looking at her curiously. 'You want to know something, Mathilde? That boss in Cannes - the one who was looking for someone in the Rue Caillebotte. He's going to have another try. Dinin told me. Some guy was down in the bar last night. The boss-man is a big fat fellow - they call him White Boy. He always wears a white suit. Seems he's actually looking for a woman. God, I pity her!'

Sandra got up and opened her handbag. 'You're owed some wages. Take this on account.' She took out a wad of notes and laid them on the table.

The two women looked at each other.

'Take it now,' said Sandra. She emphasised the `now'.

Then she walked into her huge and luxurious bathroom and shut the door.

'You're a fool', Susanna said to herself. 'An idiot. You should be getting as far away as you can. You saw what happened in the Rue Caillebottte. Run again if you have to. Run like hell.'

But when she left the Boîte Rouge, her feet were taking her in a certain direction, as if she could not resist. This time, she had some money in her pocket. Enough for the fare, anyway.

It was the only place left where she might find him.

And she did.

'I thought you'd have gone back to England,' she said.

'I thought I'd never see you again. But I waited. Don't ask me why.'

They lay in the narrow bed at the Villa Bleue, intertwined.

'I was afraid' she said. 'I didn't want you to look after me - I like making my own decisions. I shouldn't stay with you right now; I think they're after me, or us, from what Sandra told me in the Boîte Rouge. She was obviously tipping me off as much as she dared. But God knows why they want to get at us - I don't even know anything about them.'

'But you won't go away again?' he said.

He wanted to add, but thought she would find it absurdly chivalrous. 'If they get you, they'll get me as well.'

Susanna traced a line down Charlie's cheek with her forefinger. She was lying on top of him; the warmth of a day in early spring was already drifting through the windows: she could feel the warmth of the sun on her naked back.

'I don't know' she said. 'I can't commit myself to anything - not yet. It's not that I'm scared - more somehow that I can't feel very much at the moment. There's just been too much.'

He folded his arms around her narrow back which stretched along the bed in a long arabesque.

'We can't stay here' he said. 'They'll find us. But I don't understand what they want.'

'Neither do I', she said. 'How can we have got involved with gangsters in some way? It sounds absurd, like something out of a film.'

'This is film city,' answered Charlie. 'If you believe all you read about Cannes, it just exists for the film festival. The whole place is like a backdrop for a thriller. But there are real people living in it - that's the trouble! You and me, for a start. We're flesh and blood, not celluloid.'

'True.' She slid her hand down his body, and they started laughing, in spite of the tension.

Or maybe, thought Charlie, as he submerged under her salty-tasting body, maybe the sense of danger gave it an edge.

Chapter 43

Cecile gazed at the woman opposite her and tried to repress dislike. 'I should admire her' she thought to herself. 'After all, it was difficult when she was young, in that generation...'

But just because Monique Arthuis was a lesbian, that didn't necessarily mean she was an admirable character. 'The point of equality is to be able to admit their defects, to able to say they don't need special pleading, that they're just like anyone else,' Cecile thought to herself, and wondered if these were dishonest apologetics. She believed that she was lacking in all prejudice, but was she really unbiased? Perhaps it was because the woman seemed such an unprepossessing human being.

'I'd like to talk to the Arthuis woman,' she had said to Maubourg. 'And her companion as well - what's the name? Rolland, that's it. They were staying in Arthuis' house when Rosie Cashel's murder took place.'

'We interviewed them,' said Maubourg. 'They both swore they hadn't seen anything. Doubt if there's any more to be got out of them.'

'Nevertheless, I'd like to talk to them myself. And separate them. Can you get a plain-clothes man to bring them in one at a time ? Not a gendarme - and we don't want to frighten them.'

All the same, she thought, looking at Monique Arthuis's tight-lipped face, it might have done some good to frighten her. How can she be so ... so *self-righteous?*

Monique sat bolt upright on her chair. 'I've already told everything I know to the policemen. I don't know anything about the Cashel girl. Serve her right for going with the doctor.'

'You saw nothing, then, mademoiselle?'

There was no response. Cecile did not break the silence for a few moments. The woman was smoothing her light brown skirt, looking down at the material and her own stiff fingers.

Cecile restrained her anger. She must somehow find a key to turn this stiff and rusted lock.

She went on, 'You are very observant - that is in the file. The policeman to whom you spoke made a special note of it. And that you were a very intelligent witness, he commented on that also.'

These things were true, in a sense. Montvallon had actually written, 'She is clearly watchful of the activities of the neighbourhood, and a very shrewd character.'

It seemed to be working. Monique even permitted herself a tiny smile.

'I don't miss much, that is true. But on this occasion, I really did not see anything to note.'

That was more than Montvallon had got.

'So you were... observing, mademoiselle?'

Monique was a trifle suspicious, but her conscience was clear. She did not suspect irony.

'Well, I didn't see anything unusual. That's what I meant.'

Cecile let this float in the air.

'I want to ask you about something else, mademoiselle. That is really why I've asked you here.'

She opened a drawer of the desk and took out a sheet of paper.

'Do you recognise this?'

Monique seemed to be rendered indignant by the very sight of the coloured xerox. 'This picture? Certainly I do. It belongs to me!'

'It is part of the late M. Arthuis's estate? Do you have it?'

'Yes, at least, I understand it's a very valuable picture, so I have transferred it to safe-keeping. I have deposited it in a bank-vault.'

Shut away, thought Cecile, shut away from the light.

'How did your late uncle come by it? Did he tell you?'

'He didn't buy it. It was a gift, from the sister of the artist. I believe my uncle helped the family during the war - or perhaps just after, I'm not certain.' She finished rather sourly, 'He was always liable to be generous,' and emphasised the last word to make it sound like an insult.

Cecile repressed a smile.

'Do you know anything about a photograph of the picture? Did you send a photograph of it to anyone?'

'No, of course not! That stupid Washington girl - she asked me the same question. Wanting to know such silly things - about that, and the new string! As if it mattered, any of it. The painting belongs to me now and that's that.'

'New string?'

'Yes, do I have to repeat it?'

The woman raised her head and glared. Cecile felt like a stupid school-girl.

Monique continued, however. 'Doctor Durrant said that just before my uncle died the picture had fallen off his bedroom wall and apparently the foolish old man took it as an omen. Was very upset about it. Anyway, Durrant apparently told him he would put some new string on it for him, but then my uncle died, so Durrant brought it round to me the following day. He'd put the string on it. I've got it hanging on my wall now. The picture belongs to me, of course.'

She added suddenly, irrelevantly, 'It's good string,' and Cecile was reminded of the De Maupassant story, *A Piece of String*, and the Normandy peasant who finds himself caught in the web of his own meanness.

'Were you actually there when your uncle died?'

'No, well... I used to go and visit him, of course.'

'With Mademoiselle Rolland?'

'Yes, she usually came with me. She helped with the gardening. It saved expense. There is a gardener, but only part-time.'

'So were you there when he died?'

'No, as a matter of fact. He died quite unexpectedly - obviously, I couldn't spend all my time there.'

A hard nut, Monique Arthuis. I got a bit further than Montvallon, thought Cecile, but not much!

After Monique had been shown out, she opened a window to get rid of the smell of stale talcum powder. Then she rang Maubourg. Montvallon answered.

'The chief's not here at the moment, madame.'

'Well, never mind, perhaps you can give him a message. There was an artist called Leclant, in about the nineteen-thirties and forties. I'd like someone to find out about him. You could start at the Musée de Castres here - no, better ring the Picasso Museum in Antibes. They'll know who the expert is. Tell the Inspector he can go to Paris if necessary, the expenses can be authorised. And tell the people at the museum it's about a painting which probably won't appear in any of the catalogues - it's probably never been exhibited.'

'We have an art squad, madame.'

His voice sounded offended, perhaps by being asked to concern himself with something so frivolous, perhaps because it was a subject he knew nothing about.

'Yes, of course, Inspector, but their business is first and foremost to trace paintings which are known to have been stolen. In this case, there has been no report of theft, and furthermore it's a matter of suspected involvement with other crimes - at least, with one other crime. The murder of the English girl, Rosie Cashel.'

His voice carefully didn't ask quesions, but he managed to sound disbelieving. 'Very well, madame.'

Cecile put down the phone, hoping that Maubourg would not be so touchy about crossing divisional boundaries. She thought not, somehow: he was a man who hung on to things. His marriage as well as his case-load, she thought, if the gossip was right. She ran her fingers through her hair, thinking she didn't want to get involved with Maubourg's inner life, his personal feelings. If it doesn't interfere with his work ... she thought. But she knew this was a false distinction - it always did make a difference. Even in her own case, right now, when she thought she was giving the Mutilator cases all her rational intelligence, something inside her was knotting up and distracting.

All I want is to be in the country with Florence, she said to herself, and then thought fiercely, be honest with yourself! That's not all you want! If it were, that's where you would be. You want something more. It's all more complicated than that, anyway, just as Florence is more complicated than some child running through green fields in a picture-book. She has her own things, her own likes and dislikes. She's a separate person. And you want more than your child. More out of life.

But she felt so tired, anyway. And there was something she had forgotten to do, something she meant to ask for, something that needed a specialist. But she couldn't remember what it was. Dear God, did she have to take care of everything?

Chapter 44

'I'm going to Paris. Have to leave early tomorrow morning.'

Violetta raised her head from the newspaper and put down her coffee cup. She was wearing her blue dressing-gown; her brown hair was disordered and curling down her back. She was swinging a bare leg at the side of the table; from one foot dangled a tanned leather sandal. Rachelle had already left for school, her bag swinging from her shoulder, giving them both a hasty kiss as she left.

'When will you be back?'

Her voice was neutral.

What would she do? In the early years of their marriage, he had believed that she hated their long enforced separations as much as he did. But now? A phone-call to the lover as soon as she was alone?

'I may be able to get back tomorrow. Well, late at night. I'll call you.'

'I might be going out to Madeleine's,' she answered. 'It's her daughter's birthday party. Very grown up - I promised I'd be there.'

'I'll see you when I get back, then.'

She must have sensed something in his voice, because she said quickly 'You were invited, too. Remember? She asked us both, months ago. But you said you probably wouldn't be able to make it anyway.'

He didn't remember, but it was true that he could so rarely go to any social occasions that he had got into the habit of automatically turning down invitations.

'What are you doing in Paris?'

'I have to go to see an art historian.'

She looked impressed. 'At the Louvre? What about? Makes a change from drugs and dead bodies!'

'No, not at the Louvre - at the Picasso Museum. He's an expert on modern art. It's about the Arthuis case, a picture he owned. Whether it's genuine or not.'

'Sounds interesting.'

'I'll tell you more about it when I get back.'

She put down her coffee cup. 'All right. Why don't you bring Rachelle back a nice art book or something.'

'Is Rachelle going to the party?'

'She's got some meeting at school.'

'Won't the girl be disappointed - Madeleine's daughter - if Rachelle doesn't go?'

'The daughter's name is Janine. And yes, she'll be disappointed. That's why I'm going - someone from this family's got to go. They've been at school together for years.'

She took her coffee cup to the kitchen and then went into their bedroom to get dressed.

Maybe it would be all right. Maybe if he came back in time to go to Madeleine's he would call in there, and pick Violetta up, and drive her home ... they would be together like any normal family.

Violetta came back, wearing a dark trouser suit, holding a small shiny red handbag. She worked three mornings a week in a travel company.

Putting some lipstick on, her make-up bag on the breakfast table, she said suddenly, 'You don't trust me, do you?'

He was afraid of what would follow, but it was like a boil that had to be lanced. He sat down on one of the expensive dining chairs that had been a wedding-present from her parents, poured a thin dark stream of coffee into the big cup he always used.

'No. Am I wrong?'

There were tears in her eyes, he noticed with amazement, and she turned her head away suddenly. She said, 'You leave me to do everything - I have to see to everything. Rachelle - the school - oh, what's the use?'

She put the make-up case back in her bag with a click and opened the door.

He pushed his coffee-cup away and went to the phone.

'Montvallon? Get someone to book me a reservation on the TGV.'

Chapter 45

In the little room at the back of the villa, they lay and listened, to a wind getting up force across the bay, to the sea crashing against the shore, to the palm-trees rustling in the dry little winds that whirled about before the weather broke.

Susanna found herself listening, trying to hear other sounds, above the natural noises of the storm. Sounds such as cars slowing down or stopping, footsteps, doors opening.

From the tensions she could feel in Charlie's muscles as his body lay next to hers, she knew that he was listening too. Listening and waiting.

She found herself going over and over the conversation with Durrant. There was something, some small point ... something she had wanted to know ... For the first time, Susanna understood how fear can really drive out thought. Fear seemed to have destroyed her memory of what she should have said to Durrant. It was paralysing her now.

Suddenly, Charlie got out of bed, pulling a blanket round him and crossed the room. She heard the little click as he flicked the light switch. The room was suddenly flooded with what seemed terrifyingly bright yellow-white light.

Instinctively she called out 'Get out of the light! They can see you!'

Her voice trailed off, as she realised she didn't know who might be watching, nor where those eyes were hiding in the darkness outside.

'I've had enough of this' said Charlie. He was pulling on his clothes. 'This hanging round waiting till Mr. White Boy or someone doing him a favour condescends to come along and kill us.'

'What can we do instead?'

'There must be something better than staying here like trapped vermin waiting to be knocked on the head. Oh, it's not courage - I'm no hero, believe me.' As he spoke, he was looking out of the window. 'Anyway, I can't see anyone out there right now - it's still quite light. I think we should get out of here before dark.'

'But where can we go? They'll find us - they've got contacts anywhere.'

'Everywhere there are people, yes. Every bar, every street corner, every alley. But there's somewhere they haven't got any spies. For one simple reason: there's nobody there to do the spying for them. No one to bribe, no-one to blackmail - because there's hardly anyone there at all.'

They walked in the dusk towards the city limits. There was a garage where they saw motor-bikes for hire.

'I can ride one of those things. Easier to get rid of than a car - if we want to really get away.'

The oily smells, the cold feel of the bike, then the wind rushing past. As the hair-pin bends of the road got ever steeper, looking down they had seen the lights of a car gliding along below them, following the twisting and turning road up the hillside.

Charlie stopped the bike and they got off. His heart was thudding, but there seemed to be a clarity about what he had to do; it was quite simple, somehow, a series of physical actions that he had to get right. Then he told Susanna to get to the inside of the roadway, under the slope of the hillside above them. There was a crash-hat that he'd had to take along with the bike at the garage and he looped the strap over one of the handlebars and suddenly, standing beside the motorbike, turned it towards the outer edge, gunned the engine and leapt away. The machine jumped and bounded forward like a live thing and hurtled over the edge, crashing through the scrubby pines below, rolling and resonating with long metallic reverberations, till at last there was silence on the slopes below. Silence, except for the sound of a car moving closer and closer, a big powerful engine, moving easily towards the site of the crash like a shark that scented blood.

Then they were scrambling on foot straight up the hillside above the coast. Susanna's legs and arms were torn with scratches and her hair whipped around her face in the morning breeze, but she had ceased to be the frightened cowering creature in the Villa Bleue, who had listened for the merest sound of a footfall on the stairs. Below them lay the road: anything that moved along it would be as visible to them as to the hawks that soared and dropped above them, or to the gulls that wheeled out over the radiant blue water and back over the harsh and coloured landscape of the Esterel.

Looking back, they could see the car had stopped at the place where the motorbike had crashed off the road, and then a torch flickered on the hillside below. There were sounds of rocks rolling down the hillside and men crashing round in the dark: the car moved in a semi-circle and its headlights were trained on various parts of the hillside below. He pulled her down into the hillside as the headlights moved again, but the long white beams swept only across the downward slopes, picking out broken branches, a twisted fairing, a crash-hat.

After a while the men stopped crashing about in the undergrowth and the sound of car-doors slamming echoed up the slopes. The car moved so the headlights faced back down the way they had come, and at last they saw them moving down the hillside, very slowly, as if reluctant to leave the hunting-ground.

Morning came as they climbed higher and higher, a faint grey light followed by a brilliant dawn.

'There should be a village up there,' said Charlie. He had managed to get hold of a map at the garage where they had hired the bike and had it spread out, flapping in the breeze. 'We need to go a bit higher. That place must have been completely cut off in winter, I should think.'

It took them another hour or so, working slowly uphill, their calf muscles aching.

When the next dawn broke, they were crouching down beside a mass of the strange giant cubes of striated red stone. As the sun rose higher, the scents of the hillside drifted around them - pine above all, and then others, perhaps thyme, broom, wild clover. Susanna could see yellow masses of broom flowers tumbling over the crags above them. The colours of the rock seemed unnaturally vivid, running from pink, through brick colour, warm dark rose, blood-red almost, to a liver-like rusty grey, in the rays of morning light.

She pulled off the rug which Charlie had wrapped round her.

'This is the place' he said. 'The Esterel. Remember, we got a glimpse of it when we went to St. Raphael. The real Provence, inland, where the tourists don't go. I thought if ever I needed somewhere to hide, this would be it.'

'You're not the only one' said Susanna. 'This is where the convicts used to hide - the ones who escaped from the galleys at Marseilles. This is the maquis - Resistance fighters hid here. But it's a hard country. Mont Vinaigre, I think they call this.'

She looked at the dense mass of rock and scrub hanging over their heads. 'Tough landscape' he commented. 'Yes,' she said, 'but long before those towns existed - Cannes and Antibes and so forth - the places that mean the South of France today, people managed to get a living here. For centuries and centuries, before the coaches and the restaurants came along.'

Susanna broke up a bar of chocolate and passed him a bottle of mineral water - all they had managed to scavenge from the kitchen at the Villa Bleue before their headlong flight the previous evening.

After a few minutes, they struggled on upwards.

The waiter was just considering whether to call the proprietress on the phone when she burst forth from the street into the bar.

'Oh, Jean-Louis, I forgot to pick up *la gran'mère*'s bottle of Pernod... she has a glass every evening before dinner, swears it keeps her going... How odd, I think I can see two strangers coming up the path ... No one ever comes here at this time of day - and not on foot!'

Chapter 46

Maubourg sat in a small cluttered room in the Picasso Museum. The grey seventeenth-century building must accommodate many such poky corners and workrooms in its mansards and cellars, he thought, above and below the levels of airy spaces where the paintings hung, all kinds of little grey nests tucked under the roof.

There was no desk proper in this study, just a piled clutter of books and folders and several easels on which stood canvases in various stages of cleaning or framing. There was a sharp, oily smell in the air. Maubourg felt awkward, out of his depth. He had never seen a picture out of its frame, just as there some men who have never seen a woman naked. The experience, he found, was curiously unnerving.

Some empty frames lay on a table across the room, and the man he had come to consult saw Maubourg glancing at them.

'Original frames. You can learn a lot from the original frame of a picture, Inspector. About the date, the studio and so on.' As he spoke, he was holding up a small piece of brightly coloured paper; he had a curious expression on his face, compounded partly of amazement and partly of disgust.

'It's a terribly bad reproduction.'

'Of course, it's just a xerox. That's all I could do in the circumstances - take a colour xerox of a photograph. I didn't want him to know that we were interested in it - in fact, we weren't interested at the time.'

'So why did you bother to make a copy at all, Inspector?'

'I'm methodical. Very much so - it pays off in the end. I always look for the little things - the odd small things. So can you tell us anything about it?'

The other man clicked his tongue impatiently. He took a step towards the gabled window, where the light was even whiter than in the rest of the room.

'It could be right. If it is, then it's very important indeed - one of the major paintings of the century. You know, this man's work was like Vermeer's - very little of it survives. Not like Picasso - he was hugely productive. Anyway, almost all of Leclant's work was burnt by the Nazis.'

Maubourg contemplated Europe's leading expert on twentieth century art and wondered why he was dressed in a red plastic jump-suit. It looked uncomfortably hot and sticky, the detective thought, but then as André de Carcassonne lifted the flimsy piece of paper towards the light, Maubourg observed that huge armholes had been inserted in the shiny material, cut so low that pale skin and a thin rib-cage were visible at the sides.

'Where did you say it turned up?'

'In the South of France.'

'That's possible. Leclant was deported from Vichy France to a German concentration camp. Where exactly did you find the picture, Inspector?'

'This is a police investigation, M. de Carcassonne - I don't think I can give you ...'

'Inspector, don't say you can't give me any information. No art expert can establish that a picture is authentic just by looking at it, you know - all one can give is an opinion. To say that this is a genuine Leclant, we would need a provenance - we would need to establish the history of the picture, ideally since it left the artist's studio. So I can't help you unless you help me.'

'I can tell you that it came from Cannes, that it had probably been in the same house since the war. It belonged to an old man called Arthuis.'

De Carcassonne pursed his lips and considered the name. 'Arthuis, Arthuis. No, I don't recall a collector of that name. Did he have other pictures?'

'Not like this, if that's what you mean. He had a lot of antiques and some old oil-paintings, I think. Nothing modern, as far as I can remember.'

'I'll try and find out something about it,' sighed de Carcassonne and was about to say more, but Maubourg's mobile beeped sharply.

'Excuse me.'

'Oh, yes, of course, Inspector - sorry, Chief Inspector?' With more discretion than Maubourg would have given him credit for, De Carcassonne retreated to the far end of the room and stood contemplating a canvas to which, according to the legend scrawled across it in sequins, elephant's dung had been attached.

'Hallo?' It was Cecile Galant's voice. 'Can you hear me?'

'No problem.'

'Are you at the Louvre?'

'No, the Picasso Museum.'

'Oh, that figures. Well, there's been a development - the Washington girl and Cashel - they're together. And your man thinks they're being followed - this may be our chance to get moving and take the lot. I'll make any authorisation you need.'

Maubourg tried to repress the anger he felt. This was an operational decision, a police matter. Who the hell did this woman think she was?

But he knew that his anger came from injured self-regard. She was right - this might be the one chance they'd get to catch White Boy in a situation where he could be convincingly accused of criminal activity - or at least, criminal intent, if he was pursuing Cashel and the girl. And, more than that, if White Boy's henchman, Caracci, could be identified as the Mutilator, then that would be the biggest case any policeman in the South of France would ever handle.

'Ok, I'll be down as fast as I can.'

Maybe he could get to Madeleine's after all, if Violetta had in fact gone to that innocent little dinner party for their friend's daughter. And if she hadn't? If he were to knock on Madeleine's door?

'Oh, Pierre - I'm sorry, Violetta's not here. Didn't she tell you? She had to cancel. Jeanine was so disappointed.'

And the woman's curious gaze as he made his way down the steps, the husband who didn't know.

He felt sick at the thought that crossed his mind, that he might be con- spiring in his own deception by always making sure she knew when he would return. But he'd made the decision: no spying, no bugging, no sur- veillance. No fuzzy video shot from a hidden camera. This was his wife, not some criminal from the dirty side of the street. He owed her - owed him- self - some dignity. If their marriage was going to end, it wouldn't die in a welter of soiled sheets and grainy pictures.

As a matter of fact, he was fairly sure nothing had so far happened in their apartment. His policeman's eye had noticed no traces of a stranger. But his policeman's mind asked how far he could deceive himself.

As he put the phone away, de Carcassonne came back towards him. 'What a dinky thing - is it official issue? You can't buy them like that, I sup- pose? I do adore official design. Have you ever seen the uniforms of the Republican Guard in the Élysée procession?'

'M. de Carcassonne, I have to get back to Cannes without delay. Do you think you'll be able to let me have anything on Leclant? I need the infor- mation as fast as possible.'

'Tell you what, I've got a research student working on Leclant - I'll get him on to Arthuis, see if he can find out if there's any connection. But no art expert could really tell you anything without seeing the picture itself.'

'I might be able to arrange that ...'

'Do that, if you can. And, Inspector, wherever it is ... remember, if it's genuine, it's worth millions. Literally. The Japanese will buy heavily if they get half a chance - they've still got money for pictures. For God's sake, keep it under lock and key! And, Inspector, would you care for some lunch?'

Maubourg was surprised at this; he would have expected that the normal regimen of meals had no relevance to this exotic world. He was hungry; in fact, his stomach seemed a hollow void that cried out for fulfilment. There might be time to grab something before he left for Cannes.

All the same, he was cautious. Lunch here would probably mean some trifling little affair of salad, sorbets and mineral water. He longed for something solid, something that would really fill him up.

'Well,' he said, doubtfully.

'Oh, I usually send my assistant out for a hamburger about this time,' de Carcassonne was saying. 'What will you have, Inspector? - I recommend *le whoppeur.*'

Chapter 47

In the Galants' apartment, the phone chirruped sharply. Cecile turned over in her sleep, drowsily, dreaming of a child riding a tricycle and laughing, a dream of childhood happiness, yet with some dark penumbra to it, as though someone else, not seen in her dream, was watching the child too. Beside her, Daniel was breathing evenly, curled under the duvet even though it was a warm morning, where he had fallen asleep after making love the night before.

'Madame Galant?'

She recognised Maubourg's voice.

'Yes, it's me.'

'They're on the run, Cashel and the girl. They're making a break for it. I had a man outside the villa.'

'White Boy and Caracci - they'll follow them.'

'I'm not so sure.'

'Maubourg, White Boy's pride's been injured. He won't stop now. Besides, I think there's something he wants - something else, besides revenge. Otherwise, why should he have them watched?'

'We'll be ready, then.'

'Yes. And one more thing.'

'What is it?' He sounded irritated, thought Cecile. Probably thought he was going to get a bollocking on procedure.

'If there's a shoot-out, I'll back you to the hilt.'

She put the phone down.

They think there are different worlds, she thought. One where there's White Boy and drugs and gangland killings. Another where there's some lurking psychopathic monster. But they're the same world. The gangsters just make use of the killers. It doesn't matter to White Boy what the murderers do to their victims, how they kill them, whether they play with them first - he'd throw a dog a live rat as easily as a dead one.

But we all live in one world.

She thought of the Marseilles where she had grown up, and felt a shooting of an old pain, long buried, at the thought of Guillaume. He always had a child's face in her mind, the child with whom she had played on stairs and corridors and windy paper-blown open spaces. And then suddenly he had gone out of her world, and become shut away. She remembered one day running all the way down the stairs, trying to catch up with the lift, because she know he was going down in the little cage, going to meet ... she did not know, only had the sense of fear. He had got caught up with people who should have belonged in another world. But they didn't, of course. They were in his. Their drugs and their feuds had raged round the tower blocks, till at last Guillaume lay dead on a playground fence, like a crow nailed on a farmer's barn door, as a warning.

Her body jerked in the bed at the memory.

She made herself be calm, put it out of her mind.

Daniel had woken up and was lazily reaching for her under the duvet.

'No, there's something important happening. Maubourg just phoned.'

She felt guilty as he rolled away to the other side of the bed. But she had never had to say to him, as she had said to Louis, 'I can't help it.' Daniel knew that, intuitively. If he wanted her, he wanted someone with an inner drive, a compulsion. He didn't want a loser.

She was already half-dressed, pulling out slacks and a shirt. There was a row of expensive clothes in the wardrobe, black and cream and caramel for courts and legal occasions. And clothes for formal meetings, not couture, admittedly, but couture diffusion, a dark blue Givenchy suit that was like a beautiful glove, a Dior smoking jacket, a Tomasz Starzewski evening dress bought on a visit to London and considered suitable for an English Bar dinner. No 'designer' rubbish plastered with names and logos, no beige-coloured clothes 'for the life you lead,' the kind Louis had wanted her to wear, meaningless clothes for the meaningless life you lead. But it was a wardrobe for work, nevertheless, for working and networking and appearing as a suitable candidate - sometimes she felt the contents of her wardrobe were fancy dress. She loved them, but they seemed to belong to another world. They certainly weren't part of the world in which she had grown up, the tower-block in Lyons which had come before university and magistrate's college, the bedroom where Cecile's mother had nothing in her wardrobe but skirts and jumpers from some chain like Prisunic and shabby shoes with cracked uppers. There was plenty of money now, everyone was earning money, Louis and Daniel and Cecile herself, but Cecile often found that she was wearing precisely this outfit of casual trousers and open-necked shirt, almost as if by some accident of fate. I want to get a few things to go walking in, she thought, and then thought that she wouldn't be allowed to go walking, or if she did there would be one of Maubourg's men protectively following her twenty paces behind. What a ridiculous life I have to lead, she said to herself. I can afford practically anything I want, but there's no point in buying a pair of walking-shoes!

'Goodbye darling' called Daniel. 'Oh, I'll put that play-house up for Florence. She's been on about it! It'll be a surprise when she gets back.'

A few moments later, Cecile was out in the early morning light, fishing for her car keys.

Chapter 48

The peeling walls of the little bar were pale yellow in the morning sun. An old Dubonnet advertisement, its colour faded to sandy pinkish-brown, flapped on the awning. The shutters, the paint worn to the bare wood, creaked on their iron hooks.

'You can't stay here' said the waiter, eyeing the two strangers who had approached St. Émile de la Colline by a very circuitous route. Not that strangers usually approached St. Émile at all, and certainly not on foot, as Madame had commented; the place was hidden still from the main routes that streamed through the south, from the roaring tourism of coastal Provence or the expensive artistic chic of smart inland places such as S. Paul de Vence. There was no through road: the village lay at the end of a dusty track that snaked up a steep bluff of the Esterel.

These two had not even followed that route, the paved former mule-track that led through olive-groves, but had scrambled through the brush to appear, scratched and breathless, at the outskirts of St. Émile. Not that anyone in the village would have expressed much surprise - the residents of St. Émile might not have been much troubled with tourism, but they were familiar from their newspapers and television of how the world behaved down in the flesh-pots of Cannes, and treated any idiosyncrasies with aplomb.

There were some doubts in the Lion d'Or as to whether the man and the girl who had literally emerged from the undergrowth were respectable enough to be referred to the one house in the village where the occasional tourist could be accommodated in a spare room. The standards of this establishment were high - at least, in terms of demanding cash in advance and outward respectability, and it was owned by the businesswoman of St. Émile, *patronne* of the Lion d'Or bar as well as owner of the sole guest-house.

Madame Victoire Lescure was an imposing woman, even without the auburn wig. This morning she had donned it along with a yellow silk dress and an underwired bra with especially uplifting powers. Madame Lescure was, in some senses, too big for St. Émile altogether, which was perhaps why from time to time she went to Nice or Marseilles, on a kind of holiday from her native patch. She was, however, intensely proud of being truly Provençal, of the old Provence, as she put it, which had lain in these mountains for a thousand years while the outside world ebbed and flowed along the coast of the Mediterranean.

'Madame, those people were inquiring if there was a room to rent.' Jean-Louis gestured through the window at Charlie and Susanna.

Victoire Lescure looked round at this point and paid attention to the young couple, who were seated at one of the little tables under the awning. The woman was pale, smoothing down her long honey-coloured hair with an embarrassed hand, as if aware that she was being observed. Her clothes were respectable, almost excessively so. Long sleeves and a high neck were rarities anywhere in the South of France, even if sunworshipping was not absolutely universal. Madame Lescure was uneasily made more suspicious by these rather frumpy clothes - they somehow implied concealment, of more than the flesh which they covered up. But she could not attribute this to any particular reasonable thought.

The man was a more identifiable type. His thinnish face, with a mixture of awkwardness and enthusiasm, the quality of shirt and jeans, belonged to a species she had often observed in the cities of the coast, and she correctly identified him as British, but not of the lager-drinking variety. He would be polite, would speak some French - might even know some Provençal - and would pay his way. Nevertheless, the clothes looked creased and there were rents in the fabric of the shirt.

Madame Lescure advanced to the table.

'Yes, we do have a room free, I believe,' she said grandly. There was in fact only one room and she knew perfectly well it was free, having just come from checking that the pink bedspread had returned from the cleaners.

They did not look like the usual visitors who had strayed off the beaten path, in search perhaps of some *auberge* of which they could boast on their return. 'Just a tiny place - blue check tablecloths, local wine, and the most wonderful seafood - all saffron and shellfish - heavenly! We came across it quite by chance!'

No, there was nowhere of that description in St. Émile, and somehow these did not look the type who might come searching for one. Madame Lescure felt herself warming to them. But caution was still uppermost in her mind.

'But the room is five hundred francs per night' she said, carefully.

After a moment or so, the girl seemed to realise what she meant, and hastily produced a purse from which she took several large notes. Madame Lescure observed there seemed to be plenty left inside the note-pocket of the purse.

The girl spoke then, in excellent French, but with an accent Madame could not place - different from the usual English voice.

'We would like to stay for several nights' she said.

'I think that could be arranged' said Victoire cautiously.

As she led the way out of the café, the girl first after her and the man following, the waiter retreated behind the counter of the little bar. He looked carefully about and then picked up a telephone.

There was no voice at the other end, but he knew someone was there.

'I think you wanted something', he said very quietly. 'Some information.'

Chapter 49

The room was at the top of a tall house on the crest of the main street. Hooking back the shutters that had kept it cool through the warm Provençal afternoon, Susanna saw the tumbling gamboge and red-earthed hillside that fell away from the line of houses, and beyond the great blue expanse of water where the Esterel met the shore. The road, silver in the light, snaked back and forth, far below, perilously close to the edge of the cliffs on the outer side. So sheer was the drop that she could see right down into the occasional curving bays that had been cut in the rock on the inside of the road, to allow vehicles to pull over in emergency. She thought that she could make out a ragged slash scored in the rocky earth, torn downwards through the scrub at the place where the motorbike had gone off the road and the car had searched for them.

She took a deep breath of the warm and scented air.

Charlie came over and caught her round the waist.

'What are those trees?' he said. 'The ones with those strange trunks.'

Stretching up the hillside was a straggling plantation of shiny green branches with crinkled rough bark and patches of orange-rust on the trunks, the colour almost vibrating on the hillside.

'Cork-oaks, I think. They strip the bark off for the cork - it's all dull and rough on the surface and then all smooth underneath.'

'Like some people.' He teased her, relaxing. 'I don't think they can have followed us,' he went on. 'In fact, I think we're safe.'

'Charlie, who are they?'

'I don't know - the only thing I can think of is that they have something to do with Durrant. They didn't start to get after us till I talked to him. Somebody attacked me in the cemetery, and somebody ordered an attack on the house in the Rue Caillebotte - perhaps they were White Boy's men. Oh God, maybe I led them to you!'

'D'you think they were watching Durrant - and thought we were worth following too? Sandra - the woman in the Bôite Rouge - she says that White Boy's men were behind that raid in the Rue Caillebotte. According to her, it had nothing to do with the National Front.'

'But why should White Boy...' Charlie stopped, aware of the reverberations of what he was about to say.

'Why should White Boy want to kill me? Assuming that's what he wanted to do - or maybe just to get hold of me. And he'd have succeeded if you hadn't come along. But what's it to do with me? - Was it something that happened after I got back from St. Raphael - and that was on the day of the raid. The attack in the Rue Caillebotte happened before I even got there - I saw it on television when I was on my way.'

'Maybe it's to do with Rosie' suggested Charlie. 'Could be that White Boy was Rosie's killer and he's worried about my coming over here to France and trying to find out something about her death.'

'Poor Rosie' said Susanna. 'I hope they do find out who killed her.'

Charlie said nothing for a few moments. He was thinking, not only of his little sister, lying on a path with her harmless life shattered like a splintered glass, but of something that might be yet to come. He did not want to say anything to Susanna. But, thinking over the incidents since he had arrived at the Villa Bleue, he recalled his conversation with Durrant.

And he recalled the man's body in the morgue.

'A gang killing' Maubourg had said, on the way back. 'They do it as a warning to informants.'

Slash the face off.

Charlie shuddered.

He put his arms round Susanna.

Time passed and eventually the darkness was falling around St. Émile. In the distance, Susanna could hear the baa-ing cries of sheep, presumably the small troupe they had encountered earlier in the day, grazing on patches of short grass on slopes where the scent of crushed clover arose as they walked through the little patchwork of fields grubbed from the harsh and rocky soil by the ancestors of the present inhabitants of the village. The walls of rough stone were low and uneven, the old olives overgrown. Here and there an apparent cairn of loose stones indicated where some outbuilding or a sheep pen, or a dovecote, perhaps, had fallen into disuse. But the local sheep still supplied the sweet and herby little cheeses that Victoire had given them, along with a jar of black olives that swirled in a dense golden oil flecked with translucent shreds of garlic. 'You must have the special things of this region' she said. 'There are not many of them left. I can remember when almost everything came from this district - you know, we could cook anything that moved, that was what we used to say! When I was a child during the war, my mother cooked - what do you say, *l'âne*? Yes, donkey-meat, that's right. We had nothing else to eat. It was an old recipe - very ancient, I think! It was also a very old donkey!'

She was laughing as they stood in her sunny little garden.

'How on earth d'you cook donkey?' asked Susanna.

'Oh, she minced it up and made sausages of it, with a lot of garlic. She didn't tell me what it was, or I wouldn't have eaten it, because I loved our old donkey. But that was how they ate here in the old days, when times were hard. They just lived off whatever they could. People still eat rabbit here in St. Émile. But you won't get it on the coast: the tourists won't have it - not delicate enough for them. One day I'll make you rabbit and polenta - now that's a real Provençal dish - it lines your stomach, believe me.'

Victoire's house was surrounded by just such walls and fields as extended down the hillside, a rambling grey and green patchwork hanging between the rough outcrops of rock. It was possible to see, Susanna thought, what a struggle it must have been to keep body and soul together here, isolated as it must have been before the steep and winding road and the narrow track at the end of it finally connected St. Émile with the outside world.

She remembered the outside world with an unpleasant shock of recollection, and looked uneasily round the sunlit landscape as she and Charlie finished their impromptu picnic with some spoonfuls of cherry jam, washed down with wine.

'Don't worry - they can't get us here.'

Charlie sounded confident. Somehow he was troubled now by memories that made life seem fragile and precarious, so that stabs of fear twisted his guts from time to time as his mind recalled images that he thought had left him.

His sister, for instance, as she lay dead, and the somehow vulnerable way her fine hair had curled softly round her face, exactly, so it seemed to him, as it had done when she was a child, and they lay on the beach at home in England. Such a fragile thing, so unable to resist the death that had overtaken her.

Yet in comparison with the others, she had died a clean death.

He shuddered as he remembered the children terrified in the Rue Caillebotte, the door splintered on its hinges. And Durrant, who had been butchered as an example, and left as a piece of faceless meat on the grand boulevard of Cannes.

Would this chain of death extend to them, to Charlie and Susanna? He gazed out at the darkening hillside from their window in Victoire's house, and wondered if there was truly such a thing as escape.

Chapter 50

'Cecile?' It was Daniel's voice. Just hearing him, and she longed to be home.

She switched on the green desk-lamp, angling it so the light shone directly on the papers lying open on her desk, realising as she lifted the receiver and leaned back to listen to Daniel that it was nearly half-past eight in the evening. The overhead light in this room didn't seem to give a good enough light. One more dossier to finish tonight.

'Darling, I'm sorry. I'll be back within an hour.'

'It was just to tell you I've finished those analyses, the ones of Durrant's prescriptions. I compared the spread of drugs prescribed to those of other physicians in the area and then broke it across again by patient age group-ings. After all, if Durrant's patients are mostly healthy young sporting types, you wouldn't expect much in the way of long-term prescribing - not like a doctor with a heavy load of elderly patients, for example. And I faxed the results to Dr. Milliard in Marseilles - that fellow who used to run a centre for teenage addicts. Remember, I gave him some help in getting computer training for the kids? He had some interesting comments. But maybe I shouldn't have involved an outsider - these files are confidential informa-tion.'

'Problem is, I'm not sure anything here is secure. What with White Boy's network, and what seems to be a very effective bush telegraph of police gossip, I don't know if there's anyone I can be sure of. If I have to commis-sion expert evidence, I'd rather go to outsiders I can trust, like your friend in Marseilles. So was there anything strange about Durrant's patients?'

'Well, they were mostly adolescents, and they seem to have needed a lot of medication. Average age-range, fourteen to twenty-two. Of course, he could pick and chose his patients, in private practice, but he does seem to have made a speciality of youngsters.'

'Interesting! Go on!'

'There's nothing like heroin, or morphine. Nothing obvious. But he was prescribing methadone to about forty patients.'

'The heroin substitute?'

'Yes, I think so. Used to wean addicts off the drug.'

'But it's a perfectly normal thing to prescribe.'

'Oh, yes. Provided you're dealing with heroin addicts!'

Cecile took in the implications.

'You mean, he was prescribing a treatment for addiction to patients who weren't addicted?'

'Question is whether these patients had any history of previous addiction. If they didn't ... and there's no previous evidence of it in the records ...'

'If they weren't addicts, what the hell was he playing at?'

'Maybe he wasn't trying to get them off heroin. Maybe he was trying to get them on to it!'

'Using a substitute drug?'

'Yeah. Apparently it would give them a high - not like the real thing, of course, but enough to make them want some more. Amphetamines do the same thing as well - there are very high levels of those showing up in Durrant's prescription records. Then there's a substance called ketamine - ever heard of that?'

'I thought it was an American drug?'

'I got some info about it from the Web. Prescribed pretty well all over the world - known as a very safe anaesthetic.'

'So?'

'Durrant was prescribing it to kids with no previous medical history of injury or serious illness. In other words, they didn't need it. They weren't in any pain.'

'You mean, just to give them a buzz from it?'

'Sure. Ketamine was called the 'Buddy Drug' in the American army - it's so effective and easy to administer to the wounded - just give the injured soldier an intramuscular injection and he's away. But it seems it's getting a real problem on the streets in the States, because it's being taken by kids who just want the hit it gives.'

'What sort of drug is it?'

'Well, it's an anaesthetic, as I said, but it's also a hallucinogenic, according to Milliard - gives quite a trip. I reckon that's what Durrant was doing - get these kids in, give them a few minor drugs at first - something to make them feel good, perhaps something to enhance their tennis, increase their stamina - whatever. Makes them feel good, gives them a high. These are rich kids, we're talking about - they'd rarely be alone in the normal course of events. There'd always be a chauffeur or a personal trainer or someone like that with them, even bodyguards. But the one place they'd be alone would be in the doctor's surgery. What better time to get them acquainted with a few highs?'

'Get them hooked?'

'I don't suppose they'd think of it like that, although that would be the effect. More along the lines of rich adolescents having plenty of problems, needing a lot of help and discretion. Once he got their parents' confidence, the loyal and trusted physician would uncover quite a few further cases for treatment, I imagine. A politician's daughter has an abortion - maybe needs anti-depressants afterwards. A film director's son gets drunk and beats up the maid - needs calming down. Could go way beyond just looking after their sporting performance.'

'But he doesn't seem to have been giving them the hard stuff?'

'No - just what you might call the minor fringe. But I did wonder if it could be sort of introductory.'

'You mean, he helps them to feel better, and then some more, and eventually they're hooked.'

'Maybe somebody else took over the supplies at that stage.'

'So Durrant was preparing the ground, as it were. Softening the kids up so they'd be vulnerable to pushers?'

'Yes, they'd graduate from Dr. Durrant's Academy to the school of hard drugs.'

Cecile leaned back in her chair and rubbed the muscles at the nape of her neck, which had got stiff and tense.

'Anyway, his prescription pattern is different from other doctors in the area?'

'Oh, yes, wildly different. I fed four sets of records in. None of the other three doctors prescribed ketamine on a regular basis - it's used as an emergency drug, in road accidents, that kind of situation. And none of them prescribed amphetamines to such young patients. As for the methadone, you'd have to look at those patients to see whether they were heroin addicts he was trying to cure ... or whether he was starting them off.'

'If methadone is non-addictive, how could that happen?'

'It's non-addictive by comparison with heroin. But methadone makes them feel good, causes a pleasurable buzz - they're going to want to go back for more.'

'And eventually there would be someone waiting in the wings with something much bigger.'

'Exactly. Come home, darling.'

'I will. I'm getting my coat on now.'

But as she did so, she called Maubourg's office and talked to Montvallon. She needed someone to take a formal deposition from a physician in Marseilles.

She was so tired. She wanted to go home. 'You're not Wonderwoman,' she said to herself.

But it all had to be watertight. No loose ends, no loopholes.

Chapter 51

Things were moving slowly in the Boîte Rouge. It was early evening and the sky was still that strange light purple-blue, shot with neon, that hangs over Riviera city streets on warm evenings. There were a few desultory customers in the long mirrored bar, not enough to cause Bernard any exertions as he moved up and down, polishing glasses, pouring the odd drink, exchanging a little banter and small talk.

Sandra came down in a red evening dress, her heels clicking as she moved along the bar to where Bernard was standing talking to an elderly man with a deep leathery tan, who looked as if he had seen plenty of the outdoors - and not perhaps of his own free will, thought Sandra, sizing him up as an ex-convict who'd done penal labour in his time.

'That's what I heard, anyway' said the man, as Bernard turned to Sandra. '*Bonsoir*, Madame. I was just saying to Bernard here that the man who killed those Arab rats - he smashed up that nest all right - you know who I mean, the White Boy -'

Sandra said wearily 'Oh, there's no point in that anti-Arab stuff any longer - that's for the old fellows, the Algerian ex-colonists - the people who can't let go. What use is it all? Anyway, it's the Russians we have to worry about now - their pimps are muscling in all over the South.'

The old man looked sulky. 'Oh, if you know best - better than someone who lived among them -'

'Come on!' said Bernard. 'A penal settlement isn't exactly living among the natives!'

'Well, anyway, all I was saying was that I heard White Boy wasn't after the Arabs at all.'

'That's old news,' said Sandra.

The leathery cheeks seemed to pouch out in offence at this. He leaned over the bar confidentially. His old eyes watered with the bright lights of the bar.

'There's something you don't know, though. Because it's only just happened. I had it from Jean-Luc. You know, White Boy's driver.'

The others plainly didn't know, and the old man threw out his chest in

211

self-importance. 'Yes, he told me with his own mouth. He said they were after someone else when they went for the Arabs. A woman.'

'What woman?' asked Bernard, interested in spite of himself.

'Didn't you have a Scottish woman working here? So I heard, anyway. Well, this was one of the same. That's what they called her, Jean-Luc said. *Une écossaise*. White Boy thinks she knows something about his pet doctor - you know, the one who gets the kids for him. Or else he thought she had something he wanted. No-one keeps hold of something White Boy wants. So they were going to finish her off, and it seems she was living with the Arabs by then. Anyway, they know where she is now.'

He turned aside and spat on the floor.

'Damned Scottish whore!' he said. 'Fucking that Arab filth!'

'Don't use language like that in front of Madame Sandra,' said Bernard.

'And don't spit in my bar' said Sandra, automatically. 'It's a filthy habit.'

She turned and walked slowly upstairs to the telephone in her private office. She had got as far as lifting the receiver when Dinin walked in.

Sandra put the receiver down.

'Go on, make your call.'

'It wasn't important.'

'Good!'

He grinned and came towards her.

Chapter 52

There was a mobile phone squawking somewhere in the depths of the leather upholstery.

One of the men in the front of the car answered with a mutter, listened for a moment, passed it back to a fat white hand that reached out from the back of the car. There was a brief spatter of sound from the other end.

'Well, well, we know where they are! Someone who wants me to do them a favour - who wants to get out of some hillside dump and make it on the coast - with a little help, of course. Good thing we put the word out earlier on. I was getting impatient.'

White Boy was sitting in the back of a large black car. The tinted windows cast a greenish light on his doughy features. The air conditioning seemed insufficient to cool his mountainous body: beads of perspiration appeared from time to time on his forehead.

The two men in the front were turned uncomfortably towards him, awkwardly, holding the painful postures of underlings till he should finish speaking.

'Guenon, you needn't hold back when we get there. You understand me? We are going to make an example, so you can indulge in your handiwork all you like. But we don't go yet, of course. We wait till dark.'

There was a pause. The driver judged it safe to turn his head away and looked fixedly out through the window at the parade that passed along the Croisette, ignoring the difference between road and pavement, an endless procession of bronzed bodies, mostly young but here and there a thin wrinkled brown leather sack of something that long since ceased to resemble skin, clad in an expensive piece of designer towel.

The tourist season was in full flood. White teeth flashed in tanned faces, glistening almost-naked bodies bobbed and weaved through the crowds, so that there was a crazy intimacy, a closeness of the flesh, shivers of excitement at the semi-naked proximity of complete strangers, that ran through the crowds like electric currents. A kid on rollerblades came sliding dangerously through the throng which parted with a sigh and a murmur to let him through. Bodies surged round the car, shiny puce and sulphur scraps of Lycra covered bits of flesh, pricks, nipples, with sharp outlined shadows.

Sometimes a thigh, sometimes a navel was pressed tight up against the window of the car. Once, a crotch clad in a bikini thrust right against La Guenon's window, almost in his face. He stuck out his tongue and made licking movements, as the driver laughed beside him. The triangle of brightly coloured cloth was surmounted by a jewelled ring that pierced a fold of skin.

'Wonder if she's got more of those lower down!' said the driver. But the smile left his face as he turned towards Caracci.

La Guenon was fingering his knife, his face pressed longingly against the glass, like a tramp staring into a restaurant window.

Chapter 53

Martin Hollingsworth sighed impatiently. 'But you've got to get the thing to me!' he said into the telephone. 'You know what's going to happen if you don't!'

'I haven't got it!' said the voice at the other end.

Martin swore violently, but he was always a controlled man, and even now remembered that his secretary in the outer office might return from lunch any minute. So, even though he was sure that the voice at the other end was lying, he contained his rage.

Not that he thought anyone would have cause to listen into his conversation, but you never knew - someone might just overhear it and wonder.

The voice was telling him, in French, that the paper should have been destroyed at the time.

'And there is no other evidence at all of what he meant to do. I should never have agreed to giving you anything.'

'Oh, you were very wise!' said Martin. 'You say there's no other evidence, but I talked to him about it, remember. But it's done now. You agreed - we go half and half in this.'

A voice called from the outer office.

'Mr. Hollingsworth, do you want the Pyle conveyance ready tomorrow?'

'Yes, completion's at ten-thirty. We're sending Barry.'

Barry was the conveyancing clerk, a reliable drudge who could be trusted to attend sale completions without losing any essential documents. This made a change from previous employees: Martin recalled with a shudder the occasion on which a bankers' draft for two hundred thousand pounds had been discovered fluttering round Bloomsbury Gardens.

That, fortunately, had been picked up by an honest academic from a nearby faculty of University College, London.

Honest, or else he hadn't known that the piece of paper blowing down the pavement towards him was almost as good as money in the bank, mused Martin.

'Barry's sick, Mr. Hollingsworth.'

'Oh, damn it. Well, I can't come in tomorrow, Giselle' (such a silly name, blast the woman and her mother's passion for prancing ballerinas, thought Martin) - 'could you do it? It's quite straightforward - everything will be ready as soon as that conveyance has been done. Lambkin and Handbury are the other side - their clerk'll show you the ropes.'

Martin knew he shouldn't be asking a secretary to take responsibility for the completion of a sale worth a quarter of a million, but he had urgent business elsewhere. Besides, Giselle might have a foolish, feathery sort of name, but she was utterly reliable. So had Carol been, for that matter - he just didn't like to keep them too long. They got to learn too many bits and pieces. Fortunately, Giselle couldn't speak any more French than Carol could. It was just that her mother thought it was a pretty name, so Giselle had told him at her interview. He believed her: she seemed too dumb to speak two words of any foreign language. He'd rather have got someone a bit brighter, but definitely no graduate secretaries!

In any case, Carol had started to keep a pair of shoes under her desk, he noticed. And they had twice been out for a drink after work. He'd have liked to have her, to screw her, had looked at her legs and up to the shadows at the top of her thighs as she stood in a thin summer dress, but it couldn't be risked. Never shit on your own doorstep was one of his maxims, and your secretary counted as your own doorstep.

He called out to Giselle as she went back into her own office. 'I'm just going out, Giselle. Won't be long.'

She murmured something and he heard the gentle beeps of her computer starting its trawl into the files.

Martin Hollingsworth adjusted his tie in the mirror hanging on the back of his office door. Now that Carol had left, of course she was no longer his own doorstep, so to speak. And anyway, it would be a good idea to know what she was doing. Just in case she had learnt anything while working for Martin, anything that she might casually pass on to a new employer.

'Mr. Hollingsworth used to make ever so many phone-calls in French. And there was a woman from an art gallery ...'

That sort of thing.

Martin knew where she lived. Not just in the way of knowing her address, no. He had walked up and down the nondescript street in Clapham one evening when he knew she would be out, because she had told him she was going to a rock concert.

'Now don't you stay up all night raving!'

'I won't, don't you worry!'

And he had got out the A to Z and looked up the street Carol lived in, and then slipped along it that windy spring evening. Very few people about, after the commuters had come home. After dark.

It was quite near the Common; in fact, the street was quite close to it and there was a pub, the Fighting Cocks, on the edge of a dark stretch of wet grass and bushes.

Martin Hollingsworth didn't like taking risks and he was measuring them up now as he stepped out of his door into the street.

Chapter 54

There was something scrambling up through the undergrowth hanging over the hillside.

Charlie hadn't gone to bed. He sat by the window of their room in Victoire's house, unable to sleep, as the moon climbed up into the sky and the landscape beneath him changed into a strange silver and black mass tipping down towards the valley below.

He had stared out, his eyes fixed on one particular spot where the black silhouette of a gnarled olive tree hung at a slant over an outcrop of silver rock. Strange, he thought, how we remember things seen in moonlight.

Susanna was asleep behind him: he could hear a gentle sound of breathing coming from the depths of Victoire's huge old walnut-framed bed.

He looked back into the room at her sleeping shape, then out again at the twisted thready black branches of the olive.

It seemed to him that the leaves were not still. Not as still as they should be on such a clear night, when the air seemed not to move and even with the windows full open there was not the slightest draught in their room.

The olive tree was shaking against the moonlight, the branches moving slightly, silently, set in motion by something unseen.

Something behind that was sliding along the top of the rocky outcrop, slipping sideways, yet upwards, towards the house, its direction betrayed first by the branches of the olive, now by some long rough grasses that were almost in Victoire's garden.

Charlie slid back into the depths of the room crossed to the bed and put a hand over Susanna's mouth.

She woke struggling.

'Ssh, it's all right. But we may have to get out of here in a hurry.'

She was sitting up, gesturing. He passed her the dress hanging over the end of the bed.

'I think there's someone moving about outside.'

They crept together over to the window.

Charlie gestured silently to where the old olive tree stood in the moonlight.

They stared for a minute or more.

Then it came.

A swift slithering movement behind the rocks, upwards towards them. And then a crouching figure that rose up from its knees to dart over the scrubby ground.

And, to their horror, there were other movements behind the first figure, shapes creeping along the rocks, stealthy, slow.

Susanna grabbed at Charlie's elbow.

'Come on, we can't stay in this room - it'll be a trap if anyone's after us.'

They slipped towards the door, wincing as it creaked open. The long staircase stretched darkly below.

'How would they know where to look for us?' muttered Susanna.

'God knows. But if they knew we were in St. Émile, it would be easy enough. All they'd have to do would be to ask anyone in the village - and this house is the only one that lets out rooms anyway. But they don't want to be seen getting to us, that's for sure.'

They were at the bottom of the stairs now and peering out through a glass panel in the outside door.

The figure was getting nearer and nearer.

'I'm not going to wait and be caught like a rat in a trap,' whispered Susanna.

She opened the door, praying it would not alert the intruder.

It made no sound.

They slipped out of the house. A thick clump of bushes grew beside the door and gave them cover.

A thin dark shape was creeping up to the back wall, making its way towards the door which they had just left.

Charlie moved behind it.

He threw himself towards it, hoping desperately that the man had no weapon. A sudden rage, compounded partly of the fear he had just experienced, filled him with a great surge of strength and he felt ready to fight anything, leaping at the shadow near the door. He felt the solid impact of flesh and bone as he crashed into his opponent and shouted in triumph, but then he felt himself seized from behind and a blinding light flashed in his eyes. His arms were wrenched painfully behind his back, so there was one attacker behind him and another in front. He could not see past the dazzling circle of light to identify the face in front of him.

'Oh, Cashel', said a voice softly. 'Damned idiot!'

The torch was taken out of his eyes.

Blinding orange pinpricks, red-veined segments, danced against velvety blackness while his eyes struggled to adjust.

Then he saw the face behind the torch.

Chapter 55

'Get them indoors.'

Maubourg was peering at Charlie, who heard his voice hissing through the darkness. He felt himself lifted up almost off his feet and twisted expertly towards the house. Once through the door, he could hear muffled thuds and kicks close behind.

'Susanna - it's the police,' he managed to blurt out as the hand over his mouth temporarily loosened its grip.

The noises of struggling ceased.

Maubourg's voice again, in a hoarse whisper: 'No lights! See who else is in the house.'

Torch beams, dimmed, flashing round low. The sound of someone ascending the staircase with stealth and speed.

'M. Cashel, sit over there, please. You beside him, mademoiselle. Now listen, there is no time for playing games, so don't think of anything silly, you two. Do exactly what I tell you and there's a chance you'll get out alive. Try any stupidities and you'll end up on the Croisette without faces. There's a character called La Guenon who loves to slice around with a butcher's knife, and he's out there - in the garden of this house. Ah - this is your house?'

This was addressed to the terrified face of Victoire, held in the grip of a shadowy figure behind her, who had his hand across her mouth. Maubourg played his torch over her features. She nodded, her eyes big with fear.

'We are the *police judiciare* - and there are some men out there who would kill everyone in this house without the slightest hesitation. In fact, they've already tried to get Mademoiselle Washington here - but the people in the Rue Caillebotte were Algerians, of course, that time, so a lot of people thought they didn't count.'

Victoire tried to say something but it came as a deep, frightened, grunting sound within her throat.

'But they count for me,' Maubourg continued. 'Oh yes, they count for me. So I hung on. And there's a slight chance that I might be able to stop something else happening - a massacre of the innocents. Now, you must not make a sound, Madame, when my colleague releases you, and you will go to join M. Cashel and Mademoiselle Washington over there - that's right, good.'

They heard Victoire stumbling as the policeman let her go, and then she was sitting with them, and the three of them were frozen on the couch in a silent row like the occupants of some nightmarish railway carriage in an old film.

'Good' said Maubourg again. 'Now comes the hardest part.'

There was a stream of muttered instructions, a torrent of soft French in the darkness, as his underlings received their orders, then the soft creak of the outer door.

Charlie was not sure whether the two men with Maubourg had left the room: it was difficult to tell who was still there and who had gone. Beside him he could hear Victoire's frightened, irregular breathing. Susanna didn't seem to be making a sound, but he reached out and felt an answering pressure from her arm.

Maubourg had switched off the thin beam of his torch altogether, and the only light was moonlight coming through a narrow opening in the shutter. The inspector crossed to the window and opened the shutters wider. Beside Charlie, Susanna gave a soft cry of alarm as the room became exposed and vulnerable to the night.

'There is a car below the village' whispered Maubourg. 'They waited there for a while.'

There were hurried bursts of French. Maubourg seemed to be issuing instructions. Charlie sensed, rather than felt, Maubourg's two companions slipping out of the room.

He began to panic. 'Where are they going?' he asked. 'Don't we need them here?'

'Shut up!' said Maubourg. He was holding a gun. 'I'll gag you if you can't be quiet!'

Who, Charlie desperately wanted to ask, who was out there?

But he understood now that this was deadly serious business. The only safety lay in silence.

There was a slight scraping sound coming from the hillside below the garden - that was the only warning.

Quite suddenly, a man seemed to come slithering through the windows and as he moved there was a long wicked gleam low down at his side. In his other hand was a squat, dark shape.

'Oh God,' Charlie was saying to himself, 'this bastard can see us.' But he realised that the sofa where the three of them were pressed down as silently as frightened animals was hidden on the dark side of the room; the man with the long knife could not see them. Not for the moment. But that moment would pass any instant - his eyes would adjust to the darkness and then he must see that there were three terrified human beings huddled up and waiting, like creatures trussed and ready for the sacrificial knife.

Where was Maubourg? thought Charlie. He no longer had any idea of where in the room the detective might be - if he was still there with them anyway.

The man with the knife stopped as still as a cat at a mousehole, listening, staring into the darkness. He began turning his head, very gradually, as time seemed to stand still for Charlie and, by the moonlight, he watched every tiny movement of the shaven skull as it slowly rounded through the degrees.

Suddenly it froze.

Now Charlie could see the eyes, glinting in the cold rays from the window. He must see them, the cowering victims, any second now. The long thin blade was held upwards; the arm was loose, relaxed, yet somehow with an easy, practised stretch.

What the hell was wrong with Maubourg? thought Charlie. Why didn't he put an end to it?

The head suddenly stopped its quest. The face became intent, frozen, as if it had locked on to the scent of fear.

Suddenly, the silence and the darkness were both shattered. The face above the knife contorted into a snarl, the man seemed to leap in one bound across the room, and as he leapt something seemed to strike him up still higher with a great jerk and an explosion and there was a burst of flame.

The lights came on.

There was a smell in the room that caught in Charlie's throat so that he started to cough harshly.

On the floor lay a man with a stubbled head and a slender carving-knife beside his right hand. He was face down, and in his back was a bubbling wound that was frothing blood. Terrible choking noises came from his throat and his legs were kicking and drumming on the floor as the blood gushed out of his torn lungs.

Maubourg walked across the room.

There was a clear liquid pouring across the floor on the man's left side.

A petrol-can lay where it had been flung out from his left hand. There had been no cap on it.

'Caracci up to his tricks again' said Maubourg. 'But this time he was going to do something with that knife first - before he burned you all in your beds, that is to say. Damn, that makes it tricky.'

He was still holding the gun and Charlie realised what he meant. The danger of igniting petrol fumes was too great for Maubourg to risk firing the gun again.

The skinhead, La Guenon, was not dead, however. In spite of the massive gun-wound, he was beginning to drag himself across the carpet.

'Can't take any risks with this bastard' said Maubourg quietly, as if to himself. Then: 'Don't touch him!' he shouted, as Charlie found himself almost by instinct moving towards the writhing creature on the floor. 'Don't get too close!'

La Guenon had thrown out a hand. Maubourg, with one swift movement, flung himself upon the figure lying on the floor. His right hand slid beneath Caracci's neck and his left gripped the shoulder of the combat jacket in a vicious neck-lock.

There was a strange sound, subdued, yet it seemed to fill the room and echo on into the darkness. It was a sudden sharp crack.

Charlie had never heard it before, yet somehow with an atavistic instinct he knew what it was.

There was complete silence, almost awed.

It had been the sound of a man's neck breaking.

Maubourg fell back and Charlie saw in the dim light that Caracci's neck lay at an extraordinary angle. The absolute stillness continued for a few more moments.

Chapter 56

'Hallo, Mr. Hollingsworth,' said Carol. She still couldn't accustom herself to saying 'Martin.'

Anyway, it had been a bit of a shock, when the door-bell rang and there he was, the reddish lights from the stained glass in the porch falling over his cheeks.

The light came from a street-lamp: it was only just getting dark.

'Won't you come in?' she said.

There must be some important reason for him to call round to Clapham like this. He could have contacted her through the agency, after all.

He must have read this thought in her head, because he said, 'I felt a bit embarrassed about asking the agency ... I just wanted to invite you out for a drink ...' ·

They were in the hall now, and she led the way to her room at the back of the house on the ground floor. She meant to ask him why he couldn't have phoned first but forgot about it because he was saying something about the pub at the end of the road and was it all right.

Carol Bassett had just split up with her long-term boyfriend. It wasn't working with Simon. He wanted different things from her, she had decided. What she needed was some security - not necessarily marriage, but something better than saving up to get pissed in Ibiza for two weeks every year. He had called her a snobbish little cow and was angry when she said she wanted to learn a few things. That was the reason girls did better than boys nowadays, she told him. More motivated. Anyway, Carol came from a home that encouraged a bit of effort. Her mother had always been on at her about leaving school early.

Anyway, Simon hadn't wanted to be in on her self-improvement, so she needed a bit of company. Otherwise she wouldn't have thought an evening in the Old Fighting Cock with Mr. Hollingsworth something to even remotely consider. So she asked him to wait a few minutes and went into the little bathroom at the end of the landing to do her make-up. She looked round the room first but it was quite tidy - there was nothing she didn't mind him seeing lying around. Everything was put away, except for the tape she had got from the public library, which her mother had asked her to get.

Strange that he seemed to want to talk about the office - after all, she'd only been a temp. She tried not to let on she had heard anything, but it was because he was asking her now if she remembered how thin the partitions were that she did remember, exactly. Still, better to say nothing. If he'd been up to something with that droopy woman who'd called round, the one he'd shown in himself, it was nobody else's business.

So her face only showed the faintest flicker as they talked about the good old days in the office in Victoria as if Carol had been a long-serving faithful employee. She was a bit surprised when he seemed to change the subject abruptly.

'How long have you been learning French?'

She thought for a moment of explaining that the tape, 'Advanced French, Stage Two', was for her mother. But then, maybe Mr. Hollingsworth would offer Carol her old job back, if he thought she could speak a bit of French. She could always get her mum to teach her a bit.

So she said, 'Oh, I've been doing it for a while. Only I didn't want to tell you about it while I was working for you. I just wanted to make it a surprise.'

He didn't seem interested in it anymore.

While the April rain beat on the windows in the front bar of the Cocks, Martin was wondering if he should go over to France first and make sure of his property before someone else got at it.

Or finish this business here.

Chapter 57

They were sitting in the police station where Charlie had undergone his temporary imprisonment, but in an open area, not in Maubourg's little aquarium-tank of an office. Around was a vast and restless complexity of movement, gendarmes in uniform calling in, phones ringing, the constant tapping of keyboards. A huge map of Cannes adorned the wall opposite Charlie and another of the entire Riviera area covered the wall behind.

'But I don't understand about the picture,' said Charlie. 'That's why I came here in the first place - because I was sent the photograph of it. But I've never even seen it.'

'I have' said Susanna, suddenly. 'It's still in the old man's house - the niece has got it.'

Charlie fished the photograph, now crumpled and battered, out of his back pocket.

'Is it a good photograph?' asked Maubourg. Mindful of some of the lessons he had absorbed with André de Carcassonne, he added, 'Are the colours really like that? So, so ... intense?'

'Oh yes,' said Susanna. 'They're just as bright. It's not that big, either.'

She indicated a space in the air with her hands.

'And the frame?' asked Maubourg, remembering the unframed canvases he had seen behind the scenes at the art gallery. De Carcassonne had said something about the importance of original frames.

'Just a plain wood frame,' said Susanna, wrinkling her nose as she tried to visualise it. 'Pinewood, I think. Nothing special. I can't really remember anything about the frame. Dr. Durrant had put new string on it. According to the old man's niece, he was there one day when the picture fell off the wall, and he took it home and put new string on it because the old man was so upset.'

'When did this happen? When did Durrant bring the picture back?'

Susanna was surprised that the detective was so interested in such a small detail.

'Oh, I'm not sure exactly - a day or so before Mr. Arthuis died, I think.'

Charlie, who had been following this dissection of trivia without much interest, suddenly said, 'Didn't you say the picture wasn't on the wall when the old man died?'

'Why, yes.' Susanna looked puzzled. 'How strange - I'm sure it wasn't there when I was about to leave the house - but I saw it in the house when I went back to see Monique recently - so I know Durrant brought it back.'

Maubourg said nothing. Suddenly Susanna felt desperately exhausted, her legs weak. 'I want to get some rest,' she said. 'I can't tell you anything more now. I'm just too tired.'

At first she was afraid Maubourg would keep them at the police station. His eyes seemed to be staring at them speculatively, as if he thought there was a lot more to be got out of them, but suddenly his phone rang and he swung round to answer it.

There was a brief conversation and Maubourg turned again to Charlie and Susanna.

'I have to have a word with one of your neighbours, Mademoiselle Rolland. It seems that Madame Galant intended to speak to her but she wants me to make some preliminary enquiries. So get into the car and we'll drop you off at the Villa Bleue.'

The police car was crossing the nightmarish traffic of the autoroute that cut Cannes in half. They were turning left now, speeding along in the direction of the Villa Bleue.

Maubourg was calling out something impatiently into his mobile phone. Something about 'Can't you send a man now? Right away? Very well then, that'll have to do, I suppose. All right, all right.'

The Villa Bleue loomed up, its faded lobelia paint looking almost home-like in comparison with the parade of palatial gleaming villas, each in its own immaculate expanse of green and watered grounds, which they had passed. Susanna thought of the Rue Caillebotte, of how Leila had cleaned the dwellings of the rich, had polished the marble spouts and platinum taps of their bathrooms, hoovered the deep pile of their carpets, dished out steak to their lap-dogs, and come home without envy or complaint.

Maubourg cut into her thoughts.

'Here we are - I'll need you to stay in Cannes for a few more days, I'm afraid. There'll be a lot of reports to file, and the magistrate will be carrying out an investigation into the death of La Guenon - though not exactly in the spirit of utter desolation, I can assure you! You know, we have to put up with a certain amount of minor drug trading here - after all, that's the price of sophistication, you might say, of having all the glamorous creative types in music and film coming here - oh, some cocaine, some hash... but White Boy is more than that - he controls the hard drugs trade in this town. Take him out, and we get a drugs scene we can control. As for La Guenon - he wasn't the usual hit-man - the guy who's just hired to do a job.'

He turned to Charlie.

'You saw the doctor's body in the morgue. His face?'

Charlie nodded, feeling sick, trying to blot out the memory of that flayed visage and mutilated flesh.

'That was La Guenon's trade-mark' continued Maubourg.

There was a pause.

'Rosie?' said Charlie. He couldn't say anything more, he found.

He meant, but could not bring himself to frame the words, 'Was Rosie one of - what d'you call him - La Guenon's victims?' He felt he could not bear the thought of his sister face to face with that creature, of the terror she would have suffered.

But she had not been mutilated. She had been spared that.

Maubourg seemed to echo his thoughts.

'No, I don't think Rosie encountered him,' he said. 'I know that can't be much consolation to you, but whoever killed her, I don't think it was La Guenon. In fact, I don't think it was anything to do with the gangland killings that White Boy specialised in.'

Charlie opened the door on his side of the car. Maubourg added a few more words. 'We think Durrant was involved in your sister's death. He didn't have anything to say about it - but we know him a lot better now. He was involved with White Boy, after all. Doing the dirty work for them - getting kids hooked so that the dealers could step in to supply them. Anyway, we've picked up the boss himself now - he was hanging round in his fancy car lower down the hillside, waiting to make sure Caracci did his job.'

Susanna and Charlie were out on the pavement in front of the Villa Bleue. 'One more thing - I'll be sending a man to keep watch,' added Maubourg. 'He'll be here pretty quickly. There are a few minor members of White Boy's gang still running round - but I don't think they'll do anything on their own - they're like, how do you say, a chicken with the head cut off? But I'll have a man here soon, in any case. Before dark, if possible.'

The car slid off in the direction of the town. Charlie and Susanna turned and walked up the path of the Villa Bleue.

'Montvallon' said Maubourg, 'I've got to talk to the Rolland woman. 'But park further along, don't turn into the drive.'

'Rather you than me, boss' said Montvallon. 'God, they're an ugly pair - that old Arthuis witch, *vielle salope*, and Rolland, *la gouine*.'

Maubourg didn't like the ugly word for lesbian. 'Hold your tongue!' he said harshly.

'Getting soft, boss?'

But this had been said under Montvallon's breath, *sotto voce*. There were things he didn't push.

Maubourg, as it happened, didn't need to go into the house. He heard some sounds of activity at the side, and following a curving path he came upon Madameoiselle Rolland kneeling in front of a carnation bed, snipping at old shoots. Her face was rosier than ever, flushed with exertion. She rose as Maubourg came near her.

'Mademoiselle, I did not wish to disturb you.'

'Monique is in the house.'

'No, it was you I wanted to see.'

This was unusual, he suspected; she seemed flustered, brushing crumbs of earth and thin bluish-green leaves from her skirt. More than flustered, nervous, perhaps.

'Oh, well...'

Her voice trailed away. She was rubbing nervously at the sleeve of her jumper. It was a good quality one, he thought, probably cashmere, in a dark brown colour. Violetta had something in cashmere, but her's was a soft hazy thing. This looked old, worn into nubbles and smooth patches.

On impulse, he asked the Rolland woman something that didn't seem to have anything to do with the death of Rosie Cashel. It was, he realised as soon as he said it, to satisfy his own curiosity.

'How long have you.. have you known Mademoiselle Arthuis?'

She looked at him reproachfully, it seemed, but directly. Her eyes must have been quite beautiful once: they were large soft blue eyes, gentle still.

'We have been together for about twenty-three years, monsieur. You see, I can tell you exactly, because it was very important for me, meeting Monique. In those days there was a lot of prejudice - oh, I don't pretend anything, yes we were lovers. I know how people gossip, so I might as well tell you myself. It was all over some years ago, but we stay together. We need each other, it's as simple as that.'

A lot simpler than it is with me and Violetta, thought Maubourg. They stay together without the cement of marriage or sex or children, these two, so why might Violetta and I break apart? Because she can't be faithful and I can't live with her infidelity?

'You met here, in Cannes?'

'Yes, I had come here for a holiday - although I could barely afford it. I was a typist in a government bureau in Paris - and I met Monique, who was visiting her uncle.'

'So you know the district well?'

'Quite well.'

'Did you know the English girl staying in the Villa Bleue? Rosie Cashel?'

'Only by sight - I had come here with Monique before old M. Arthuis died, so I saw her once or twice then. And after he died, well, we moved in here, so I saw her across the road and spoke a little sometimes, just to pass the time of day, but I didn't really know her.'

'You don't know anything about her death, Mademoiselle?'

'I have been asked before, and I told them then, no!'

'But I am asking you again, Mademoiselle. Can you remember anything strange happening on the night Rosie Cashel was killed?'

'No, I don't know anything about it. Nothing at all!'

'And Mademoiselle Washington. The housekeeper in this very house. You must have known her.'

Mauburg had a curious feeling. The big eyes in the anxious little face seemed to retreat from contact. Something was disturbing her. He looked down and saw that she was shredding an early carnation bud into tiny gleams of pink.

'Of course, I met her on a few occasions, when I came here with Monique to visit M. Arthuis, but I can't tell you anything about her.'

'I've talked to Mademoiselle Washington. She came here to see your friend, Monique Arthuis. I gather a lot of the old man's possessions have been sold off - except for the picture, the painting of the cemetery.'

Was there now a definite edge to her mouth, the lips pressed together as if holding something back, something that was just on the edge of being said? Was it the mention of the picture? Curious. He probed further, pressed on the sore tooth.

'Strange, mademoiselle, I would not have thought it is to Mademoiselle Arthuis' taste. A modern painting - and of a rather morbid subject.'

Her eyes were now fixed on his. She dropped the shredded flower-bud and put her hand up to her mouth.

Yes, definitely the picture. He had scored a hit, but how to follow it up. Maubourg racked his brains to recall what he had been told about the Leclant when Susanna Washington had seen it in Monique's sitting-room. Something about the cord. Trivial, but no matter, the important thing was to keep on the subject of the painting.

'Yet Mademoiselle Arthuis presumably likes the painting very much - I gather she has even had new string put on the back.'

Suddenly she blurted out 'I can tell you nothing', and before he could say anything more she had turned and was hurrying to the house.

He called after her 'The *juge d'instruction* wants to interview you,' but she had disappeared indoors. Damn, thought Maubourg. Shouldn't have asked her so much about Monique Arthuis. Probably upset her - we won't get anything out of her now.

He walked along to where Montvallon was seated in the car. 'Old biddy tell you anything, chief?'

'Not really.' How to explain to Montvallon the tension he had felt in her at the mention of Susanna Washington and the picture? He didn't try. 'Poor old creature.'

'Why say that, boss? Seems she's on a cushy number here. Look at the house she lives in!'

Montvallon indicated the elegant building and expensive grounds of the Arthuis mansion with a sweep of his stubby thumb.

'I feel sorry for her, all the same.'

But he couldn't say why.

It was a change from self-pity, anyway. He hadn't called round at Madeleine's when he got back from Paris. He'd picked up the phone, put it down, sworn at his own cowardice.

Violetta had come in an hour or so later, asking him about the Picasso

Museum. Was it interesting, did he get something for Rachelle? No, he hadn't, there wasn't time.

Violetta didn't say anything about her party. She smelled warm, musky, as she brushed past him to make a *tisane*. He'd wanted to go to bed with her, an act of possession, perhaps.

He forced the ensuing fruitless moments, the image of his hands on her brown skin, of her hand with its pale varnished nails pushing him away, out of his mind.

'Let's get back into town, Montvallon.'

Chapter 58

She was there, in the kitchen. Somehow, Charlie wasn't surprised; it had been there all along, he thought, some underlying knowledge, a person who'd been overlooked, something that said the woman's name, right at the back of his mind.

She sprang up as soon as they got into the kitchen. 'The police - I thought they would come into the house - I saw the car and the Inspector talked to me - he frightened me, to tell you the truth. I think he knows things... He wanted me to go and talk to that woman, the *juge d'instruction*, but I ran into the house. I expect they'll come back with a warrant, though; people say she's very determined. The magistrate, I mean. Listen, I want to talk to you - to ask you for something - if you'll help me get away ... There's something I can do for you in return.'

'Susanna, I think there's a bottle of Scotch in that cupboard behind you,' said Charlie, fishing three tumblers out and setting them down on the scrubbed wood of the table before continuing, 'All right, Mademoiselle Rolland, what is it?'

The other woman sank onto a chair, her soft brown-grey hair falling from a grip which held it in place, stumbling even in her sensible brogues. As Susanna poured the whisky, she waved it away.

'No, thank you. I don't touch the stuff, Monsieur Cashel. You're entitled to the truth. You were her brother, after all, even if it was only her half-brother and you didn't seem to care what happened to her.'

There was a long pause. Charlie found there was nothing he could say in his own defence. Somehow, he had only come to love the grown-up Rosie too late.

The woman continued, almost remorselessly, as if she sensed Charlie's shame. 'Dr. Durrant did love her, I think. He told me once he didn't want some thin-faced harpy with gold chains - he'd seen enough of that type hanging round the sports club. She was so young, she wasn't cynical, you see. She believed he could still do something ... She thought he could still be a real doctor, that's what he said.'

Charlie felt sick. He thought of Rosie's innocent face. 'She thought she could reform him, did she? Well, it didn't do anything for him in the end!'

'She believed in him!' said the other.

'And I know what it meant for her! Ending up in a morgue, that's what it did for Rosie!'

'Charlie,' said Susanna, 'let her say whatever it is she's come to say. Otherwise she'll never get through the story.' She turned to Madame Rolland. 'What happened? You won't have long to tell us - when the police come to look for you again across the road, they'll probably call here on the chance we've seen you.'

'Monique told me about it. And some of it was from the doctor. When he was looking after the old man.'

Chapter 59

The old man, Arthuis, lies in his bed. There are few distractions left to him now; his niece does not call often and in any case she gets bored with his stories of the past and she doesn't read the papers, so she can't tell him what's going on, as he so often asks.

He prefers practising English with the housekeeper, Miss Washington, enjoying her clean Scottish accent and her calm good sense, but she is often busy. And besides, he likes to talk about other things, about expeditions, for instance, and the analysis of moon-rock, things that distract him from pain and the four walls of his room in the tall grey house just opposite the Villa Bleue. These things, he finds, his doctor has often read about in some scientific magazine, and the doctor is willing to sit down at the end of a morning of visits, and share an aperitif with his patient. That weary pump, Arthuis' heart, cannot carry on for much longer, as both men know. It has already functioned valiantly for eight decades, and by rights even the slight excitement of a Dubonnet sends too vivid signals coursing through the old man's veins, but there is little point in banning it now.

Their talk turns sometimes to other things. Today, for example, to art. They are discussing the sale of the Duchess of Windsor's effects, taking place in Paris, and that leads on to Arthuis's own collection of antiques. 'Ah, yes, I bought most of the pieces many years ago - when prices were not insane, as they are now! But, you know, probably the most valuable thing I have is not an antique at all! In fact, I got it by accident - I would never have thought of buying it, though I have grown close to it, over the years!'

And he gestures to the painting opposite his bed. A small oil, with patches of vivid blue, and white rectangles in the foreground, amidst a burning dark emerald mass of cypress trees.

'It's a Leclant. Oh, yes, everyone has heard of him now. Jewish, murdered in the concentration camps. No-one knew anything of him then, when I was given the picture. It was his sister, you see - she escaped, but she had somehow managed to hide this painting and store it under the floorboards - and then... well, I helped her and their mother at the end of the war. Have you ever seen starvation, doctor? Real starvation?'

The old man falls silent.

A few days later the doctor reads about Leclant in his morning paper. There has been a retrospective exhibition in Paris. But few pictures by this artist, whose work was destroyed as decadent, are known to survive. The last Leclant to be sold at auction fetched more than ninety million francs in New York.

'It must have seemed so easy,' said Mademoiselle Rolland, almost wonderingly.

'What did?' said Charlie, but Susanna broke in. 'Yes, it must have been! I understand now.'

'Doctor Durrant was called to the house ...' said the other woman.

'Yes,' said Susanna. 'I called him, remember? The night the old man died. I phoned for you to come straight away. And you did.'

'And he went up the stairs and into the room and saw that Arthuis was dead. It only took a few minutes to examine him. He'd had a heart attack, just as everyone expected. But he didn't leave straight away.'

'I understand now! Because when I went into the room after Durrant's visit, the picture had gone from the wall! Before Monique or anyone else had gone upstairs. So Durrant took it!' said Susanna, fiercely. 'He took the picture, with the old man lying there in the room! And who would ever suspect a doctor? That was the best safeguard, wasn't it? A respectable doctor, stealing over the dead body of his patient. Who would believe it! He would have got away with it!'

'How can anything so small be worth so much?' said Mademoiselle Rolland, wonderingly. 'Because that's what it meant to him, not just money, not just millions of francs. It meant enough to go away with Rosie Cashel.'

'Except Rosie wouldn't go away with him!'

'Not difficult to guess that,' said Susanna.

'He showed it to her - that was his mistake. He came to the Villa Bleue that evening - he didn't tell her where the picture was from, of course, but she must have guessed it was stolen. She might have visited the old man sometimes, and even seen it there, though it's curious - if you're not interested in art, you don't really notice pictures, do you? I mean, if they're removed you just sort of notice the empty space on the wall, and you say to yourself, 'oh, where's that gone?' Anyway Durrant took it to Rosie Cashel, and I don't know what he said. I suppose he said they could go away together and he would sell it, something like that, and she said 'No! No! Where did you get it?'

'How do you know that, Mademoiselle?'

'I heard it, or part of it, and Monique told me the rest of the story. I was there across the road with my window open and I heard your sister's voice. She was speaking very loudly, very fast. I couldn't see them, by then. They'd moved up the path and close to the house.'

The woman paused. She was pressing her hands to her eyes.

They were talking in English, but it was easy to understand. It was all very simple - she was saying `No, no, take it back!' And he was saying `Please, Rosie, come with me.' It's funny how at times like that - when people are really feeling everything - they use such simple language. Just a few short words. `Please. No.'

Susanna sat back in her chair, looking at the woman's elderly face, the veins on the hands that were now dabbing with a handkerchief, and thought 'This woman has known how it is - to ask and be rejected.'

She took a long breath. Charlie said, very quietly.

'She wouldn't go away with him, was that it? After he had risked everything for her, after he had stolen the picture, broken every professional oath, every taboo - taken it from a dead man - put his entire world at risk - Rosie wouldn't go away with Durrant! And so he killed her!'

'Then and there,' said Susanna, 'outside this house, standing in the garden.'

'I suppose so,' said Mademoiselle Rolland, with a great sigh, as of relief. 'Although I didn't actually see it. But I never saw her alive after that. And I was sure Dr. Durrant hadn't really been here with Monique just before Madame Ferrier found Rosie's body - that was his alibi. Monique said he had been with her all the time - because she wanted him to give her back the picture. It was a kind of agreement they made and I had to keep quiet about it. Oh, I feel so terrible about it, so sad. What do you think I should do, M. Cashel? The magistrate wants to see me.'

'Tell her the truth', said Charlie. 'You can't do anything else. Why didn't you go to the police earlier?'

'I was afraid to say anything, because of Monique - she gives me a home, you see. I have no money of my own - nowhere to go. I was hoping -if I helped you, you might get me to England.'

There was a pause while they took in the realism of these simple statements, and what the admission of poverty must have cost in defeated pride.

'I don't know if we can do that, though we'll help you if we can. But why should Monique Arthuis cover up for Durrant?' asked Susanna, eventually.

'There was a reason... he knew something. He had been the old man's doctor, after all. I can't say any more.'

'But that's not all he did, was it? He must have brought the picture back - probably because Monique had noticed it was gone.'

'Yes, he brought it back - and they agreed no more would be said! He even had a story to explain what had happened. Apparently, he said that the string had broken and the picture had fallen off the wall - just before the old man died. Arthuis was terribly distressed about it - so Doctor Durrant took it as an act of kindness and put some new string on the back. Such a little thing - the policeman knew about it, though. I felt he was telling me he knew really what had happened. Anyway, according to the story the doctor made up, his next visit was when he was summoned after Arthuis' death, so that didn't seem an appropriate moment to arrive with the picture. He just brought it back, with the new string, at the earliest possible opportunity, and handed it over to Monique. But that was just the story for public consumption, in case anyone noticed the absence of the picture. Durrant even went so far as to put new cord on the back, in case anyone should check. You noticed that, Mademoiselle Washington; Monique told me so. She didn't believe a word of the story - but it suited her book not to draw any attention to the picture immediately after the old man's death. As long as she got it back quietly, that was what she wanted.'

Susanna was silent, puzzled. The Monique Arthuis she had met seemed like a vengeful harpy. Why should she so meekly overlook an attempt to deprive her of her rightful inheritance?

'He killed Rosie! But he'd taken a photograph of the painting,' said Charlie, with sudden inspiration. 'That was it! But why?'

'Because he knew he'd have to find a buyer for it! You can't take an original painting like that down to your local second-hand shop!' exclaimed Susanna - 'and he didn't know anything about the art market. So he was going to send the photograph to someone who could help him to sell it. But he never did that. And someone else sent it on - to you.'

Chapter 60

Charlie found his mind was full of confused, irrelevant thoughts. Such as, now that he was sitting in a chair in the solemn office of the *juge d'instruction*, he found himself observing that the woman opposite him had fine clever eyes. This was the famous examining magistrate, of whom Maubourg had spoken, the tough ball-crusher who ran her office with an iron hand. But she was wearing a nice suit in some plum sort of colour, and she had some make-up on. That seemed to be the only human touch in this room, that and a small gilt-framed mirror hanging in a corner, where presumably she had applied the discreet touches of lipstick. Everything else was official, impersonal, the property of the state.

Damn, he mustn't forget. This woman might not look like a battle-axe but she had a lot of power. She could, as he understood it, do pretty nearly damn well what she liked with Charlie himself, for instance.

He tried to get his attention back to what she was saying. The chair in front of her desk was not very comfortable. Maubourg sat on his right and on their left was a clerk, a man who was taking notes as they talked. There was a tape-recorder running as well: she had asked Charlie if he objected. And she had asked him if he wanted a translator. The interview was mostly in English anyway, Mme Galant speaking it well, if rather pedantically, Maubourg translating when it came to difficult moments. It hadn't seemed worth getting a special translator.

And they'd told him that he didn't need a lawyer, not at this stage, anyway. 'You are not yet being charged with anything, M. Cashel. You are simply assisting the investigation. This is not even the *interrogatoire de première comparution*, when any charges would be laid.'

She waved a hand in the direction of the note-taker. 'This is *le greffier*, the clerk. He will make a record of what we say. And I hope you will co-operate with us, M. Cashel.'

He sensed he didn't have much option.

They went through his account of what he had witnessed at the house in St. Émile, which was muddy and confused, but what he could remember was down on record. He stated quite positively that he thought that they were in serious peril from Caracci, even after the man had been wounded, and that Maubourg's shot that had terminated the killer's life at the end had been totally justified.

'Would you even go so far, M. Cashel, as to say that the Inspector might have been placing your lives in danger if he had not made sure that Caracci was eliminated?'

'Oh, quite certainly.'

There was a pause, as if she were satisfied about something. Mauburg leaned back in his chair. The clerk looked up with interest. Charlie felt he had said something important, though he wasn't quite sure what. Anyway, it was true - thank God Maubourg had shot the bastard! Thinking about the possibilities, Charlie began to shake.

'But there's still the problem of who sent you the photograph,' said the woman, after a few moments.

By this stage the interrogation had a curious effect, as of enforcing reality inside his skull. Charlie was now sitting on his chair with his head hidden between his hands, as he tried to come to terms with what had happened. His body seemed suddenly to be shaking with a post-adrenalin rush, his hands as unsteady as if he had some malarial fever.

'For God's sake, we've been through it all now' he said.

'Yes, but it's not the end of the story, Monsieur Cashel' interjected Mauburg. 'For one thing, as Madame says, there is still the question of the photograph. How did it get into your hands?'

'Damn it, that's for you to answer! How the hell do I know?'

His mood changed again as a paralysing kind of fear, a retrospective fear that he had somehow kept at bay, struck him. And he was suddenly exhausted, truculent with the reactions of anger and fright. All he wanted was to sleep.

Chapter 61

'It was you.'

Cecile Galant put down the dossier of the Cashel case.

The woman opposite, who had been waiting with bowed head for the investigation to begin, looked up with her surprisingly large brown eyes, set in a scrubbed and weatherbeaten face. She was wearing a black blouse and skirt, flat-heeled black shoes. Cecile could picture a black head-scarf over her head, completing the image of the traditional Mediterranean widow, a type surviving even amid the topless tourist traps of the Riviera, living alongside them but in a different world.

'It must have been you,' repeated Cecile. 'I've been through the dossier - there was no-one else who might have cared about the Cashel family. And you found Rosie's body - the police reports describe your distress. Who else could have sent the film? But why did you do it? I can't understand. What were the Cashels to you?'

The woman's lips began to move, but the voice was so soft and nervous that Cecile had to lean forward to catch it.

'I scarcely knew her - Rosie Cashel, though she was always nice to me. We never talked much. But I'd worked for Madame Anna - her mother. It wasn't right, what was going on. It just wasn't right, you know. I saw what happened, with the film.'

'What happened, Madame Ferrier?'

'Why should I tell you?'

'Because I've guessed right once, haven't I - I've guessed it was you who posted the film to Charlie Cashel in England. You see, the report just said that the photograph of the cemetery picture had been posted to Charlie Cashel. 'The photograph' - I'm quoting. And if that had been the case, then very few people would have realised the significance of it and thought it would have been worth sending on. But when I talked to M. Cashel, I discovered the wording had been inexact. It was not the photograph itself that had been sent - it was the roll of negatives. So they could have been pictures of anything, the person who sent them wouldn't necessarily know what they were photographs of.'

Cecile looked across the desk. She didn't think the woman was really following, but she needed to rehearse all this so as to get it straight in her own mind.

'And that, Madame Ferrier, means that we were not just confined to people who knew about the cemetery painting. The negatives could have been of anything - someone could easily think that they were photographs of Rosie Cashel herself, for example.'

There was a long pause. Then the other woman said:

'Yes, that's exactly what I did think. And I saw them arguing, Dr. Durrant and the girl, Rosie. He had a camera case in his hand and he opened it up and there was something inside it - something black and shiny with a bright yellow tag. And then I realised it was the roll of film - he tried to hand it to her and she pushed it away, shouting at him. Then I couldn't see them any more. They were going up through the garden, at the side of the Villa Bleue.'

'And what did you think it was about?'

'What else, in this town? What does a roll of film mean here? That she had some photographs taken, I suppose - some publicity pictures, you know, like the girls at the beach do, for the festival. Anyway, then they went round the side of the villa and I couldn't see them again. But I could see the film - lying in the driveway. And I went and picked it up - I was going to give it to her, you understand. I thought Durrant had somehow got hold of it and was challenging her about it - that he was angry because he was so jealous of her. I didn't follow them then - God only knows, Madame, how I wish I had, because I might have prevented... at any rate, I thought I shouldn't be there, when they were quarrelling. I am not an eavesdropper, like some people round here. I am loyal, madame, they trust me, the employers. But then I came back a couple of hours later and I found her lying there, poor little thing.'

Cecile let the woman pause for a few moments. 'I saw her lying there and I touched her poor cheek and she was so cold, madame, so cold. Well, I ran in and telephoned the police, but I didn't want to give them the film, because if it was what I thought it was...'

'If it was shots of her in the nude? Soft porn or something like that?'

'Yes, if it was that, then I didn't want people to know about it. She was a nice girl, you know, very kind... I know it's very old-fashioned, but it was important to keep her good reputation - I thought the family would have wanted it.'

'So you didn't hand the film over to Maubourg. And you didn't tell him about the quarrel with Durrant that you had witnessed.'

'No, but I thought somehow that it wasn't right that Durrant should get off, if he had been involved in the murder, and the police didn't show any signs of arresting him. So I thought, when I learned that Rosie had a brother, that if I sent him the film it would be safe with him, whatever it was, and besides, he might want to find out who had killed his sister. The police, well, they just do their job, don't they? But when it's your own flesh and blood...' The voice trailed away.

Cecile got up and walked round the room, then back to her chair.

That's exactly how it would have been, in the world this woman had been born into, some little village where everyone knew everyone's business and the family took care of everything. Don't give things away to officialdom, keep silent, but trust your own kith and kin. Rely on them alone - and rely on them for vengeance.

That was part of the old Provence, too. The jealous, blood-soaked country, where a vendetta could continue for generations, where a brother would avenge his sister's murder, or protect her honour to the death. It lay only a little while back in time, that old South of France, inland from the soft life of the coast, with its own brutal, strong-tasting existence. No good telling this woman that her ideas were absurd, outdated.

'How did you get Charles Cashel's address in England?'

Antoinette Ferrier looked up in surprise.

'Oh, that was easy. I asked the undertakers, the people who arranged for her body to be flown back home. I said I wanted to write a letter of condolence. There was no problem.'

'Do you know what the photographs showed?'

'No, I still don't know. I've never seen them.'

When she told the woman she was free to go, Cecile heaved a great sigh. All that mystery over who had sent the photographs and why, and there it was, a nosy old woman who had seen something she had thought and fantasized about until it became some lurid tale involving pornographic photos and lovers' quarrels. And yet, it had been a violent and lurid act in the short life of Rosie Cashel that the woman had witnessed, only it had been a prelude to her murder, not a stage in a blue movie.

But all the same, she thought Cashel had been hiding something. In his

244

position, most British people faced with questioning by a *juge d'instruction* demanded to see the British Consul, asked frequently when they would be free to return to the safe bosom of their own country, worried about their flights home.

Charlie Cashel hadn't betrayed any anxiety to return to London, none at all.

Which presumably meant, thought Cecile, that there was something he didn't want to get home to.

Lenoir put his head round the door.

'Anything else, madame? Will you see the Rolland woman now?'

'No, will you take down a preliminary statement from her? Cashel told me her story - I think it's plausible enough. Monique Arthuis is next on my list - but we don't want to give her any warning.'

Lenoir raised his eyebrows, but didn't ask questions. 'She's been weeping into her hanky, poor old Rolland,' he said. 'Had to send out for a box of tissues. Says she doesn't know what will become of her.'

His voice sounded sympathetic, not cynical, as she might have expected. Did I misjudge him, thought Cecile? His kindness?

A thought flashed across her mind. Perhaps Lenoir was gay, perhaps that was why he felt sorry for this sad, lost and lonely partner. A kindred sympathy. Or was it just a kind heart?

You are too suspicious, she told herself. Why would he need to keep it a secret, in this day and age? But she knew the reason, thinking about the phone call from the Commissaire and the attempt to discredit Maubourg because of his family problems. This was a real bureaucracy here, with a repressive atmosphere of conformity. The message to any employee who wanted to get on was 'keep your nose clean'. And that meant being straight, being married, staying married. And toeing a political line that wouldn't upset the Chamber of Commerce. Did Lenoir have an inner life that made him more than a spiritless clerk?

'Well, there's something I can do for her,' she said aloud. 'I'll remind Monique Arthuis that she'll need a friend, someone to look after the house and pay the bills. It may be in her interests to make sure Mademoiselle Rolland stays here and is comfortable.'

Lenoir smiled. 'You're a subtle operator, if I may say so.'

'You may, I give you permission.'

Chapter 62

They were sitting round the kitchen table in the Villa Bleue, eating those little cakes called *religieuses*, one small bun on top of a large one, filled with caramel and chocolate cream and covered with chocolate and caramel icing. Susanna had just brought them back from the pâtisserie and the blue and white striped wrapping paper lay on the table, serving as a plate.

Suddenly Charlie leant forward over the table. 'Susanna, if we're ... If there's going to be any future in this ... there's something I've got to tell you.'

Oh God, he had thought, there's still Imelda. That's what I've got to tell her about. Imelda, the police sirens in the street. It can't be much longer before they trace me here.

He found himself trying to stammer out a version of events to Susanna. It was difficult, explaining to anyone who hadn't known Imelda, just what she had been like. He went over things, the shoplifting, the rows.

'It's all right, Charlie' she said, several times, but he didn't think it was. How could it be? 'They'll be after me. Who else? They always go for the husband or the boyfriend - they'll think I put her up to it. Besides, she won't try to keep me out of it - we had quarrelled - over that damned photograph.'

Charlie was overcome with a sense of disbelief. How could he have been trapped so that he was here, at this moment, looking at a woman he wanted to spend his entire life with, yet tied to the past by that old stupidity?

'They can't be long now,' he repeated. The English police, he meant. He thought again about the *juge*, the woman in whose office he had been sitting a few hours ago. Had she guessed that he had been fleeing from something in England - that the photograph and its supposed connection with Rosie hadn't been enough to bring him back to Cannes? He had really come to save his own hide, not to investigate poor Rosie's murder.

It was dark now. He couldn't think, except to wonder if it was worth struggling any more. It was possible to make one last attempt to get away, he supposed, but he was so tired. Every muscle in his body seemed to ache and his mind was refusing to operate, 'Give me sleep,' it screamed at him, 'Give me sleep!'

Peering out of the window, he was aware that there seemed to be some kind of movement on the path of the Villa. 'Not the police again!' said Susanna. 'Surely Maubourg doesn't want any more from us.'

There was a knock on the door.

'Can't be Maubourg and his merry men' said Charlie. 'They'd have banged like the last trump.'

He got up and walked slowly, reluctantly, into the corridor.

He had a moment of recognition as the figure outside the door pushed past him.

'Martin!' he said, disbelieving.

But there was no doubt.

Martin looked distinctly out of place in the kitchen of the villa, still in the suit and waistcoat he must have been wearing for his day in the London office, his neat professional solicitor's garb, tie knotted under white collar. The collar was looking a bit wilted and Martin had heavy stubble on his cheeks - that was the only sign that he had not just stepped out of his office. But then, Charlie found himself recalling irrelevantly, Martin always did have a heavy beard.

'Hallo, Charlie. I've invited myself in.'

'No need to ask you, then.' It was almost like being in a Marx Brothers comedy, this exchange, thought Charlie. Almost, because the expression on Martin's face was deadly serious. Normally he had an affable suggestion of Nigel Hawthorne as Sir Humphrey, his iron-grey hair close cut, his face lined with something approaching smile-lines - at least, they could pass for them from a distance. His face was now contorted, his mouth jerking the words out. And his eyes, grey eyes that ought to be so trustworthy - they suddenly seemed so small - why had he never noticed before how they nested in folds of fat and wrinkles?

'Have you still got that photograph? The picture that brought you on this wild goose chase in the first place.'

'But it wasn't a wild goose chase, was it, Martin? Because they've found out who killed Rosie.'

Funny, there was a time when Rosie hadn't seemed important to him.

And when Martin had seemed - well, just plain straightforward Martin, good old Martin, the mainstay of the family.

Why did I ever think that about him?

'Thought I'd just stay the night here,' said Martin, casually. 'Any objections?'

Somehow, Charlie hated the thought, but there was no reasonable objection he could make. But he was saved from having to say anything at all.

Martin was about to sit down at the table when there was a loud commotion outside and a hammering on the outer door.

'I'll go' said Susanna.

They heard her open the door and then suddenly the room was full of people. The woman, the judge, followed by Maubourg, and behind him some other copper whom Charlie recognised - not the one who had roughed his wrists about in the police station, a younger one, less tough-looking.

The woman spoke straight to Martin.

'That is your car outside, Monsieur? Good, please follow me.'

She moved quickly outside and they all followed her; Martin moved reluctantly and Maubourg had to come up behind him in a meaningful way.

There was a dark blue car, dusty, road-stained. British licence-plates.

Charlie noticed that the two policemen had taken up positions next to Martin, blocking his movements.

'Your car keys, monsieur.'

Then suddenly things were happening - Martin was blustering, something about his rights, that he was a lawyer - was trying to pull away and the young policemen had him in an arm-lock, while Maubourg experly slid his hands into the Englishman's pockets and emerged with a set of car keys.

Cecile nodded.

The car doors were opened. Nothing on the seats, the interior innocent.

Nothing in the glove compartment.

Maubourg moved round to the boot.

Martin was still protesting. No-one took any notice.

It gleamed and glowed even in the grey interior of the boot, the oils fluid and shining, the colours vibrant with life.

Maubourg was speaking.

'There will be a charge of theft. And of trying to smuggle a work of art out of the country. They are very serious charges, you understand.'

Martin was screaming with rage now. 'Shut up, M. Hollingsworth,' said Maubourg, equably. 'You are disturbing the conversation here.'

Martin opened his mouth to shout again and the nice young policeman jabbed a fist into the lawyer's stomach. He doubled over, gasping in a spasm, and a trickle of green vomit dribbled out of his mouth and down the side of his waistcoat.

'And clean yourself up', added Maubourg, pushing a white handkerchief into Martin's hand. 'Madame has something to say here and she must have some respect.'

'I came next door, to visit Mademoiselle Arthuis,' said Cecile. 'Normally, of course, I would have her brought to my office for interview, but I wished to look at the painting for myself - after all, it is not everyone involved in a murder case who has an original Leclant hanging on the wall! Art must be respected, must it not? The picture is too valuable to be moved around like a sack of potatoes, so in this case the magistrate has come to the picture instead of ordering the picture to be brought to the magistrate. Anyway, Monique Arthuis couldn't show me the picture. She made all kinds of excuses, but I was sure she couldn't produce it. And when I saw a British car parked in the drive of the Villa Bleue and I heard a loud English voice from inside, I thought I would pay a visit here. Fortunately, I had an escort, because I expected not only to interview Mademoiselle Arthuis but to issue a warrant for her arrest.'

'Monique?' said Susanna. 'But what had she done? It was Durrant who killed Rosie.'

'The warrant is not for murder - for theft. In fact, she and M. Hollingsworth conspired to steal the picture - he was to take it back to England to be sold there. And she has committed a most serious civil wrong. The suppression of a document.'

She turned to Martin.

'I believe you can enlighten us, Monsieur Hollingsworth. I would advise you to help us.'

Martin's rage seemed to have subsided. He was handcuffed now. Charlie didn't deny himself revengeful pleasure as he looked at Martin's wrists.

They were all inside now while the young policeman spoke urgently into his mobile phone.

Cecile went on speaking.

'It was when I realised that you were a *notaire*, Monsieur Hollingsworth. A solicitor, who would be familiar with legal details. And so, what more natural than that M. Arthuis, when he desired to be reassured on a point of British law, should ask to have a word with the most respectable relation of the family opposite, who happened to be visiting in order to settle some matters arising from the death of Rosie Cashel.'

Charlie broke in here. 'Why should old Arthuis want to know about it?'

'Because he wanted to make a legacy. And he wanted it to be valid according to your law. He wanted to be sure there would be no problems with carrying out his intentions - in case the beneficiary had returned to Britain when he died. I could not understand it for a while - why should he think there would be any complications. Then I realised. Because Scottish law is different from English law, isn't it? We have heard quite a lot about that recently, because there is much discussion of devolution in the news-papers - every time Corsica or Brittany, for example, wants to secede from France, such issues are discussed. Is that not so, Monsieur Hollingsworth?'

'Yes - but, of course, it would have made no difference!' said Martin.

'Tell them,' said Cecile, and there was a certain tone in her voice that made Martin tell them.

'He wanted to transfer something to Susanna Washington - by a codi-cil, that couldn't be challenged in law. The will left everything to Monique Arthuis. But he wanted... I'm not going to go on.'

Martin's voice dwindled away, as if he were obeying some deep legalis-tic instinct of self-exculpation. The young policeman came close and raised his fist again, but Cecile was speaking again.

'No need, I will finish the story. He desired to reward Susanna Washington for her services. So far from dying an ingrate, Mademoiselle, Monsieur Arthuis had appreciated your care very much. Enough to leave you his most valuable possession. The painting by Leclant. But he wanted to be sure that he had complied with all legal formalities so he asked you, M. Hollingsworth, whether there would be any difficulty under Scottish law about the possession of such an important art work passing to Mademoiselle Washington, assuming she would want to return to Glasgow. And you, of course, informed him that there would be no problems, but you guessed that the picture was worth a fortune. The sale of a Leclant in New York had made the front pages of the newspapers - so the expert in Paris informed Chief Inspector Maubourg.

'And you were determined to get it. You had two problems - where was it, how to sell it. You had an arrangement with Mademoiselle Arthuis - you knew that her uncle had left the painting to Susanna Washington, and Mademoiselle Rolland says Arthuis even gave you a copy of the codicil, so you were in a position to get her cooperation. You came out to Cannes to find the picture. So then there were two factions after the Leclant, because there was someone else besides you who wanted it. White Boy was after it, because he'd demanded something from Durrant to compensate him for loss of business, and Durrant promised him the picture. Perhaps he was desperate, just trying to stave White Boy off. Anyway, when he couldn't deliver, White Boy had to punish the defection, and he put Caracci on to Durrant. So Durrant became the sixth victim of the Mutilator - but this was a business killing, not for private pleasure.

'But you, M. Hollingsworth, you had to make plans to deal with the second problem, assuming you got hold of the painting. How to put the picture up for sale without arousing suspicions once you had got hold of it? Of course, London is one of the centres of the illicit art market. To do that you would have to get some contacts in the art world - I don't know exactly who, but the British police can find out. They've checked your telephone contacts. We've been in touch with them and they've already made certain inquiries checking up on a gallery in - I believe it's called Cork Street?'

'Oh, God!' Betrayal loomed sickeningly in Charlie's mind: he knew what had happened, in the sickness of his stomach, before he had thought it through.

'Imelda', he said. 'She works in an art gallery there!'

'I'm not saying anything more.' Martin produced this like a trump card.

'Mademoiselle Rolland made a statement to my clerk that she saw Monique Arthuis destroy the original document after the old man's death,' continued Cecile. 'But it doesn't matter, Monsieur Hollingsworth. There is plenty of evidence against you in London. Miss Imelda Shoesmith has plenty of information to give us. They searched her room, you see, Inspector Willis and his assistant. And they found - well, stolen goods, but not what they expected. And she's very angry with you, Mr. Hollingsworth. She thinks you betrayed her shoplifting activities to the police. Her statement says you had threatened her that you would tell the police she was a thief - unless she helped you with what you wanted from her.'

Charlie rubbed his face with his hands, remembering how he had confided in Martin about Imelda's frightening little obsession. Well, so Imelda had given Martin away before he could throw her to the wolves.

The biter bit.

Chapter 64

'So Durrant killed the poor Cashel girl. But he was involved with White Boy and the drug racket, pushing ketamine to kids.'

Cecile looked at him and waited a moment or two before answering. 'People can fall in love in very stupid ways.'

She added hastily, as Maubourg's face semed to tighten.

'Like a middle-aged minor drugs dealer falling for a totally innocent young girl. It can happen. It did happen in this case.'

'Yes - well, that's Durrant taken out of the equation. And we can conclude the Mutilés dossier as well. Caracci, La Guenon, he was responsible, sometimes on White Boy's orders, sometimes for his own gratification.'

Cecile Galant responded sharply to Maubourg's statement. They were sitting in the canteen in the municipal offices late in the afternoon, a pile of notes on the table, between their trays with the debris of green salad and microwaved fish in mushroom sauce. We eat like the rest of France, thought Cecile, and tonight we'll probably have a Macon Chardonnay, because that's a nice light wine that takes our fancy. We don't need to drink the fruit of the local soil any more, we can pick and choose from all over.

She said, 'No, we can't close that dossier.'

'But there's no doubt that Caracci was the killer! Forensic evidence can show it was the notched knife we found on him that inflicted the wounds on all the victims. The first of the mutilations happened shortly after his arrival from Corsica. Besides, White Boy will testify against him.'

'White Boy would testify against Jesus Christ to save his own skin. But that's not the point - I'm as convinced as you are that Caracci was the Mutilator and we won't get any more attacks like that.'

'What's the matter, then? Excess of police force during arrest? I had to stop him, the air was full of petrol fumes and a single shot could have set the place alight. They'll all testify to that, Cashel, the Washington woman, Victoire. I didn't dare fire for fear of the petrol fumes and Caracci was a dangerous animal. I didn't intend to break his neck but I did the world a favour. Anyway, he was probably dying as it was.'

'No, that's not a problem. I'll get all their statements and no-one's going to mourn for him. The general verdict will be that you did the world a service. No, the matter is this: it's not enough for you and me and a few other officials to be convinced that Caracci was the Mutilator. Don't you understand? This is a high-profile case.'

'Oh, you want to play politics with it!'

He was contemptuous and it flicked her on the raw. She had thought they were understanding one another, beginning to work together as she wanted, but he would only follow her part way.

She would have to go the rest of the distance alone.

'Playing politics, as you call it, means that we get the funding we need, it means that we get the public on our side, the press supporting us - you - instead of hammering away at the incompetence of the judicial system!'

'It's the timing, isn't it?'

No, she thought. I can't do anything about the timing. It's Easter and the city's filled with the holiday tourist avalanche already for the weekend, and I want to get away to be with my daughter. She's only five-years-old, for Christ's sake. Is that so wrong, to want that?

'I want more evidence. There must be some, and I don't specially want it to be scientific, if you understand me. I want something really obvious, something the papers can pick up on with no trouble at all - no brains needed.'

'What can we do about it? We haven't got anyone we can put a squeeze on.'

'No, we have to do it more rationally - by the way, I sent the Rolland woman home, if the Arthuis house is home to her still. There was nothing more to be got out of her. Anyway, I've been thinking about the next stage: nailing Caracci's guilt, which is a different matter and a damned sight more difficult than killing Caracci himself. I've been reading up about the psychopathic mentality.'

'Psychologists' theory isn't evidence.'

'No, but it can tell us how to find evidence - or rather, what sort of evidence there will be, the physical evidence, I mean. We don't focus on the victim, we concentrate on the mind of the killer himself, and on the phenomenon that the psychologists report, trophyism. The way that these psychopathic killers steal parts of their victims - pieces of skin, hair, things like that. They almost inevitably keep them, you know - they masturbate over them, relive the crime, sometimes it's as if they need proof of what they've done, or want to boast about it. Jack the Ripper sent a kidney to the police investigating the Whitechapel murders - it was taken from one of the dead women. Had a piece of renal artery attached that corresponded exactly with what was left in the body, so they knew it was him all right. Still didn't catch him. Anyway, the point is there's a compulsion to keep some part of the cadaver.'

'So what do you want - a butcher's shop?'

'That's exactly it. Where did Caracci live?'

'Everywhere and nowhere, like the rest of White Boy's gang. They lived in hotels, with the tarts they were pimping for, over the bars they were extorting money from. It was a circus - they were moving on all the time. Caracci dossed wherever it suited the boss, basically.'

'So there isn't anywhere that was his, his alone, I mean?'

'The Monster's Lair?'

He was laughing derisively now.

'Pure, blind fantasy. You should be writing headlines!'

Chapter 65

'The taxi-driver?'

'What about him, boss?'

'The one who was killed - one of Caracci's victims. The taxi-driver. Didn't he come from Corsica, same as Caracci?'

'Yeah, I think that's right. They don't even think they're French.'

Montvallon scratched his head. On the wall beside him a film company's calendar of pin-ups as Cannes understood them, which is to say without benefit of air-brush, was marked with successive battle-plans in stages that counted down towards the film festival, with its attendant nightmares of crowd control and bodyguarding. Only five weeks to go. Like a sort of Advent Calendar really, thought Maubourg, enjoyably.

'Someone went out to his home, didn't they? Interviewed the widow and so forth.'

'Think it was Dupont. It'll all be in the file.'

'I just want to check.'

'He's in the back office if you want him. Trying to grease his way onto Sharon Stone's protection unit - that's going to be the plum job!'

'Someone ought to tell him it's not like the movies!'

Dupont was a tall man, gangly, anxious. His brown hair stood up in permanent twists. He had a strong, slow Provençal accent - a country boy, thought Maubourg, in the city.

'Barsi, the taxi-driver? They had an apartment - very small. I went over it - real thorough. We were looking for evidence that he'd been involved in something, so we were looking for drugs and stuff. I'd say we took that place apart - couldn't have hidden a flea, time we'd finished.'

'Was there any mention of any friends of his who'd stayed with them? Anyone he knew from Corsica, for example?'

'His woman didn't mention anyone, boss.'

'But did you ask her?'

'Yes - well, we asked if he had any special friends who'd come to the apartment. No-one she could remember - seems like he'd dumped his old mates when they got married. She was on at him to get a proper job and all that. Said before he met her he'd been...'

'What is it?'

'I just remembered. She said he'd been living in a real dump. An old caravan somewhere up in the hills.'

'There's no caravan mentioned in the report.'

'No, it didn't seem to matter - hell, it was before they were married. Long before the murders.'

Chapter 66

Cecile settled herself more comfortably behind the wheel of the silver Alfa Romeo 155 and put her foot on the accelerator. She put on a jazz tape, the old MJQ, as the kilometres towards Toulouse rolled away. It was almost time to get rid of all the rubbish lying about in the back of her head, the muddy residue and silt of her working life, the images that recurred in her head. This journey was a chance, a space that alllowed a decent gap between the world of the magistrates' office, and that of her daughter.

Things were more or less cleared up, anyway. The thing couldn't yet be fully made public - if Maubourg didn't make progress towards finding definite proof that Caracci was the Mutilator, they would have to hold a press conference and convince the media. The political types in the municipality wouldn't like it, but she needed more evidence, and that meant more time and more money.

There was still a kind of nausea in her stomach at the thought of Caracci. Even Louis, when she had rung up to arrange to come to Toulouse, had asked her over the phone if she was feeling alright, so it must have even crept into her voice, somehow. Odd that Louis should have noticed it, but that was always the way it had been: just as she thought he was the same all the way through, an utterly insensitive commercial lawyer with a heart of solid wood, he used sometimes to show a sudden flash of insight or sensitivity and she would think, 'No, he's not like all the others after all. I'm making a mistake.' But she had realised in the end that his occasional sensitivities were a deliberate indulgence, as if he allowed himself to be affected when the matter was unimportant. As in the case of what she was feeling.

She pushed Louis out of her head for the moment, concentrating on the road. In an hour she would be with Florence and they could walk together, with the child hanging on to her hand and hopping in excitement as she always did on any outing. 'She's an adventurous little creature,' thought Cecile. 'I suppose I was the same at her age!'

But there was something that was still tugging at the back of Cecile's mind. There was something she had overlooked. Something fine... just a trace... as fine as a hair...

The silver Alfa screeched off at the next intersection, circled down a fly-over, spun back up and on to the opposite carriageway, making back on its tracks.

CANNES 60 KM.

Cecile felt something breaking inside her.

She called Maubourg from the first lay-by.

'They found some hairs on Durrant's body, didn't they? Animal hairs. Can you remember whether there were any on the other victims?'

'I can't remember now, but I think there were. They were probably just pet hairs... at least, that was considered likely at the time.'

He's being tactful, she thought. The previous examining magistrate didn't think they had any significance so they were ignored. That's what he means.

'Were they ever analysed?'

'I did suggest it - but no, I don't think it was ever done.'

'Probably considered a waste of public money,' thought Cecile angrily. 'And as a result here I am heading down a motorway in the wrong direction, away from my daughter, away from our weekend together.'

Aloud, she said, 'Can you line me up an analysis? Assuming the hairs are still in the lab?'

Maubourg answered quickly. 'None of the evidence has ever been destroyed. I made damn sure of that. But I don't know who we'll get to do it - not at the Easter weekend.'

'Try to get someone - even if you have to go to the zoo!'

Maubourg chuckled. 'After big game, are we? Well, I'll do what I can. By the way, one of the victims, the taxi-driver, Barsi, came from Corsica and so did Caracci. There may have been some special link there - they tend to stick together, though Barsi's widow says her husband quarrelled with all his old friends, round about the time she was persuading him to stay straight. Still, we're following it up.'

'Good. But keep me informed, won't you, before you take any major action? And, by the way, no point in trying to contact me at the Toulouse number. I'm on my way back to Cannes.'

Cecile pulled back on to the motorway and put her foot on the accelerator. The signs flashed past.

CANNES 40 KM.

'I'm a fool,' said a voice inside her head. 'I should have spotted the failure to analyse the hair. Go through everything, check out every single detail yourself - you didn't do it, Cecile, and as a result your daughter is going to have to wait to see her mother and you might as well call this weekend finished, and Louis will be triumphant at what a bad mother you are.'

CANNES 25 KM.

She wondered why there seemed to be tears trickling down her cheeks.

Chapter 67

The hillside smelled of thyme and loomed above them, a greyish-green mass. Here and there were the quick-moving forms of a flock of goats, scattered out along the escarpment.

The jeep was racketing up the slope, bumping over the rough terrain. Distant bleating came from the goats.

'He brought her here before they married. In their courting days, apparently. Good spot for a bit of...'

'OK, Dupont.' The young man's legs were furled up, even in the comparative space of the jeep.

'She obviously remembered it, anyway.'

'Looks like you'd remember it more for the goats.'

'For cheese. Supposed to be very good - sells for a fortune in the delicatessens down on the coast.'

The caravan was decayed, the plastic fascia boards split and rough coarse grass growing round it in clumps.

'Go slowly. I want everything noted. Everything.'

'Looks like it hasn't been touched for a while, boss.'

'There's a fair old stink up there. Worse than the damned animals.'

They were down wind of the caravan now, as the driver stopped the jeep at the end of a rutted track a few minutes walk from the caravan.

'Have to do the rest on foot, boss. Looks like someone was shitting up here, anyway, - looks human to me, but nothing fresh.'

Dupont had gone ahead, stretching his long legs as he got out of the vehicle, striding up towards the abandoned caravan.

'Hold on - wait where you are for a minute. I've got a call to make.'

He got out the mobile phone. Should have no difficulty from up here.

Cecile's voice came clear through the pepper-pot of little black holes.

After a minute, he called out to Dupont to carry on, to wait for him outside the caravan. 'And talk to that lad over there. Find out if he knows anything about the place.'

Dupont's long legs went lolloping off in the direction of the goat-herd, who was standing still and staring in the direction of the jeep. Snatches of conversation were carried on the wind, in an accent so thick Maubourg doubted whether he could follow it.

'The boy says he hasn't seen anyone coming here for a while. He didn't much like the look of the bloke who comes up here. Saw him carrying a mattress or a sleeping-bag - something rolled-up, once, but he doesn't come that often and only seems to stay for a day or two. Anyway, he doesn't have any objections to the goats wandering round, apparently. The boy says a lot of people do, because they eat everything in sight, rubbish, washing, plastic bags, the lot! But the boy goes all around the hills, wherever the goats wander off, so he's not sure how often the bloke comes here anyway.'

When they got up to the top of the slope, they stared at the grimy windows, peered in. Everything seemed tightly shut, sealed against the sun.

Dupont looked at Maubourg questioningly.

'Yes, do it!'

It was easy enough to burst open the door. The frame didn't smash - it just flew open.

'Jesus!'

'You're not to go in.'

'But boss - '

'Those are the instructions.'

Maubourg moved away, out of Dupont's hearing, took out the mobile again, spoke, listened. Lenoir's voice came out of the plastic, echoing over the scrubby grassland.

'She says you wait. She's gone to get into the car - she's on her way.'

'We wait,' said Maubourg, pushing down the aerial of the mobile.

'What the hell for, boss?'

'Those are the orders. Shut the door again. As tight as you can.'

So they sat, silently, on the hillside, as the bells around the goats, necks tinkled away into the distance, and they swatted occasional flies. Until another vehicle appeared up the track and screeched to a halt beside the jeep, and the film crew got out and started running up the slope.

Cecile's chauffeured car was behind it.

Chapter 68

'In the Den of the Mutilator.'

'Mutilator caught at last.'

Maubourg tossed another newspaper down on to Cecile's desk.

'God, you're ambitious! You must have warned the camera crew to get there first!'

He had abandoned formalities, angry and disgusted. 'Cold bitch,' he thought as she answered him in her clear level voice.

'Look, you can have what you want now. Equipment, manpower. Listen, Maubourg, we got that computer analysis of Durrant's prescriptions done because the *juge d'instruction* happens to be married to someone in the business - not because you had a unit capable of doing it! But just now the municipal council love you. It was on the television news last night. The cameras have got it all. Mind you, they can't show it all. Too horrific. But it puts it beyond any doubt. Only the genital areas from the women had been kept. I signed the permits for the analyses on the hairs to go ahead, by the way and that zoologist you got hold of phoned me half an hour ago.'

'What did he say?'

'Goat hairs. We can only make a guess at what he did with the clothes, and the parts he didn't keep and whatever he used to wrap the bodies in.'

With a lurch of his stomach, Maubourg recalled the goatherd, speaking of his charges. 'They eat everything, rubbish, plastic...'

He said, 'But ... Christ, it was so obscene! How can you imagine any human being with a mind like that ... To do that. And cut out ...'

'You haven't read very widely, have you, Inspector? In 1864, in the American West, a certain Colonel Chivington commanded a fine cavalry regiment. They attacked an Indian encampment, killed the women and children, cut the sexual parts from the squaws and fastened them to their saddles. They were never disciplined nor reprimanded. Trophyism is a well-known phenomenon - it's common enough with hunters. Of all kinds.'

'But you can't compare..'

'Can't you?'

Maubourg said nothing.

She said, 'He came here looking for somewhere to stay, just as his fellow Corsican, Barsi, moved out of the caravan and got married. I suppose he let Caracci stay in the caravan. There'll probably be some women missing in Corsica, from the early part of Caracci's career. You can send someone there to check.'

I've silenced him, thought Cecile. What was lying in that caravan - yes, it was the work of a sadistic lunatic.

But it was also the work of a human being.

What is there, what could there be, that lies between the world of my child and this? That's what Louis will say to her one day. 'What a world your mother lives in!' And he'll tell her. What I do, and what it's like. That's how I'll lose her.

Chapter 69

The crowd was circulating in front of the scrap of canvas hanging by itself on the white wall. Beyond, the bright blue of the sea was visible in the distance and the room shone with the dazzling clear Riviera light.

One of the waitresses the Museum had employed for the opening of the new exhibition - well, an unusual exhibition with one exhibit only - proffered a glass of wine to Maubourg. He would rather have had a handful of the canapés that he could see circulating in the distance, but there were too many people in the way. He recognised various dignitaries, the mayor and a spread of chamber-of-commerce types, the president of the festival committee, even a white-faced young American film star with a body guard close behind.

There was no-one he knew enough to start a conversation with, though, so he began to manoeuvre his way through the crowds, the cloying perfumes tickling his nostrils, towards the wall where the Leclant gleamed alone in the great expanse of white.

A large shape loomed up. clutching a glass. 'Ah, Maubourg, it was an excellent piece of work, discovering where this picture was. I've just given some information to the art critic of *Le Figaro* on the subject - they're going to do an article about Leclant. Very gratifying.'

'Thank you, Commissaire.'

The other man gazed about the room.

'Your wife here, Maubourg?'

'No, sir.'

'She's not interested in art, perhaps?'

Damn the man.

It was painful, Maubourg found. A kind of public humiliation.

'No, sir, it's not that. She ... she just had another engagement.'

'Ah, Inspector!' It was André de Carcassonne. He was wearing a cravat of green rubber, but was otherwise quite normally clad. Maubourg greeted him with relief, and introduced him to the Commissaire, noting with satisfaction that police ranks appeared to mean little in the art world. De Carcassonne looked unimpressed. Nevertheless, the Commissaire made a social effort.

'Welcome to Cannes, M. de Carcassonne!'

'Yes, well, this is such an important occasion I thought I must manage to tear myself away from Paris. An unknown Leclant - and an unknown benefactor!'

He looked shrewdly at Maubourg. 'Or benefactress?'

The policeman smiled non-committally, though it was more or less an open secret among the art crowd, he supposed.

'Yes, it was a most generous gift.' Doubly generous, he thought to himself, since it was the donation of a penniless Scottish housekeeper, but Susanna Washington had been insistent after the civil tribunal had awarded ownership to her.

'No, I don't want a picture of a cemetery hanging on the wall! Too morbid for words!'

She had been laughing, of course, but perhaps she had some feeling the painting would be unlucky for her. She could have sold it and never had to worry again, as the saying went, but it might mean that she would never be free of worry again.

'It belongs here, Inspector. In Cannes, where it was painted.'

And Cashel had looked at her in a certain way; perhaps she felt she didn't need anything more than that. She should have a lesson in realism from Madame Galant, thought Maubourg. Still, time enough for that, and anyway, Madame was away. On a family holiday, she had said. Montvallon had surprised Maubourg.

'Not so tough as she sounds.'

Was it true? Come on, admit it, Maubourg said to himself. You'd like it to be true. You don't want a woman to be as tough-minded as Cecile Galant.

A familiar face surfaced out of the crowd, and pressed close against him. 'Ah, Inspector!' said Victoire Lescure, 'how lovely to see you!' A cloud of scent arose from her powdery cleavage. 'You know, I was a bit of a detective myself' she continued. 'I've sacked that waiter of mine in St. Émile, Jean-Louis. I worked out he must have been in the pay of that terrible man - the gangster. Really, it is like something from Hollywood! Otherwise, how would they have known which house to attack, I mean out of the whole village? Someone must have told them. Answer me that, I said to him! And of course, who else could it have been? So be off and take your traps with you, I said. He's always wanted to get to the coast anyway - thinks some gorgeous blonde American will be all over him in five minutes. But how are you, Inspector?' She squeezed closer.

'Ah - did you really sack him? Well, what a coincidence. Because I thought I saw him serving drinks here in the Museum - over there, at the bar. Perhaps you'd just go and have a look to make sure.'

Her eyes opened wide and, heaving with excitement, Victoire shouldered her way through the throng.

God forgive me, thought Maubourg, it just popped into my head. He suddenly felt absurdly cheerful and pleased with himself - the effect of champagne. The crowd was getting noisier by the minute. A flash went off and Maubourg recognised the photographer from the local paper, squinting through a lens at the glitterati.

Suddenly, there was a tiny figure in front of him, an elderly woman with short iron-grey hair. She was wearing spectacles, the upswept sort that were fashionable in the nineteen-fifties. There was something familiar about her, but he couldn't place her.

Bloody good sort of policeman you are, he told himself.

'Inspector Maubourg?'

'Yes, Madame, what can I do for you?'

His heart was sinking. He wanted to get away, not to stay here and be polite to some old biddy. He wanted to get home, longed for it like an animal seeking for a bolt-hole.

She was saying something.

'I am Madame Rigaud.'

Ah, the widow of the previous *juge d'instruction*.

'I thought you might be here, Chief Inspector. I'm a member of the Cannes Fine Arts Society, in any case, so I have an invitation ...'

His policeman's eye automatically noted her agitation, the hands twisting round the stem of her wine-glass, her wrinkled upper lip trembling slightly.

'There's something I should have said. About my husband. Something he told me just before I died. I always thought I should have passed it on to the authorities, but that new judge, she seemed - well, I thought she would be hard to talk to, you see.'

Her voice trailed away, invited agreement, but he didn't say anything and she continued.

'But I think I can tell you, Chief Inspector, and you won't be cross with me for not saying anything before now. It's about some photographs. My husband said - you see, he was having a lot of bad dreams - he didn't want to see them anymore whenever he opened the file on the Mutilator. He said they were such horrible pictures, you understand? So he put them in another cabinet, a locked one, where they weren't staring him in the face all the time. But he knew it was wrong, that he shouldn't just have taken them out of the file. It troubled him to do anything that was against procedure. I always meant to say something about it, but somehow ...'

'Don't worry, Madame Rigaud. She found them.'

She found them, and now perhaps she can't sleep at nights either. A hard one, that, but only on the surface. They were getting to understand each other, she and him. A long process, but it was coming.

Time to go. He'd come again, another day, when things were quiet.

'I'm afraid I have to leave, Madame.'

'Ah, yes, Chief Inspector, you must have so many important matters to attend to. Goodbye.'

'*Au revoir*, Madame.'

He still hadn't seen, it the focus of the whole exhibition.

But the picture would keep.

Chapter 70

At home in the apartment, Maubourg watched the television with a sinking heart. His light-hearted mood had evaporated. Violetta had not returned.

The news was on.

'And we now bring you a report from the lycée that has been at the centre of the row over whether Sayida Mahmoud, aged sixteen, should be allowed to conform to Muslim custom and wear a scarf covering up her hair when she attends classes.'

Such a little thing, thought Maubourg. Such a tiny thing, a scrap of material.

The head teacher of the school, a man who looked like a sixties liberal, insisting he had to defend 'our national culture'.

'But we are French Muslims!' Sayida's great bewildered brown eyes. The imam of the mosque behind her. A row of teachers in front of her.

Then a group of schoolgirls. One of them his daughter.

'She should be allowed to wear it,' insisted Rachelle. 'Why are other girls allowed to wear crosses or crucifixes? Why can't we be more tolerant to the Muslim girls?'

The reporter again.

'It will interest the viewers at home to know that this young lady is the daughter of Chief Inspector Daniel Maubourg. Of course, we cannot ask the Chief Inspector for his views - as a public official, he cannot take sides in such a dispute. But it would be interesting to know what goes in the household of one of our most prominent officials - and we have already heard his daughter's views. Perhaps such opinions are pretty general in the Maubourg family - at any rate, we have someone else who might be able to tell us, because here, I believe, is Madame Maubourg coming especially to collect her daughter from school.'

'Bastard', thought Maubourg, helplessly watching as the camera panned towards the Renault drawn up next to the kerb, where Violetta, clad in a silky grey dress, was sliding her long legs out of the driver's door. The lens dwelt lovingly on Violetta's delicate face.

She crossed over to her daughter and they stood face to face, but the obscene fuzzy padding of a microphone shot up in between them, in front of Violetta's mouth. The reporter had followed her, one step behind. Now the camera was showing a whole battery of other cameras, someone crawling on their hands and knees holding up a mike.

'Madame Maubourg, what do you think of your daughter's action in this case? And can you tell us what your husband thinks?'

Maubourg braced himself for the betrayal.

Violetta turned and looked directly into the camera with her magnificent eyes. The camera lens adored her eyes, even in this hard-news location focus; it made love to them, lingered on them.

'We do not have arguments in our household' she said, crushingly. 'We are a happy and close family and I am taking my daughter home. That is all I have to say.'

She put her arm round the girl and led her to the car.

Chapter 71

In an office in Victoria, the 'phone rang.

'Hallo', said a female voice. 'I'd like to speak to Mr. Hollingsworth.'

'Mr. Hollingsworth isn't here', said the police officer who had picked up the phone. 'Who is that speaking?'

'Oh, it doesn't matter. I used to be his secretary - well, the temp. I suppose he's got someone else now.'

'He won't be in the office for a bit.'

'Well, it doesn't matter. It isn't anything important.'

Carol Bassett replaced the receiver in the hall of the house in Clapham.

Funny, that he hadn't turned up for that next meeting in the Cocks. He had telephoned - so he must have had her number after all, registered some part of her mind - and asked her particularly to meet him. She had sat there like a lemon for half an hour before she had decided that he wasn't going to turn up. Had two Martinis while she was waiting, and felt a bit annoyed when the barman evidently thought she was feeling lonely. Or on the prowl.

Well, no matter. She didn't particularly want to see him again anyway. She might have had another week's work out of him, that was all. He certainly wouldn't have got any more out of *her*.

Lucky thing, really, she thought.

Charlie picked up a newspaper from a stall near Martin's office and handed over some change. He hoped there would be nothing about Imelda in it - she was being prosecuted for shoplifting at Bow Street Magistrates Court. Charlie had enough affection left for her to hope there wouldn't be a reporter in court, but she probably wouldn't care much anyway. He turned back towards Susanna, and they paused in the dusty street., tourists banging past them with suitcases along the narrow pavement.

Charlie was scanning the pages of the paper, fanning them over rapidly.

On an inside page, there was a small item.

'Mutilator's Lair Discovered.' She peered over his shoulder.

'The Riviera, playground of the rich, is safe once more! The Cannes murderer known as The Mutilator has been identified beyond all doubt. Luigi Caracci, a small-time gangster with an evil reputation, was killed in a shoot-out with police in a picture-book Provençal village and police raided the caravan where he had lived to find a horrifying collection of pieces of flesh and skin cut from the bodies of his victims.'

'If anything, they've toned it down a bit.'

Charlie continued to read, as if transfixed by the crude print and clichéd prose. 'The city can now breathe again, as it struggles to keep its image as the Riviera's premier glamour resort. The film festival, due to begin next week, will be the usual gorgeous parade of sizzlers - and don't forget, day by day, your favourite newspaper will be bringing you the Topless Tops of Cannes!'

The two of them vanished into the crowds at Victoria.

END